OUR LAST FALL

A NOVEL

LYVIA MARTINEZ

Bywater BOOKS
2026

Bywater Books

Print ISBN: 978-1-61294-347-3
Library of Congress Control Number: 2026937965

Bywater Books First Edition: September 2026

Printed in the United States of America on acid-free paper.

Cover designer: TreeHouse Studio

Bywater Books
PO Box 3671
Ann Arbor MI 48106-3671

www.bywaterbooks.com

For June, godmother to all my characters.
And for Caroline, whose belief in me keeps me going.

CHAPTER 1

4:23 p.m.

EVA VARGAS LIES FACE up on the surprisingly cold parking lot asphalt, waiting for her breath to return to her lungs. She groans in pain as she shifts her leg out from under her, staring at the orange sky, afternoon sun low in the clouds. Ignoring her stinging palms, she pulls the strap of her messenger bag away from her neck, which helps her breath return more easily.

Unfortunately, it does nothing to help ease her humiliation from tripping over her own feet. She does her best to sniffle away the prick of embarrassed tears from her eyes. Swallowing a few times also prevents that lump from forming in her throat at the thought that her brother Javi would've picked her up right away if he were here, Band-Aids at the ready somehow.

A mortifying whimper escapes her lips as Eva sits up. She checks her bag's contents: house keys, wallet, giant water bottle—good, nothing broken or spilled. Hopefully her phone didn't skid too far away when it slipped from her hands as she fell. She better get up soon before a stranger approaches to ask her least favorite question in the world: *Are you okay?*

"Me cago en . . ." Eva curses as she wobbles back to her feet.

She brushes most of the dirt off her bomber jacket and looks herself over. Pink scratches on her palms and a tear on the knee of her brown Dickies pants are the worst of the damage.

Frustration bubbles and overflows almost immediately, and Eva lets it out as a long, exasperated breath. Of course, just one more thing to add to this terrible month. She stamps her sneakers on the ground as hard as she can and kicks at a rock, as if that might hurt gravity back.

She finds her phone finally. Worry makes her hesitate before she glances at the screen. The same lock screen photo she's had for the last year looks back at her: Javi, mop of messy brown hair and smile as wide as can be, pulls a reluctant Eva into the picture with one strong arm around her shoulders. His other side is cut off, his arm reaching and holding onto someone out of frame. All that's visible of the other person is a bit of puffy golden-brown hair, and a brown freckled shoulder.

Eva swallows hard, tears and throat lump fighting her again. She couldn't bring herself to change the photo, so cropping it was the next best option.

Focus. Don't break down right now.

Shaking out her shoulders helps a bit. She checks her phone over. Good, no new scratches or cracks. No calls from her mom, either. Annoyingly, the clock on the lock screen now reads 4:25 p.m., reminding her she's still late. Knees sore, Eva stumbles into her first few steps until she's able to break into a jog.

Farther ahead, a large, bright yellow canopy marks the entrance into the Los Angeles County Fair. A surprisingly large number of people are still making their way to the congested, multilane security checkpoint. Her spirits sink. Late afternoon on the last day of the fair should've meant a smaller crowd to contend with. No luck there.

Anxious to get to her friends quickly, Eva dodges and weaves ahead of adults, children, and enormous strollers. If she thinks only about what she can do and control right now—just keep moving forward—she won't think about how big and frightening tonight feels.

This is the first time everyone in their friend group is getting together without Javi. They were a mishmash group, her friends and his, all brought together by his charisma and unmatched people skills. But now it's just her.

Eva won't think about how tomorrow the fair will be gone until the next year. She won't think about how she's not sure she could keep the group together for a whole year, let alone after that. Not the way Javi could. On top of that, his friends will have graduated from high school and be off to college or work.

They have to do it this year. Tonight. He'd already bought his county fair season pass, had gotten everyone to agree on a day to go together.

And then they all attended his funeral instead.

The back of her neck grows clammy with the overcast afternoon chill. She bumps into someone as her steps stutter. No, no, don't think about how terrible things can go tonight, how they could get banned or fined or arrested. How that could affect the rest of their lives forever. And everyone would blame her . . .

Don't catastrophize; nothing's happened yet. Don't freak out, don't freak out.

Eva breathes in deeply. She reaches into her jacket pocket for her teal-colored guitar pick and redirects her nervous energy into spinning and flicking it between her fingers.

Following her therapist exercises, she tries to focus on what she can sense. The bright yellow welcoming canopy. Neon lights and spinning rides, tall palm trees that grow into the skyline. Heavy, fatty smells from the deep fryers that have been boiling all day. The familiar sounds of the fair: several genres of popular music combining together into a terrible blaring mashup. Javi used to call it the best mashup ever and try to sing along to all of them at once. The roar of rollercoaster gears blends with people's shrieks and laughter. She even recognizes the extra-loud screams of riders falling on the Big Drop, the one ride she's always been too scared to try.

She grits her teeth against it all. These sights and sounds used to mean the most fun day of the year. A day to spend with just their friends, no adults or responsibilities—just thrills, laughter, and unhealthy food. Now it all twists her stomach and gets under her skin.

Javi would've told her to drink some water or wear warmer socks or stretch. Those small everyday things, he'd say, are normally the real cause of a bad mood. But he's not here and she's not in a *normal* bad mood. She hasn't felt normal for a month, not since—

"Eva!"

"Hey, hey!"

She jolts toward the familiar voices.

Off to the side of metal barriers, her best friends Hyun and CJ wave to her, all smiles and wide sweeps of their arms. The kind of silly way you greet someone you've known since middle school band class and all you ever do is be embarrassing together.

"Heeeey," she breathes out with relief, little sparks of nerves easing as she jogs to them like an exhausted marathon runner reaching her family at the finish line. "Soooorrryyyy."

"It's okay," Hyun says with a bright smile on his tawny cheeks. He opens his arms wide and crouches into a crab walk to meet Eva at her height, made all the funnier with his baggy maroon sweatpants and loose-fitting mustard cardigan. She rolls her eyes with a smile and raises her arms in preparation. He wraps her up in a hug, lifts her against his tall, skinny frame, and squeezes hard enough to crack her back in several places. It's a move he picked up after his older sister became a chiropractor. Eva groans at the pops, but her shoulders hang more relaxed after he sets her down.

Eva blurts out her explanation in one breath. "I know I said four o'clock, but Mom was particularly smother-y today. She kept asking me what I'm working on in therapy, and it took her *fooorrrever* to go take her Sunday nap so I could run to the bus and—"

"You're good, you're good!" CJ steps in for her own milder hug, wisps of her blonde hair escaping her high messy bun. Her soft powder-blue hoodie is comforting even if it clashes with her short shorts and flip-flops. "*We're* only on time 'cause I told Hyun we had to be here at three-thirty."

Shocked, Hyun stands to his full height, almost a head taller than Eva. The bangs of his perfect tied-back, feathery black hair swish as he glares at CJ with an accusing point of his finger. "I could've had *more* time to do my hair?"

CJ laughs and pushes Hyun's shoulder. "Oh, do you need help making it even *more* elegantly disheveled?" She reaches for the large, shiny, maroon hair clip holding half his hair back. But he knows her fighting style and dodges expertly.

Eva welcomes their distraction, the casual lightness that reminds her of life before. How they'd compose on-the-spot joke songs of random things they saw, or design friend tattoo sets for them to get once CJ finally became a tattoo artist. They always know how to make her laugh. She's noticed them amping up their silliness around her in the past month, but she's not going to complain.

Being with them is the only time she feels semi-normal. The only time she's able to think of other things besides how much she misses Javi. She just might be able to play her guitar again or watch an obscure niche documentary, or even play Mario Kart.

"Hey Eva!" Another voice, this one not as familiar, calls out from the bathroom stalls. It takes Eva a moment to recognize Greg, CJ's cousin. He only visits once a year.

"I thought you said you wouldn't have to bring him?" Eva whispers at CJ, unable to hide her frown.

CJ huffs. "I *tried*, but what was I gonna do? Mom and Dad

had another date night tonight, and he was sitting there eating a whole jar of olives by himself and I couldn't stand the look of him. I took pity. Plus, I only have my learner's permit and Greg *somehow* has an actual license despite his parents not believing in cars. But don't worry, I didn't tell him what we're *really* here to—" Greg steps within earshot and CJ's tone immediately changes to high-pitched and chipper. "—Hey, Greggy! You ready to have fun tonight?"

"Boy, am I ever!" Greg beams brightly. "Usually you've already been to the fair by the time I'm in town. I'm hyped!" He does a little jig, pumping his fist into the air. It's really easy to forget he's older than Eva, sixteen years to her fourteen. His hand-me-down clothes add to his younger look, with his faded cargo pants and blond hair that looks like his mom still cuts it for him. He always wears the oddest T-shirts with outdated references, too. His current shirt has frogs promoting Budweiser on it.

"Glad you could join us, Greg," Eva says through thinly pressed lips.

"Yeah! Should we go in then? It's already kinda late in the day."

"Uuuum . . ." Eva stalls, glances at CJ and Hyun for backup. "W-we have to wait for Bless and Frank."

"They're seriously not here yet?" Hyun looks at the crowd. "She usually keeps him on time."

Eva glances down at her phone. *Dammit, 4:34pm already?*

"Nope. No texts either." She knows they can't do this without them, even if a part of her kind of dreads it. She's never spent time with them without Javi before. They're in his same grade, older and therefore intimidating.

"Aw, c'mon, time's a-wastin'!" Greg says, arms raised in excitement, already looking past the security checkpoint at the fairgrounds beyond. "They can meet up with us!"

Eva stiffens and grips the strap of her bag tightly. Greg

joining last minute is bad enough, but now she has to figure out how they'll execute their plan without him figuring things out.

Should they tell him? But what if he freaks out and reports them? She doesn't know him well enough to be sure he'll be cool. It takes good planning to get to everyone's rides, and they've had a few run-ins with park security in previous years. There's a high chance they'll get in some serious trouble tonight.

As if through some telepathic best-friend connection, CJ places a steadying hand on Eva's shoulder before she turns to Greg. "Actually, Greg, can you go get my entry ticket?"

He laughs, but his brow dents in confusion. "Didn't you get it online?"

"I always get it *at* the fair. It's good luck! If I get my ticket right before we go in, that means we'll have a good time."

"Oh, okay then!" Greg says, tone all too eager to please. He takes her bundle of cash and walks off to the ticket booth.

Eva, CJ, and Hyun stare after Greg, then release a collective sigh of relief once he's out of earshot.

"How are we going to do this with him around?" Eva talks to her shoes.

"It'll be okay," Hyun says. "We'll keep him distracted. Greg's clearly kind of oblivious."

"Oh totally! Easy to distract." CJ's tense laugh comes out a little too loud. "He's like a dog, colorblind and easily excited by high-pitched voices."

"Is he really colorblind?"

"You've seen how he dresses."

"Yeah . . ."

Eva focuses on her breaths and her friends' warmth surrounding her. Their contact and silly conversation help keep her crawling anxiety at bay somewhat.

Hyun clears his throat and draws Eva's attention to him. He bites his lip, like he's nervous to ask something. "So Javi's . . . you brought . . ."

Eva squeezes both hands on the strap of her shoulder bag. "Yeah."

CJ and Hyun glance at each other and swallow hard. Sometimes they're both so synced up it's weird.

Eva breathes out a nervous laugh. "Wouldn't it be funny if I forgot him after all this headache, getting everyone to come out here tonight?"

"That would've been tragic," CJ's smile is thin, forced, like she doesn't want to admit she's uncomfortable. She glances at Eva's bag, gathering the courage to ask. "So . . . how did you actually . . . you know . . ." She winces. "Bring him."

Eva breathes in deeply through her nose, out her mouth.

She holds her bag out toward her friends. They both release a small gasp as she opens it, clutching at each other in exaggerated wonder. Maybe a little fear, too.

Once they get a good look inside the bag, their eyebrows furrow in synchronized confusion.

"Is that a . . . a . . ." CJ stutters as if she can't believe it.

"It's a water bottle," Eva responds flatly, looking into the bag with them. The large metal water bottle used to be a solid bright red color, but now stickers cover almost every inch of its surface. Javi loved showing off his favorite things: national parks, inspirational quotes, puns, basketball teams, and video games. She knows the faded ones and the ones covered by newer stickers: Her fingers have traced the giant dent on its side countless times.

"I can *see* it's a water bottle, Eva." CJ twitches, her usual humor dropping away.

Hyun slaps a hand on his forehead. "Did you actually put your brother's ashes in his giant *sports water bottle*?"

Eva shushes Hyun loudly just as CJ clamps a hand over his mouth, but they still draw the momentary attention of a few passersby. Exactly what they were trying to avoid. Please no, they can't get caught before they've even made it inside.

"What was I going to do? Bring the urn?" Eva tucks the water bottle deeper into her bag. "The lid doesn't screw on; it would be way more obvious, plus my mom would've noticed immediately and—"

CJ rubs at her temples. "I'm sorry, I don't know why I'm crashing out over this."

"I can't exactly google 'Most Respectful Way to Smuggle Your Dead Brother's Ashes into the County Fair,' can I? I did what made sense to me and, anyway, he loves this water bottle."

Eva holds her bag close, like a small child hugging a stuffed animal for safety. Embarrassment feeds irritation at their questioning and judgement. Did she make the wrong choice? Was there even a right choice?

Hyun forces out a laugh that cuts the tension. "It's a pretty good idea actually. No one'll suspect a thing. It'll be fine. Totally fine!"

"Okay!" Greg announces his return before the group sees him, causing them to jolt.

A mixture of annoyance and relief mix in Eva's chest at the interruption.

"Are Bless and Frank still not here?" Greg asks as he hands CJ her physical ticket.

"They should be here any minute," Eva says quickly, throat dry. She glances at the crowd passing them by.

"And Clare?" Hyun asks.

Eva exhales, still looking around, attempting as casual a tone as she can. "She's not coming."

"She's not?" CJ tilts her head, confused. Something in her eyes makes Eva feel like she's trying to dig into her brain for details. Damn that best-friend ability to read into her.

"Really? She was Javi's best friend; she should be here." Hyun states the obvious.

"She said she couldn't make it." Eva shrugs, looking away.

She can't explain more than that as she's always been terrible at lying. She'll twist up her words and say the wrong thing. They need to get going, get inside the park already. In an hour or so her mom will wake up, check the shrine she built for Javi's ashes, and notice his urn is empty. And then Eva will never get the chance to commemorate him the proper way.

Javi was never stationary. He was always moving, dancing, jumping, running. She'd have spent her entire days inside the house if it wasn't for his "wouldn't it be fun if" ideas. He deserves more than a funeral, more than somber music and dark clothes.

She won't let their mom turn their mantel into his tomb. In Eva's opinion, Mayra wants a stagnant commemorative place where he'll be stuck forever. But that's not what he would've wanted. It wasn't a night with Javi without fun, laughter, and a bit of fear.

Eva's phone buzzes in her pocket, shooting nerves of worry up her fingers.

CJ and Hyun tense alongside her, as if her anxieties feed theirs.

Eva reaches into her pocket. Please don't let it be her mom, please don't let it be her mom.

She inhales deeply and looks at her phone.

"Frank and Bless are here." Eva breathes out her nerves along with her words.

"Hell yeah!" Hyun pumps his fists in excessive celebration.

"Where are they?" CJ stands on her toes and looks through the crowd.

"They're closer to the security and bag check. Must've walked right by us." Eva pockets her phone again. The relief that they don't have to keep waiting for them is overshadowed by the conflicting feeling of worry at having to spend time with Javi's friends without him.

"We should get going, yeah?" CJ nudges Eva's shoulder.

Eva nods and grips the strap of her messenger bag.

"Whoa," Greg interjects, laughing awkwardly like he's

afraid to ask. "This is the most serious I've ever seen you all. We're riding rides and eating junk food, right?"

Eva exchanges a quick, guilty look with her friends.

"Right," Eva says, not sounding convincing even to herself. "It'll be fun."

CHAPTER 2

4:46 p.m.

FRANK AND BLESS ARE fortunately not too far away from where Eva and her friends (and Greg) are waiting. Eva notices them first, standing right before the security check.

They're hard to miss really. They look like complete opposites from each other: Bless is small, thin, and mousy, wearing an oversized flower-print dress and lavender cardigan that make her russet brown hair and skin shine.

Frank, on the other hand, is tall, rounded at the top, with light brown skin. His large black hoodie, buzzcut head, and permanent scowl add to his imposing vibe. He always makes Eva think of a scowling, sour lollipop.

The groups notice each other as they walk up, and the waves and awkward hellos are a marked difference in closeness between them. Eva's glad they actually made it, even with the aching tension growing in the back of her neck. The reality of having to lead and keep this group together tonight feels like a weight over her head. She doesn't know how Javi did it, all of them from different grades, with different ages and interests. Eva at fourteen would've never had the bravery to approach a seventeen-year-old. And yet they all gathered around him, drawn into his orbit by some irresistible gravity. Everyone meshed around him. How could Eva begin to compare?

"Bless!" Hyun steps up to her, bright mood undampened. "I saw your post. Congrats on USC!"

"Ah, thank you," Bless responds as she tucks a long thin braid behind her ear, cheeks darkening with the attention. Her fingers are barely visible under her long cardigan sleeves. "I was so nervous." Her voice is quiet and timid, with a slight lisp in her s's.

"If anyone was getting in by early action, it would be you!" Hyun throws up his hand, and Bless meets it with a soft high-five.

CJ's lips thin into a flat smile, shoving her hands into her light blue hoodie pockets and rocking back and forth on her heels. Eva can't help but notice how uncharacteristically quiet she is, usually one to join in with anything Hyun does or says.

Eva wishes Hyun hadn't reminded her what Bless is putting at stake by being here to spread Javi's ashes with her. Could getting caught and arrested make USC cancel her acceptance?

"Glad you're both here," Eva says, shaking her head to dislodge her worrisome thoughts.

"And so sorry," Bless says. "I tried my best to get us here sooner."

"She really did." Frank's voice is its usual, grating, deep monotone. "I didn't want to come, and it took her twenty minutes to get me out of my house."

"Frank." Bless huffs as if correcting a small puppy that keeps biting shoelaces.

Eva frowns up at him. Frank's irksome sincerity will be a lot to deal with tonight without Javi. He's always kind of scared her, contributing to how she never understood why he and Javi were friends. They were basketball teammates, but beyond that? A mystery. When she told Frank of her plan for tonight, he said he wouldn't come, that he didn't see the point. Eva had secretly been relieved. She hadn't counted on Bless persuading him to join them.

Still, she'll need to help them all get along if they're going to do this for Javi. For all of them.

"Yo." Hyun flashes his brightest smile at Frank. "Someone need one of my amazing back-cracking hugs?"

"You want me to pull your hair clip out?" Frank's voice is so even and low it takes Hyun a moment to realize the threat that it is. Hyun's smile fades, and he takes a step away from Frank, placing a protective hand over his lovely hair clip.

Frank's eyes focus on Eva, then flicker down to her bag hanging from her shoulder. His scrutiny intensifies the tension in her neck.

"So!" Bless pipes up, voice squeaky with the attempt at more volume, which only makes her lisp more pronounced. "We're just missing Clare then?"

Oh no. Not this again.

Eva swallows hard. "She said she couldn't make it."

Bless turns to her, nervous look changing to concern. "We can't do this without her, can we? She was Javi's best friend."

Eva cringes at both the use of the word "was" and at the thought she'll likely keep getting this question all night. Instead of answering, she shakes her head and shrugs at Bless as if it's all out of her hands. Hiding the fact that she has orchestrated all of this to purposefully leave Clare out. She messaged everyone individually and chose a night Clare would be busy elsewhere rather than working at the fair like she does every summer.

She just couldn't stand to see her, not after everything. They need to get past this and get moving.

"We have about six and a half hours until the fair closes at eleven," Eva says with as much authority as she can muster. She can do this. She can lead. "It's going to be tight, but if we focus, we can get to everyone's rides before the end of the night. Like always, first let's get inside and we'll draw straws to decide the ride order." Javi always liked the slight chaos of a random order, and she can keep that tradition alive.

In an awkward unison of nods and shrugs, they all turn to the fairground's security checkpoint.

Ahead of them, the crowd sorts into several security lanes, each staffed with a set of security personnel. Attendees walk through tall metal detectors one at a time as a security guard looks at a screen for any flags from the machinery. Some people are waved on through while others are asked to step to the side to have the contents of their bags checked.

Javi's never brought his giant, metal water bottle to the fair before so Eva doesn't know if it'll trigger the detectors.

"It'll be okay." Eva hears CJ whisper at her, leaning in. "If we walk through with confidence, like nothing's wrong. I bet they won't even stop us."

"You scared, Eva? You trying to sneak in some booze or something?" Greg's attempt at a joke garners no laughter and instead makes Eva cling to her bag even more.

"Who even says booze anymore?" Hyun mutters.

Bless looks questioningly at Eva, then glances down at her bag. Her focused stare draws Frank to also look at the canvas messenger bag.

When they meet her eyes again, a small nod from Eva confirms what they've likely assumed: Javi's in there.

"If we stay calm, they won't suspect a thing," CJ says, placing a light, comforting arm on Eva's shoulders. "And if they do suspect, we cause a scene and distract them."

Eva looks over the different security lines, trying to assess which one might let them through safely. Some of the security guards are more focused and keep a close eye on those stepping through, while others seem less interested, practically checked out.

One particular guard catches Eva's attention: an older

woman with a crisply ironed navy uniform and graying light brown hair pulled into an excruciatingly tight bun. She waves guests over with sharp, no-nonsense hand movements, a chunky watch rattling on her wrist.

The group must've all seen the female guard at the same time because they let out a chorus of groans and throw their arms up in defeat. Except Greg, who has no clue what's going on.

"Are you *kidding*?" CJ exclaims in disbelief. "Seriously? Palchuck? Today?"

"Yep, we should just go back home." Frank turns and walks away.

"Stop being a jerk." Bless gently grabs him by his hoodie and keeps him in place.

"We'll pick a line far away from her." Eva's voice comes out squeakier than she means it to.

"She targets us every year! It's over!" Hyun rubs his hands down his face dramatically.

"She does?" Greg asks, looking from the group to Palchuck and growing more anxious with every turn of his head. "Why?"

"Well, we can sometimes have a little *too* much fun, you know?" CJ answers.

"Like what?" Greg's tone shakes, like he's almost afraid to ask.

Hyun steps in, all too eager to answer. "One year I missed every bottle in the hoop toss, but I *really* wanted that stuffed fake bag of Takis."

"Oh, one year," CJ continues for him, "I really wanted to hold one of the winning pigs from the pig race. The race was over when I ran onto the track, but they still yelled at me!"

"One year, we all had Icees right before getting on the tilt-a-whirl." Bless's grimace is enough to convey how that story ended. "Clearly, traditions we could stand to break."

CJ's brow furrows and lips purse at that last comment.

Eva has to focus everyone back on their current problem. She reaches in her pocket for her guitar pick, tracing the sides. "We just have to hide among a big group and avoid Palchuck's security line. We're not going to quit at the first roadblock, are we?"

"Do we get to quit at the second one?" Frank says with a laugh to himself.

Eva whips her head to glare at him, determined to say something totally cutting that will shut him down. But then her eyes follow his pointing finger all the way to the gate.

From over the crowd, Palchuck stares right at the group, eyes already squinting into a frown that deepens each one of her forehead wrinkles. Her rounded, stocky face makes her look like an angry bulldog.

Oh great. She's noticed them.

"We're not quitting," Eva looks at Frank, putting as much resolve into her voice as she can.

"Oh, idea!" Hyun says as he bumps Eva's side. "She's always nicer to Bless, right? She could carry the bag for you!"

"What? Haaaang on." Eva takes a short step away from the group.

"That's a great idea, Hyun!" Greg raises his arms again. "Give the booze to the nice quiet one!"

"I don't know about this . . ." Bless looks as worried as Eva feels.

"Hey, don't pressure Bless." Frank glares at Hyun, stepping in front of Bless defensively.

"It's only an idea." Hyun's tone is prickly.

Eva clicks her nail against the guitar pick as the group squabbles around her. This isn't good. They don't have time to argue tonight. But she doesn't know what to say to stop it. Javi always knew how to get everyone to agree on what to do or eat or ride next. He always found a way to make everyone happy, feel like they were considered and listened to. The fair gave them a liberating chaos, and Javi somehow kept it all under control.

She can barely keep herself together, never mind their group of friends.

A gentle weight settles on Eva's shoulder. She expects to see CJ, but finds herself looking up at Bless instead.

"I—I can do it if it would be helpful." Her hand on Eva's shoulder shakes. She's always seen Bless as the quiet shy one in the background. Seeing her put herself in potential danger stuns Eva. Is it for Javi? For her?

"What do *you* want to do, Eva?" CJ asks, diverting everyone's attention back to her.

Eva nods, accepting CJ's support. It's a small gesture, but it props her up somehow. It gives her enough space to take a deep breath, plant her feet more firmly.

"*I* have to carry hi—the bag," she says, finally, with as much firmness as she can muster.

The group around her quiets. She glances at each of their faces, from Hyun's disappointment to Bless's relief. She can't let them see how much her legs are shaking.

"Okay." Frank huffs loudly, turning away with an exaggerated drag of his feet. "'Cause we don't look suspicious at all right now." He walks toward the security line.

The group hurriedly falls in line behind him: Frank first, followed by Greg, Hyun, Bless, and then Eva and CJ bringing up the rear.

Eva tries to calm her breathing, to still the electricity in her nerves telling her to run home instead. She catches her nail on the guitar pick and flicks it a few times.

"I'm sorry," she whispers to CJ. "I couldn't let someone else carry him . . ."

"It's okay." CJ gives her a small but sincere smile. She places a hand on Eva's arm. "You're allowed to be selfish with this one."

Eva nods appreciatively and pulls CJ into a half-hug.

Ahead of them, Frank steps up to one of the middle security

lines. Good. It's far enough away from Palchuck that she probably won't notice them again, but not so far that, if she does see them, she would think they were trying to avoid her. Even though they totally are.

The security guard checking bags in this line is younger than the other guards and seems completely bored with his job, only glancing quickly in each bag brought to him. Eva breathes a small sigh of relief. Surprisingly, Frank did pick a good line. Was it an accident or is he paying more attention than he lets on?

"Uh oh . . ." CJ says through gritted teeth.

The warning immediately sets Eva on edge again. She looks a few lines over, makes eye contact with Palchuck and quickly wishes she hadn't. The way Palchuck scowls—deep, square lines setting in—makes Eva's stomach churn. She brushes at her hair, tightens her nubby ponytail, and tries very hard not to look at her again.

Their line feels like it moves the slowest it possibly could. No one in their group speaks, no joking or chatting or pushing each other around like they usually would. Eva wonders if Palchuck is still staring at her, but she's too scared to check.

Frank is only six people away from the detector. They're so close.

Eva can't help one more glance over at Palchuck.

She's not there. Eva looks around for her, but can't see her anywhere. Maybe she stepped to the side or bent down to tie her shoe?

No.

She switched lines. Palchuck is now right at the end of their line, taking over the spot for checking bags from the younger guard.

Frank is a couple of people away from her now.

Eva's chest rises into her throat as worry overtakes her. They're going to get caught. They'll get in so much trouble none of them will ever speak to her again. With shaking legs, she takes a step back and bumps into CJ.

"It's okay." CJ speaks softly. "Keep going. I'm here." CJ nudges her forward as the line moves.

Eva bites her lip as Frank walks through the detectors. Nothing flags.

Palchuck steps in front of him before he can pass by. He's taller than her, but Eva would put money on the old security guard in a fight.

"Hey, Palchuck." Frank holds a hand up and waves.

Palchuck nods stiffly, more of a sizing up than a greeting. "Francisco."

"Aww, you remembered." his deadpan tone barely carries the joke.

"Oh, I couldn't forget. Your group means I'm about to have the shi—" Palchuck notices small children in line nearby and clears her throat. "—crap. Crappiest night."

"Well, we're not here to crap on *your* night specifically." Hyun's laugh is way too loud. He slinks back again when Palchuck squares her glare at him.

"I should kick you out right now, save myself the trouble." Palchuck's words are a threat Eva is inclined to believe.

Frank holds up his hands. "I don't have a bag. Can I go through?"

Palchuck grumbles and waves Frank past her. "Pat him down, Tyler."

The younger bored-looking guard half-asses the pat-down.

"Every year." Palchuck talks to herself. "Every single year I hope I don't see you. Almost thought I'd finally lucked out this time. You don't usually come this late." The bulldog of a security guard motions to the rest of the group, looking down the line at each one. "But here you are. All seven of you, like the seven plagues."

"It was ten plagues, actually," Bless corrects in the quietest tone.

But Palchuck seems not to have heard her as she glances at

Greg, then does a double take. Her head nods and lips move as she counts their group.

"Come on, Palchuck." CJ leans on the railing with her best attempt at sincere innocence as Hyun steps forward. "We're just here to eat some bad food and ride rides that are below-safety-standard regulations. Same as everyone."

"Oh, just that?" Palchuck laughs, though there's no actual joy to it. Hyun and Greg pass through the detectors. Palchuck waves them through, still counting members of their group.

Eva can't swallow past the lump in her throat. If Palchuck checks the water bottle, it'll feel weirdly light and won't make a liquid sound. What if she insists on opening it? Eva can't decide if she should run and jump the line or turn back and find another way in. Her indecision leaves her rooted in place.

Palchuck keeps glancing at her. Or at least that's how it feels to Eva. She's probably figured it out already.

"I think . . . yeah, a girl's missing. Clare was it?" Palchuck's words make Eva's stomach feel like she's dropped from the tallest roller coaster.

"She couldn't make it." Bless answers simply, offering up her opened bag.

"Right. She couldn't make it." Palchuck continues to look up and down the group. "Well, something's still not right." She leans into Greg's space and points at him. "This one's new."

"You're holding up your own line, Palchuck," CJ yells from behind Eva.

Palchuck waves Bless through. Eva can only grit her teeth, regretting not giving up her bag like Hyun suggested.

And now Eva's next.

She stands in front of Palchuck, holding onto her bag tightly. She'd never noticed before how someone's stare could hold such tangible weight.

"Open your bag." Palchuck's voice makes the request feel like a threat.

Eva's hands are slow and clunky as she lifts the bag in front of herself. She doesn't need to look up to know that Palchuck's eyes are boring right through her.

She pulls the cloth flap back and holds the bag open. The large water bottle is nestled under her wallet, house keys, cell phone, and a bundle of old receipts and candy wrappers.

"It's your brother, right?"

What?

Eva's eyes pop wide open. How could she possibly know? How could tonight be over already? They didn't even make it inside the park.

"Hello?" Palchuck waves her hand to get Eva's attention. "Your brother, Javier? He's the other one missing from the group, right?"

Oh my god, oh my god. Nerves ping-pong under Eva's skin. Palchuck hasn't figured it out; she doesn't know.

Eva breathes out, swallows, then looks up at Palchuck. She's had to tell so many people so many times, but it never gets easier. There's no good way to say it. No gentle, sugar-coated words to explain why her brother isn't here tonight. And even if there were, Eva would not use them for other people when she can't use them for herself.

"He died a month ago." Eva's voice shakes, fading to a whisper on the last word. A deafening silence follows, like the mute stillness after a blaring alarm. Her own words ring in her ears as if they came from an amplifier.

Palchuck glances at the rest of her friends, as if unsure if this is a joke or some prank. Their general somberness must be convincing as her challenging stance slackens.

"Oh . . ." Palchuck's voice is scratchy and dry. She takes a slight step away from Eva. Surprisingly, it makes her half as threatening, almost as if she's shrunk an inch.

"I'm sorry," Palchuck says, finally, harsh voice a little quiet.

Eva still holds the bag open, arms and hands growing shakier with every passing second. "It's okay," she says. The words she uses when she wants to absolve people of their pity toward her. She hopes she sounds more sad than nervous.

Palchuck clears her throat, glances inside the bag, then waves her through.

Eva closes the bag carefully, saving any look or gesture of triumph for later, and walks to her group. They feel like an oasis after a walk through a harsh desert.

"Hold it right there!"

Eva freezes in place as Palchuck barks from behind her. She turns slowly, sure she won't get away with this a second time.

But Palchuck isn't looking at her. Instead, she pats down CJ's hoodie pocket, reaches in, and pulls out a nail file.

CJ lowers her arms with an exasperated sigh. "What am I gonna do, annoy someone real bad? File down their nails against their will?"

"And now you can't." Palchuck is all too satisfied as she tosses the nail file in the trash. "Alright, go."

CJ walks away, wide eyes conveying her surprise and panic as she approaches Eva. She puts an arm on Eva's shoulder and they both try very hard not to run to their friends (and Greg).

Eva shakes her nerves out through her hands and mouths a silent *shiiiiiiit*.

"I can't believe that just happened," Hyun sings at them, high-pitched and frantic.

"We really freaking did it!" CJ says, squeezing Eva close. "We're in!"

Eva's not sure how she even survived that. Sure, they've gotten away with stunts in previous years at the fair, but this one feels different. Somehow it fills her with nervous hope that maybe tonight will be the magical night she has been imagining after all, like in the movies where teenagers run around and scream and find themselves. A resonant but fun way to say goodbye to her most important person.

They jostle around, the excitement of being inside the fairgrounds electrifying. A spark of excited anticipation passes through each one of them. Contagious and energizing. Even Frank cracks a half-smile.

Eva chances a glance towards security, at Palchuck.

The older woman looks back at her, brow furrowed and eyes intense. And yet Eva sees an unexpected softness in them.

Palchuck gives her a slow nod, and Eva could swear there's something like understanding behind it. She's not sure what it means. A part of her feels too seen to want to know.

With a quick nod back, Eva turns to join her group.

CHAPTER 3

5:07 p.m.

IF THERE'S ONE TRUTH Eva knows for sure, it's that county fair entrances are where human reason goes to die. People enter and forget their common sense, milling about in groups, walking slowly because they can't decide where to go, what to do next, and how to get out of the freaking way. Sunday afternoon on the last day of the fair only makes the chaos worse.

Javi would've loved it.

"This way!" Hyun's voice is loud enough to be heard over the crowd's chatter and the fairground's thumping music. His tall frame is the easiest for everyone to follow, so he takes the lead. Not that it helps Eva all that much. She can't see past the shoulders of the people around her. She extends her elbows, trying to keep the meandering crowd from closing in.

They stop by the entrance set of porta-potties. It's not the most glamorous or nicest-smelling meeting area, but they're at least tucked away enough to be able to talk without anyone bumping into them.

"What are we riding first?" Greg asks, his enthusiasm clear as he bounces on his heels.

"We always draw straws so we can decide the order," CJ answers, and Eva's glad she can count on her best friend to carry some of the burden of wrangling Greg.

She doesn't want to leave the group or have them stand around here too long. This feels like the kind of mission that could fall apart if they lose any momentum. A quick glance at her lockscreen confirms it: 5:08 p.m. They already have only six hours left.

"I'll get the straws," she says to everyone, sounding to herself like a captain about to leave her crew for a dangerous solo mission.

"Wow, you sound like you're taking the ring to Mordor," Greg says with a long, loud laugh as if encouraging the others to join in. When no one does, he peters out.

"What's Mordor?" Hyun asks with genuine confusion.

Greg mutters something Eva can't hear, his cheeks turning the reddest she's ever seen. She also has no idea what he's talking about, but they don't have time to get into what is probably one of his weird, outdated references.

"Want me to come with you?" CJ asks, but Eva's quick to shake her head "no."

"I'll be faster alone." They exchange a firm nod as if passing on and accepting the responsibility of keeping the group together while Eva's gone.

Taking a deep breath, Eva steps back into the river-like crowd that could easily sweep her away if she's not watchful. She dodges and weaves, pushing through with her elbows out.

She makes it to the nearby snack stalls with large menu signs full of cluttered images of fried, sugary foods. They always attract long lines because people enter the fair, see how long the wait is, lose all sense of critical thought, and jump in so they don't miss out. Amateurs. They could get the same food if they went farther into the fair. Most stalls have multiples all across the large fairgrounds.

Eva heads to her target on autopilot: a small fresh-made lemonade and corn dog stand with bright neon-colored stripes. She doesn't bother with the line and heads for the table with napkins and straws. Strange as it sounds, she likes their straws best. They use thick paper ones that don't get soggy too quickly. They'll be easy to trim down for the draw.

She waits for the family in front of her to collect their napkins and condiments, then notices the box of straws is near-empty. Damn. She takes the four remaining and waits anxiously for refills.

Brown curly hair in her periphery makes Eva freeze. A closer look and she confirms, no, she doesn't know the girl taking orders at the lemonade stand. She breathes out the leftover nerves and shoves a hand in her pocket, twirling the guitar pick again.

She's being ridiculous. Clare wouldn't be working here today. She doesn't work Sundays because she spends them with her dad. So it's actually *good* she didn't tell her they were coming tonight so she didn't have to change her usual plans. And if Clare were here, she'd probably be working at the stall by the not-so-scary haunted house ride, which Eva will make the group avoid tonight at all costs, just in case. It'll be easy since that's Clare's favorite ride, and she's not here to draw a straw for it anyway. It's fine. It's fine. She's got it all worked out.

"Eva?"

A cold shiver runs from Eva's fingers to her stomach at that all-too-familiar voice. The surprise and jolt of anxiety make her wobble on her feet, and the weight of the bag on her shoulder threatens to knock her off-balance.

It can't be. After all her careful planning.

Of course Clare would find some way to mess up her plans.

Eva closes her eyes and scratches her nail into the guitar pick. She turns slowly, knowing she has no choice but to face her.

Clare stands there like a creature of myth that was summoned by the mere thought of it. But she's no mythical creature, only a normal sixteen-year-old who triggers Eva's fight-or-flight response. Her short nose and rounded face, usually brightened by her wide smile, now twists up, shock giving way to a deep frown as she takes Eva in.

"Glad you didn't leave your jacket behind again," Clare says, tone unusually biting. That one dimple on her left cheek also appears when she scowls. Eva hates noticing that.

While she would prefer to look anywhere but at Clare, it's hard to redirect her gaze from the atrocious uniform all lemonade stand workers wear: a button-up shirt with green, pink and blue colored stripes, and a baseball cap sharing the same hideous design. Clare's made the outfit her own by tying the bottom hem of the shirt into a knot just above the waist of her jeans, allowing for a peek of chestnut skin at her stomach. Her cloud of golden-brown hair has been wrestled into the horrendous hat, but it poofs out of the sides as if trying to escape. Most ridiculously irritating is how pretty she still manages to look despite that abomination of an outfit—a thought Eva has had an embarrassing number of times before.

"What the hell are you doing here?" Clare shakes her head as she drops the substantial box of straws onto the table.

Eva considers her escape options. She could throw her handful of straws at Clare's face and bolt blindly into the crowd, but then good luck quickly finding her way back to her friends. She could run through Clare, hope the force knocks her out and she forgets she ever saw her, but Clare's taller and sturdier than her, with arms like . . . *stop that.* Or she could pretend she's just some look-alike. But Eva's never been that good at being herself, so how could she pretend to be someone else?

As usual, her brain can't decide on anything at all. She needs to at least *say* something.

"Clare, I—" *I hate myself so much every time I even think about you.* Eva shakes her head, breathes in through her nose. Talking to Clare feels like punching a fracture that had just started to heal.

"I thought you didn't work Sundays." Eva's voice is flat, the cumulative result of all her reasoning distilled into a single, brainless statement. *Great job.*

"Dad's busy tonight." Clare scoffs, letting her right arm rise then fall limp at her side, smacking her thigh. Her go-to gesture when she's already disappointed in you. Clare has every right to refuse to explain herself, yet here she is, indulging Eva anyway. "Plus, it's the last night of the fair. They needed extra help at the front stall, and I like to be helpful and make money."

Eva nods to avoid having to say anything else.

Clare's eyes squint. "I thought I saw Hyun in the crowd earlier . . ."

Another concern worms its way into Eva's brain: if she takes too long, the group will wonder what's keeping her. If they think she's gotten lost, they might come looking through the stalls. Then they'll notice Clare and ask questions and probably toss Eva into the petting zoo goat pens once they find out the truth. A fate worse than death, some might agree.

Breathe.

If Eva can keep her cool, she might get through this. She got past Palchuck. All she needs now is to get the rest of the straws and run back to the group. Lemonade stall workers can't just leave mid-shift, right?

Clare glances at the straws in Eva's hand, and her dark blue eyes squint in growing suspicion.

"A handful of straws, no drink. I thought I saw Hyun . . ." Clare counts through the thoughts, laying them in order and studying them. Eva can practically hear realization hit Clare, like a gear clicking into place.

This cements Eva's decision for her. Grab and run it is.

Eva dashes forward and grabs whatever straws she can. But as she tries to twist past Clare she bumps right into an older man, knocking and spilling his large lemonade.

"I'm so sorry, sir." Clare steps in automatically with her customer service voice, offering him a bundle of napkins. "You can of course get a refill."

Ohnonono. Eva looks down at herself, checking if any lemonade spilled onto her messenger bag. Realistically, it wouldn't affect the water bottle or its contents, but she checks it every which way all the same. Most of the drink missed it, fortunately—a few napkins will do the job.

Her relief is short-lived as Clare's familiar strong hand grabs her forearm.

"Let go!" Eva pulls and wriggles, but she's no match for Clare's rock climber grip.

"What, forgot to text me the invite for tonight?" Clare asks, her voice intense.

Eva shrugs, easier than trying to come up with anything. Even if she knew what to say, she can't risk it. It would come out completely wrong anyway if she tried.

"It's pretty shitty to leave me out of something like this." Clare's chin shakes, but her lips purse tight, keeping it all in.

Eva wants to pick at the scab. "I don't have to invite you to anything."

"You're all here as some kind of goodbye, is that it?"

Crap. She's always been too damn smart, too good at reading her. Eva pushes away memories of late-night conversations after Javi fell asleep, sharing thoughts with each other they'd never told anyone else. Thoughts as silly as Eva's latest niche documentary hyperfixation to heavier things like Clare's worries over her dad's loneliness.

With Clare this close, Eva can smell her hand lotion: Japanese Cherry Blossom from Bath and Body Works. She prefers it because it's the easiest one to find and it's so popular they'll never discontinue it.

Eva grips the strap of her messenger bag with her free hand, willing the right words to come to her. Some kind of excuse that would get Clare to back off. The group can't find out she never invited her. Even knowing it was wrong, Eva couldn't bring herself to talk to her again.

She's avoided Clare for almost a month now She can't imagine suddenly spending a whole night with her, even surrounded by other people.

Eva knows the right thing to do would be to apologize and smooth this over, allow Clare to join them so she can say her goodbye to Javi, too. But Eva feels the selfish urge to open her mouth and do what she always does: say the wrong thing. Make the silence go away, make Clare unleash her anger at her the way Eva deserves. After that, she probably wouldn't ever have to worry about seeing her again.

"I can't believe you," Clare says through her teeth.

Eva purses her lips to keep the instinctive "I'm sorry" from coming out.

"Clare!" One of the lemonade stand employees calls out from inside the stall. "We good on straws?"

"Just a minute, Emma!" Clare calls back. She moves them both to the side, out of view.

"Let go." Eva pulls against Clare's grip. It's futile; she knows she can't get out of it. "God, I forgot how freakishly strong you are."

"You're taking me with you."

"What?" Panic rises in Eva's chest, bad decisions catching up to her so much faster than she'd expected. "N-no! You can't—"

"Because you told everyone I couldn't come?"

Craaaap. Of course she'd figure it out. Eva's eyes dart around, looking for anything she could use as an excuse. "That's not—"

"You're *not* going back without me, so stop stalling and lead the way." Clare looks back at her with intense determination.

"I still need space—" Eva's excuse feels flimsy even as she says it.

"I gave you space, and you locked me out. You're not pushing me away this time. You can't ignore me if I'm right here."

The words send Eva's dread overboard. Embarrassment and fear congeal into anger. She spits the words out before she can help it. "Why do you even care?"

"Of course I care. He was my best friend—"

"*Was* he?" Oh no. She really needs to stop talking. "Then why didn't you go *with* him?" The words burst out of Eva, the crack of a whip. They both still, the raucous noises around them fading behind the ringing echo of Eva's words passing between them.

Clare's chin shakes. "That's not fair." Her frown slowly crumbles, and Eva feels like she could too, knowing she's the cause of it. She did it again. She opened her mouth around Clare and something vile crawled out.

Eva was right not to invite her tonight.

"You're *such* an asshole," Clare says with one final stabbing glance as she turns away.

Eva scoffs, holding back tears. "I know," she mutters to herself.

"Emma, I need fifteen," Clare yells to the lemonade stand employee, then turns and rushes into the crowd.

"Hey!" Eva calls after her.

Oh no. The crowd's gotten bigger already.

"Clare, wait!" She runs after her, shoving her way through with her elbows.

Clare's longer legs and sturdy, taller form help her navigate through the throngs of people easily. Eva struggles to keep up, like battling a stormy tide that's pulling them apart. The crowd fills the growing space between them.

"Clare!" Eva calls out again, the name almost making her throat close up.

Someone turns too quickly and smacks Eva in the face with their backpack, the peril of being shoulder-height to most people. She catches glimpses of Clare's hair in that hideous hat moving farther away. Then Eva's swallowed up, unable to see past the people directly around her.

All this over some stupid straws. She could've gone to *any other* stall. Why did she have to go to that one?

If she can only find a landmark, something that'll tell her where she is and where she needs to go. Her skin crawls, fear bubbling in her veins. Her stomach twists into her chest. No, no, she can get through this, feel the ground, feel the jacket. Just push through the crowd. Get out of here in any direction. She holds her guitar pick in her pocket, snapping her finger against it.

Get out, get out. *Snap snap.*

A strong hand grabs her jacket and pulls her forward through the swarm of bodies.

Eva turns around and looks right into Clare's glaring face. Even as the look cuts right to the heated, angry core of her, a small part of Eva is glad to see her.

"They're all by the porta-potties, right?" Clare asks.

"Clare, please—"

Clare hauls Eva to what surely will be a very terrible fate.

"What excuse did you give them for why I didn't come?"

Eva doesn't want to answer. She looks away, drags her feet while Clare drags her. Finally, she responds, "I just said you couldn't make it, which you *clearly* couldn't since you had work."

Clare scoffs and keeps them moving.

"Oh my god, is that Clare?" Hyun's voice rings out like an airhorn. Curse his tall stature. There's no chance of covering this up as they all turn their heads, processing Clare's presence with something between surprise and delight.

Hyun is the first to get to them, pulling Clare into one of his back-cracking hugs.

Eva tries her best to calm down and prepare for the questions that will inevitably follow. At least she has a moment while everyone excitedly greets Clare.

Except for Frank, who crosses his arms over his chest. Eva can't help feeling a sense of camaraderie with him, like they're both upset about Clare joining the group tonight.

"Is this why you couldn't make it?" Bless asks, looking at Clare's uniform. "You had to work?"

"I, um . . ." Clare glances at Eva, and all she can do is take a deep breath and wait for Clare to decide her fate. It feels like an eternity. Her head is heavy with the fair's noise all around, or maybe it's the palpable weight of Clare's eyes on her every time she looks at her.

Clare responds at last. "Yeah. It's the last night of the fair. They needed extra help."

Eva fidgets with her pick, thumb and pointer finger pinching it and rubbing against it. Of course Clare would be a freakin' saint and not tell them the truth. It makes Eva feel even worse.

"Are you able to get off, though?" Hyun asks, sweetly pleading and holding Clare's hand to his heart.

"Yeah, I'm surprised you didn't call in sick so you could come with us," CJ adds.

"It's wrong to lie, CJ," Bless chides.

CJ rolls her eyes as she turns away from Bless and scrunches her nose in distaste, moving her lips in mock repetition.

Eva glances back at the lemonade stand where Clare's co-workers struggle to get through the never-ending line of customers. She's not sure which is worse, Clare joining or not joining their group. She knows Clare *should* be a part of this. Javi would want her to be, but Eva can't help the deluge of guilt and resentment she feels when she even thinks of Clare. If Javi were here, he'd probably pull Eva aside and tell her she's being irrational, thinking only of herself. But, just this once, is it so bad if she is?

"So you're joining now, right?" Hyun asks, as if there is no other option.

"No pressure, though," Bless offers with a small smile and a hand on Clare's shoulder.

Clare looks at Eva again, and Eva purposely avoids looking back.

"I'll get my stuff," Clare says finally, thumb pointing back at the lemonade stand.

"Yeah! Now it's a party!" Hyun celebrates. "Let me come with you. I can help you come up with a great excuse to get off work. My fee is one extra-large lemonade."

As Clare and Hyun head back to the stall, Eva distracts herself from her own thoughts of how awful this night is going by ripping the paper straws into different lengths.

"Just happened to bump into Clare, huh?" At some point Frank's made his way to stand beside her, and Eva can't interpret his tone as anything other than smug.

"Yeah." Eva doesn't look at him, merely crossing her arms. "It's great."

She waits for Frank to say whatever else he's going to, but instead he pats her on the shoulder—twice, comfortingly, which is even weirder—and walks over to Bless. Eva rolls her eyes and sighs.

It's almost no time at all before Clare and Hyun return. Clare now has her backpack and a T-shirt with a happy rock that says 'you rock!' Hyun skips happily next to her drinking from a large cup of lemonade.

"Right," Eva says, more for herself as she gathers the straws, breaks them apart in different heights, and shuffles them in her hands. She arranges them so they appear all the same height, her hands covering their true lengths. She considers whether they should make this moment more ceremonious, maybe say something or—

Then Frank steps forward with an exasperated "Ayup" and takes the straw closest to him. From there, everyone crowds around Eva and takes their straw.

"Alright, settled," CJ says once everyone's done comparing.

"Order will be: Greg, Hyun, Eva, Frank, me, Bless, and lastly, Clare. Any complaints?"

"Nope!" Greg chimes in, already walking off. "It's caterpillar time!"

"It's in the other direction, actually," Bless corrects, and Greg turns on his heel.

"I mean, this is my first time here so you really shouldn't follow my lead." Greg brushes off his embarrassment as the group follows after him.

Eva hangs back from the group, a sense of unease crawling up her skin, like she's being watched. She glances around, readjusting the strap of her bag over her shoulder.

They'll have to keep their guard up all night.

CHAPTER 4

six weeks ago

"AAAALRIGHT!" JAVI'S VOICE BELLOWED right at Eva from across the beige laminate kitchen counter. She squealed in fright, jolting and knocking her notebook and pencil away. Gravity was also against her as Eva's sudden jolt made her tall wooden stool wobble precariously.

Thankfully, a strong hand grabbed her by the shoulders before she could tip over.

"Whoa!" Clare exclaimed as she made sure Eva was safely sitting back on her stool. "Careful."

Javi doubled over in laughter, grabbing the U-shaped counter for support. Eva wanted to reach across and smack him, but she knew her arms wouldn't reach. Plus, she might knock something over, and that would be a travesty for their mom's carefully decorated pastel-yellow kitchen.

"Javiii!" Eva pulled her noise canceling earbuds out of her ears. It felt like a crime to stop Prince's falsetto mid-song. "What was that for? You're standing like two feet away from us!" She clutched at her chest, trying to keep her heart from beating out of her ribs.

"Sorry, sorry." The way he laughed around each word confirmed he was not all that sorry. "I can't believe how you were *both* lost in your own worlds."

"We were *busy.*" Eva motioned to the evidence of their interrupted work. Her and Clare's notebooks, papers, and pens flung away. Clare's huge precalculus workbook crumpled and bent on the floor.

"Well, *I* personally don't mind the interruption as much . . ." Clare said unhelpfully.

Eva jabbed her elbow lightly into Clare's side, earning her an "oof" followed by a laugh. That's when Eva noticed Clare's arm was still wrapped around her shoulders. She tried not to think too much about how Clare's fingers brushed against her arm, leaving behind nervous little goosebumps.

As Clare bent down to pick up the thrown items, Eva was too keenly aware of the way her body moved. She cleared her throat, trying once again to settle her heart, now beating hard for a completely different reason. It was hard not to notice how graceful Clare was, completely in charge of the movements of her toned arms. And yet Eva's favorite things to notice were her softer areas. Clare's cheeks were still rounded, especially when she smiled brightly and her stomach rolled and pudged whenever she hunched over.

Eva cleared her throat, fully aware she shouldn't stare. Clare deserved better than that, but damn. She was only human. Covertly, she got one more look, then turned back to the counter.

Javi grinned at her with a wide pleased smile. Chills ran through her skin. Did he notice her looking?

"Sorry again for scaring you," Javi said, turning back towards his work. "I did have a very good reason."

Javi's arms worked with practiced, easy flourishes. He spilled only a little as he transferred his work from the rice cooker into two bowls. The counters held the evidence of his messy process: dirty bowls, cutting boards, spices, and cooking utensils. He looked comically both at home and out of place in his usual baggy basketball jersey and their mother's bright yellow, lemon-patterned apron on top.

"I'm a little nervous to be honest," Clare whispered beside her.

"I think he got it this time." Eva said, more with hope than conviction.

Javi placed two heaping bowls in front of them.

The smells hit first: savory, earthy, and aromatic. The familiar scent of a dish cooked with plenty of sofrito, a common Puerto Rican base consisting of the perfect mix of onions, peppers, and garlic. The cut-up Vienna sausages stood out amid the yellow-colored rice.

Eva frowned at the green peas mixed in what should've been a perfect plate of just rice and sausages.

"Why the peas?" Eva had to ask. She loved their mom's arroz con salchicas just the way she made it. Any departure from perfection felt like a betrayal.

Javi's enthusiasm didn't wane despite her question. "I saw it in a recipe online and thought it could be fun to try something new."

Eva pursed her lips at the bowl. Being a little sister meant having a healthy amount of suspicion over anything her older brother declared was "new" or "fun."

"We're not getting away from this one." Clare reached over the counter, opened the silverware drawer, and grabbed two forks, handing one to Eva.

Javi clapped his hands and rubbed them together, nervous energy radiating from his tense shoulders. "Dig in and let me know what you think!"

The acrid flavor hit Eva's tongue as soon as she took a bite. Which then turned into a weird shiver from her shoulders down to her stomach. One eye fluttered closed as she struggled to stop herself from spitting out the incredibly salty mouthful.

"What?" Javi's bright smile dropped immediately, shoulders

hitching up to his ears.

"Bruh!" Clare said after spitting her mouthful and unpuckering her lips. "How much *salt* you put in this?"

"A pinch, like Mom's recipe said!"

"What's a pinch to you?"

Javi, with all the confidence of someone who knows he's right, brought over the salt bowl. He dipped his fingers in all the way and came out with an entire handful of salt.

"That's a *handful*, Javi!" Eva couldn't believe her throat still worked after swallowing the brackish food.

"My fingers are pinched! I'm pinching it!" Javi holds up his closed hand indignantly, delicate streams of salt slipping out between his fingers. "A lot fell out though so I put in a little more."

"*More?*" Eva and Clare yelled in synchronized disbelief. He did everything with such confidence, Eva found it hard to believe he would mess up this much.

Javi clicked his tongue and waved his hands in a dismissal. "You're both messing with me. This is fine." He took Clare's fork and shoveled some rice and a sausage into his mouth.

He froze, pursed his lips, then shook his head and ran to spit in the trash can under the sink.

While Javi dealt with his situation, Eva handed Clare her bottle of Malta, and she took a long drink from it. The carbonated malt beverage, a Puerto Rican staple, was an acquired taste, mostly enjoyed by those who grew up drinking it. It gave Eva an endless amount of joy that Clare liked it.

"How do I fix it?" Javi asked, turning back to them as he wiped his lips. "What if I add sugar? Would that help?"

Before either of them could advise him against adding sugar to his disastrous meal, they saw headlights from outside and heard a car pulling into the driveway.

Eva and Javi glanced at the mess covering the counter, then shared an all-too-knowing look.

"Mom!" The siblings exclaimed in unison.

"We'll help you clean up," Clare said, already jumping to action.

Outside, a car door slammed closed.

Eva's skin ran cold. There was no time at all.

Javi placed a strong, kind of damp hand over hers. Gross. But up close he smelled like cilantro, which she loved.

"I got this," Javi said, corners of his mouth up in a crooked smile. "She's gonna yell either way, so may as well be at me."

"Javi." Eva paused as if she was about to insist on helping, but then she patted his hand and nodded. "This is totally your mess so yes you should take the blame for it."

He laughed and pinched her wrist in retaliation, then stepped around the counter, a brave knight facing a dragon he might not survive.

"Both of you. Go."

A key jingled as it entered one of the front door locks.

Clare's hand grabbed onto Eva's as they pulled each other down the hallway and toward her bedroom, the farthest door on the right. The front door locks clicked open and the door creaked just as they jumped into Eva's room and quickly shut the door.

They tried to calm their quick, excited breaths, both waiting for what would come next. Mayra could be unpredictable depending on what mood they caught her in. Her returning after a long day of work and errands was likely not going to work in Javi's favor.

Clare pressed her ear to the door, one side of her hair flattening out against it. She met Eva's eyes, and her parted lips formed into a small smile that warmed Eva's insides. Her smiles always made Eva forget where she was or what she was doing. They were the kind of smiles that made you feel like you were in on some secret joke, just the two of you.

"¡Jaaaaviiiiii!' Mayra's yell from the kitchen broke the spell between them. "You did this? ¡Qué revolú!"

Eva snorted a laugh, and Clare shushed her with a light push.

Mayra and Javi's voices were quieter from the kitchen. He was likely winning her over already by asking her cooking advice, telling her how he had tried her recipe but he couldn't get it as good as hers, promising he'll clean it all up tonight.

"He's gonna be okay," Eva said confidently, hoping she could redirect them away from the door. She didn't always get Clare to herself, but when she did, she wanted to make the most of it.

Eva's room wasn't a common hangout spot, reserved more for nights without plans when Javi was away at games or at Frank's. Still, Clare always took it in like she was trying to commit its current state into memory. The bed was unmade, clean laundry stacked on top, waiting to be put away. Eva's desk was stacked high with color-coded notebooks: journals, schoolwork, poetry, songs, sketches. The only carefully organized area was the corner where her guitar lived.

Clare was as comfortable in Eva's messy room as she was in the rest of their house. And she demonstrated that by casually picking up a T-shirt from the clean laundry pile on Eva's bed and folding it.

"Oh, you don't have to do that," Eva said with a nervous, shaky laugh.

Clare shrugged. "I'm in here for a bit, so let me help."

Eva could never say no to Clare, so she nodded and pretended to grab a pair of jeans to fold when really she was pulling her underwear out of the pile, to avoid the mortifying instance of Clare seeing it.

They worked in enjoyable silence. As much as she liked spending time with her brother, he did bring a lot of chaos and noise with him.

"What song are you on now?" Clare asked as she set down a pair of Eva's Dickies on the folded pile. She motioned to the notebook Eva had been writing in earlier, before the salty rice debacle.

"Raspberry Beret." Eva answered as casually as she could, hoping not to give away how much she wanted to talk to Clare about her current thoughts on Prince's discography. Clare had been the one to recommend that Eva give him a listen. He was apparently one of Clare's dad's favorite artists and she had grown up memorizing and performing his songs. Eva could never admit imagining small Clare painting on a beard and singing her little heart out.

"Ooo, want to put it on?" Clare leaned closer to Eva, a small smile on her lips again.

Eva wished she had something to fidget with and to direct all her nervous energy into. It was a lot, Clare in her room wearing those summer shorts and touching Eva's clothes. Would any of them take on Clare's cherry blossom moisturizer's smell?

With a nod Eva connected her phone to her small waterproof speaker. Spending most of her time with Clare and Javi meant a lot of her things needed to be sturdier.

That distinctive drumbeat and count-in sounded out, and Clare swayed to it as if on instinct. She bounced on her heels and danced along. Eva bobbed her head, fingers ghosting through quiet guitar chords even as she held her unfolded La Brea Tar Pits shirt. They enjoyed processing music like this, listening to it and miming the instruments, even though she had a perfectly real guitar next to her bed.

Clare danced around, hopping on one foot, twirling Eva's hoodie around her head. When she reached out her hand, Eva took it without a thought. They danced and spun around each other, or Clare did, as she was clearly more athletic and therefore comfortable in her movements. Eva twisted side to side to the rhythm and let Clare pull her along.

The walls of Eva's room were covered in posters of her favorite bands and singers. Clare's performance was so good and committed, Eva could see her pictured among the posters of her favorite bands and singers on her bedroom walls. Clare's long curly bangs fell across her face as she finished with a flourish and a bow. Eva wanted to reach up and brush them away.

"Fun, right? You like it?" Clare asked, breathing hard as the music went quiet before the next song started. She dropped into a sitting position, jostling the pile of clothes.

"Yeah, it's good!" Eva said, with a little more enthusiasm than she felt for the song, finding it hard not to agree with Clare.

"How would you rank this one?" Clare lowered the volume of the next song, which Eva appreciated.

"I think, um . . ." Eva hesitated, nerves bouncing in her stomach and chest as she prepared to share her honest thoughts. She picked up her notebook and flipped to a page. "Number nine, above 'The Beautiful Ones.'"

"Nine? *Nine*?" Clare thumped her hand dramatically over her chest, as if she'd just been stabbed. "It's top five for me, up there with 'Little Red Corvette.'"

Eva laughed, bumping her foot against Clare's calf. "You always go for the upbeat songs. When I made you listen to Taylor Swift, your favorite was 'Shake It Off.'"

"I like something I can really dance to!"

"And I still can't believe how low you rank 'Purple Rain.' It's, like, his best! Everyone agrees."

"You and my dad can be disappointed in me together, I guess. In my opinion, it's a good one to fall asleep to." Clare shrugged, an *I don't make the rules* gesture.

Eva shook her head in pretend disappointment. "Suit yourself. Me, I can't resist a good power ballad."

"Enjoy your naps."

"It's so emotional!"

"Okay then, enjoy crying while you nap."

"How dare you!" Eva playfully smacked Clare with her notebook.

"Hey, I'm doing your laundry for you!" Clare held up her hands in defense and grabbed hold of the notebook the next time Eva swung it. In their laughter, Eva didn't notice at first that Clare wasn't letting go.

Clare smiled up at Eva, dark blue eyes crinkling as that single playful cheek dimple made an appearance.

"Can I read your notes?" Clare's lips quirked mischievously.

Eva's breath caught in her chest, ready to give Clare whatever she was asking for. "I—it's gibberish, I haven't really gathered all my thoughts yet."

"I'd still like to see." Clare tugged at the notebook, signifying her interest without being too forceful.

Eva took a deep breath and let go. She stood back, her hands twisting her Eras Tour hoodie much too tightly.

Clare opened her notebook to the page marked by her pencil. There was no way to distract herself. All she could do was focus on the cute little changes in Clare's expression as she read from it.

"Eva," Clare said with a burst of incredulous laughter.

"I told you I'm still gathering my thoughts."

"This is all just other words that rhyme with beret."

"Well . . . it's what came to mind so—"

Clare read them off. "Parfait. Duvet. Bidet?!"

"It's funnier if you sing them as part of the chorus actually." Eva jumped onto her knees on the bed next to Clare, bumping her legs as she reached past her to pick up her guitar.

She strummed a clumsy version of the song and sang the next line. "Raaaspberry buffet!"

Clare threw her head back in a laugh, the kind that shook her shoulders and made her hair sway like a willow tree in the wind.

Eva would do anything to hear that laugh again, so she continued. "Raaaspberry sorbet!'

"You're making me hungry!" Clare scolded playfully,

throwing Eva's strumming off when she shifted closer. Eva blamed the soft, unsteady nature of her mattress on that move.

She shook it off, continuing the game. "Try one!"

"Raaaspberry dismay!"

They laughed and sang an endless chorus of rhymes, each more ridiculous than the last. Eva would smack Clare's arm lightly at particularly bad ones, and Clare would lean her weight on Eva's shoulder in retaliation, singing them even louder.

They wrote them all down in Eva's notebook.

Javi had to knock a few times on Eva's door before she finally heard and let him come in.

"Did I miss something?" Javi poked his head in, surprised at seeing the two girls completely weak and spent from their giggle-fest.

"Raaaspberry delay!" they sang at him.

After they finally regained their breath and the proper use of their limbs, Clare and Javi talked through their weekend rock climbing plans at Joshua Tree National Park. Soon after, it was time for Clare to go home. Her dad was pretty lax about her curfew when she was at their house, but she never abused that freedom.

As was routine, the siblings saw Clare off at the door, watching until her bike disappeared down the street.

"Did Mom ground you for making a mess?" Eva asked as Javi closed the door.

"No, it's all good. I showed her my pinch of salt mistake."

"What did she think?"

Javi gave Eva an all-too-self-satisfied smile. "She thought it was so-dium funny."

"Noooooouuugh." Eva laughed even through her groan at his bad pun.

They worked in comfortable silence, tidying up the rest of their mess as they moved through the living room. A practiced choreography after years of trio hangouts. Javi had taken care of most of the kitchen himself, which Eva appreciated.

"So what artist are you going to make Clare listen to once you're done with Prince?" Javi asked as he set the dishwasher to run.

"Probably Rosalía. Clare said she wants to hear more stuff in Spanish." Eva smiled to herself, looking forward to translating the lyrics for Clare while they listened.

"That's cool," Javi said with an oddly heavy exhale.

Ready to head to bed, Eva turned off the kitchen light and walked down the hallway to the bedrooms.

Then she realized Javi was not following.

He stood at the entrance to the hallway, running his hand through his long curls, which he did when he was lost in thought. She should remind him he was due for a haircut soon.

"Eva." Javi's voice was quiet as he turned to look at her. "You like Clare, right?"

The question froze her in place, the hallway lights the only thing illuminating Javi's face. She wished she could see him more clearly, read what was going through his mind. Could he know? Was she being that obvious, how Clare's bright eyes made her insides feel like they were melting?

"W—what do you mean?" She asked, not wanting to answer directly in case he was talking about something else.

"Well, remember when I first brought her around, and you were so upset. You used to put your stuffed animals on every seat and tell her the house was too crowded so she should leave."

"Stoooop, I was, like, ten," she mumbled, embarrassed.

"You haaaated her, and you used to yell at us when we climbed the tree in the backyard."

"You kept knocking leaves and acorns on me while I was trying to read!" Eva lowered her voice when Javi put a finger to his lips to shush her.

"But you get along with her now, right?"

"What are you trying to get at, Javi?" Eva asked, side-stepping the question.

Javi took in a deep breath, bracing for something big.

"I really like her." A little smile curved his lips, accentuating the cleft in his chin. "And I think I'm going to ask her if she wants to be my girlfriend."

Eva's stomach dropped.

Oh.

Of course. How could she think she was the only one? This was Clare Morris they were talking about. Anyone who'd ever met her would agree she had the kind of smile that could make flowers grow.

"You think she'll say yes?" Javi hunched his shoulders as he dug his hands further into his pockets. This was a very uncharacteristic sign of nerves for him.

Conflicting feelings swirled in Eva's chest, overwhelming her, keeping her silent. She'd always cared about his happiness, same as he did for her. She would never get in the way of that. Clare deserved the best, and wasn't Javi the best? They'd be perfect for each other. Besides, there's no way Clare felt the same way about her.

That constant insecure voice in her head reminded her Clare would probably never see her as anything more than Javi's little sister. And she could be content just seeing the two of them happy with each other. Not like she'd ever get in the way—

"Eva?" Javi's voice brought her back. He sounded almost pleading, like he wanted to push for her thoughts but also wanted to give her space. Why did he sound worried?

"Of course." Eva's voice came out with a croak. She cleared her throat. Overcompensated with an enthusiastic, "Of course she'll say yes!"

Javi's sigh of relief lodged a lump in Evas throat. His smile was bright and pearly, brown cheeks rounding out his squared jawline.

"You're the best." He pulled Eva into a breath-squeezing hug. "I gotta start planning how I'm gonna tell her." Then he bounded off to his room.

Eva stared after him. Only when he was out of sight was she able to release her crushing grip on her guitar pick.

CHAPTER 5

5:31 p.m.

"THIS IS RIDICULOUS!" CJ's voice is loud with indignation. "Fifty dollars and it's not even unlimited rides anymore?"

"Miss." The weary older woman working the booth rolls her eyes and rubs at her face. "You should've checked online for where to get discounted tickets before coming to the fair."

"Come on, you can give us a deal. We come here every year."

"Sorry, I have no clue who any of you are."

"We're regulars!" CJ smacks the counter. Hyun rubs one of her shoulders as he intensely sips his lemonade. Eva isn't sure if he's trying to goad her or calm her down. Probably some weird combination of both. "And furthermore—"

Eva has to turn away. It's too embarrassing when CJ pulls stuff like this. Not that anyone ever stops her. Who doesn't love a discount, after all? Especially if someone else acts like a fool in your stead.

This is taking precious time, though. Eva can't help glancing at her phone to check the time. Just a little over five hours left until the fair closes, and they haven't even gotten to any rides. Will they be able to get to all of them?

She can feel someone's eyes on her and absentmindedly glances up to notice Clare looking down at her phone, frowning. Eva was so focused on the clock she'd forgotten about the lockscreen picture: Javi pulling Eva in for a photo, his other arm around someone cropped out of the picture. Clare cropped out.

Eva shoves her phone back in her pocket and looks away as if she didn't notice Clare looking. She can't meet her gaze even when she can feel Clare's eyes still on her. She's always been the type to stare right through you, into your innermost thoughts. Now it makes Eva feel uncomfortably exposed.

Javi's funeral. That was the last time she'd seen Clare. That awful night exactly twenty-seven days ago. They'd argued and yelled at each other. Or, really, Eva had yelled at Clare. She'd screamed at the top of her lungs, said things she doesn't know how to take back. The lingering anger and embarrassment make her doubt she would take them back even if she knew how. And after all that, Clare still texted several times to check in on her.

Eva never replied.

And now here they are, having to pretend everything is fine as they spend time together with friends. Clare might be planning some big moment of revenge where she reveals to the group that Eva lied and never invited her. Even knowing that's not the kind of person Clare is, Eva can't help worrying.

"Miss," the disgruntled ticket lady's stressed-out voice brings Eva back to the embarrassing scene. "The only group discount pass I have is for families."

"That sounds perfect." CJ leans forward, as if she's found her winning card to play. "We're *like* family."

The woman, tired and done with CJ, looks to the group for help.

"We can just leave her here and then she's your problem, ma'am," Frank says casually, but it may as well have been a violent threat for the fear in the woman's eyes.

"Fine," she says, relenting. "Two dollars and fifty cents

off each, how's that?"

"Well, if that's the best you can do," CJ says with an eyeroll. She pays the woman and steps toward the group with the ride ticket cards.

CJ's mood switches instantly as she hands the paper cards out. "Hell yeah, bargaining queen strikes again. You're welcome!" she sing-songs, doing a happy little dance.

Hyun bumps her shoulder. "That was absolutely awful. Javi would've been proud," he whispers, loud enough that Eva can hear. CJ smiles and Eva nods in approval.

"Let's Caterpillar it up!" Greg yells out once everyone has their ride passes.

"You like it that much, huh?" Clare asks him, amused.

"It's just so freakin' cute, you know?" Greg pinches his own cheeks and walks backward so he can face the group.

"Greg, you're yelling," CJ complains.

"Hyun gave me some of his lemonade."

CJ turns to Hyun. "You gave him that? The sugar drink with some lemonade flavor?"

"Uh, he asked to try it," Hyun responds innocently.

CJ looks back at Greg as he skips and hops his way to the ride. "Shit."

"Are we sure he's not twelve?" Frank asks.

"His parents are total health freaks who don't believe in sugar."

"Well, no one told *me* that!" Hyun's tone is defensive.

"Ooo, look," Bless says, pointing to a path to their right. "The garden center's pretty close by, maybe we can check it out if we have time—"

"Please no!"

"Nonono!"

Hyun and Greg shout at the same time, then pause and stare at each other in confusion.

"Geez, okay," Bless mutters and keeps walking.

They make it to the line for the Caterpillar ride. It's a low-stakes ride that whips the riders in a circular track as it bobs up and down. Each car is modeled after a segment of a green caterpillar's body, with the front car sporting a pudgy face with antennae and a maniacally excited smile. It's mostly families with smaller kids in line.

This isn't one of their "must rides" every year, just one they occasionally do if everything else has a long line. They especially avoided it after that vomit incident a few years back. Still, Eva smiles, knowing Javi would've been all about Greg's enthusiasm for it. That's how he was; he got on board with whatever you were into, like your enthusiasm fed right into his. So while this isn't part of their yearly routine, it somehow feels right.

"So it's all two-seaters," CJ calls out as they're getting closer to the front. "Anyone okay with sitting alone?"

"I'll do it." Eva says, happy to volunteer. She wouldn't mind some time to herself, even if it's on a ride that makes her dizzy.

As they get closer to the passenger loading area, Eva recognizes the skinny older teen in baggy clothes working the operator controls. She's seen him working the fair almost every year, even though his constant bored expression suggests he'd rather be anywhere else. His flat shoulder-length red hair somehow matches his droopy and uninterested eyes. A listless beanpole with acne and an overbite.

He holds his hand up to stop Greg before he rushes to a seat.

"Hold up, dude. How many in your party?" the ride operator asks with a sniff, voice low and lethargic.

"Seven."

The teen counts their group, then counts the number of open seats. "Alright, go on."

Greg cheers and dances as he makes his way to one of the open seats. Bless and Clare enter the ride next with no issue, but the teen puts his hand up to stop Hyun.

"No drinks allowed on the ride," he says, nodding at the large cup in Hyun's hands.

"I know, I know." Hyun drinks his large lemonade faster. "I'm almost done."

"He *just* got it. How is he almost done?" Frank mutters next to Eva, and she stifles a laugh at his disbelief. She'll never forget the year Hyun tried to set a group record of most lemonades drunk. At number five, he'd said he could see into tomorrow.

"And you should take that hair clip out." The ride operator points at Hyun's hair, and Eva tenses. Messing with Hyun's hair never goes well.

Hyun laughs in response as if the request were nothing to him. "I run with this clip in, and it never falls off."

"If this is the time it does, you could hurt yourself or someone else."

Hyun's smile flattens a little. He towers over the ride operator, but this doesn't seem to intimidate him.

Eva nervously glances at those already on the ride, then looks back at the long line behind them. They're making people wait, and that's going to upset them and draw attention to their group, and if they get any sort of negative attention, she knows it'll make its way back to Palchuck. The clock on her phone reminds her of the time they're wasting, Javi's smiling face helping broadcast that it's already 5:47 p.m.

"I ride with this thing on every year." Hyun doesn't back down. "No one's ever made me take it off."

"Sounds like they didn't know the rules or cared enough about you and other people's safety." The older teen's words would seem almost caring if it weren't for how flat and unfeeling his delivery is.

"Everything alright?" CJ says from her seat on the ride, a hand on the bar and moments from stepping out and joining the argument.

"Hyun." Eva's anxiety at inconveniencing strangers pushes

her to inconvenience her friend instead. "Just take it off. You can redo your hair after the ride."

The sharp look of disappointment Hyun gives Eva makes her chest sting. Yet another moment Eva lets her anxiety push her into making the wrong choice. Before she can apologize, Hyun shakes his head and plasters on a bright smile.

"Hey, it's okay!" Hyun says loudly. "I got this." He holds his lemonade out to Eva, and she takes it. He turns back to the operator, fingers steepled like he's ready to argue. "Listen, um—"

"Kevin," Frank and the older teen respond at the same time.

Eva and Hyun blink between them, nonplussed.

"What? He's here every year," Frank says with a shrug, as if obviously they should all remember his name.

"Yeah, I'm here every year," Kevin adds, wiping his nose with his sleeve.

"Okay. Kevin." Hyun takes in a deep breath, centering himself. Calm, smiling Hyun is a rare, eerie sight. "I've ridden roller coasters way bigger than the caterpillar with this hair clip in and no one got hurt, maimed, or killed. I think it'll be fine in the caterpillar, a baby ride made for literal babies."

"Just take it out, let's go!" Greg yells from his seat.

"Shut up, Greg!" CJ says like she would've smacked him if he were within range.

"Kevin," Eva says, handing Frank the lemonade so she can focus as she steps into the argument. She tries really hard to keep the frustration out of her tone. "Tonight is a very special night for us, okay? It would really mean a lot to us if—"

"It's dangerous to wear that hair clip on a ride, sorry." Kevin leans back against the railing, arms crossed, unintimidated and unmoving. If he wasn't actively being a pain, Eva would admire his lackadaisical approach to a situation she is so close to crumbling under.

Frank sighs, scratches his free hand through his buzzcut hair, then gives Kevin his most judgy shrug. "Why do you even care so much, man?" He shrugs in that way that says *be cool.* "It's a hair clip."

Kevin directs his half-lidded gaze to Frank. "I don't know what kind of chill, no-structure household you come from, but here we take rules seriously."

Frank's posture goes ramrod straight. The only sign that Kevin realizes he said something wrong is the bob of his Adam's apple.

Frank rolls his eyes and hunches back behind Eva, turning away as he clearly gives up being a part of this argument. Oddly, he takes a sip from the lemonade, then flinches as if realizing his mistake. "Ugh, too sweet," he mutters.

This is not a roadblock Eva had anticipated. Hyun is usually so ready to please, but his one hard line is anything that will mess up his hair. How can she get around this? Hyun won't budge, and for some reason this Kevin guy really cares about the rules no one else does.

She reaches into her pocket to run her fingers along her guitar pick. What would Javi do in this situation?

"Kevin." Eva steps forward and draws his attention. She tries to channel Javi's easygoing, charming tone that could convince anyone to do what he wanted. "We really appreciate the hard work you do to keep everyone safe. If this were any other ride, I'd be more worried, but it's the caterpillar. People don't even take their hats or sunglasses off on the caterpillar."

Kevin stares at her, chewing the inside of his lip, unimpressed.

Okay, time for a different Javi tactic: bribery. "Is there anything we can do to make you change your mind?"

Kevin glances at the lemonade still in Frank's hands. "I *am* thirsty."

Hyun gives an aggrieved squeal as Frank hands the lemonade over to Kevin without hesitation.

With a shrug, Kevin takes it and steps aside to let them through.

Eva lets out a deep breath, tension easing.

And then a buzz in her pocket stops her just as she sits in the ride.

It's a text from her mom: *Dnd estas? Pq cuando te llamo va directo a voicemail? Call me!*

Eva's chest constricts. Her mom always bombards her with questions whenever she's going out, which has only gotten worse recently. The only way to do this was to sneak out, even if she knew it would only be a matter of time before her mom noticed she was gone. And if her mom's noticed she was gone, it's only a matter of time before she figures out where she is, and only a matter of time before she—

"You shouldn't use a phone while on a ride." Kevin's voice makes Eva jolt, and she quickly shoves her cell into her pocket.

"Thanks, Kevin," Eva grits out.

She sets the messenger bag in the empty seat next to her and massages her sore shoulder, glad to have a break from its weight. Other riders fill in the few remaining empty seats.

Kevin lowers the safety bars and makes sure everyone is secure. He walks back to the control panel, locks eyes with Hyun, and takes a big gulp from the lemonade.

Hyun's indignant squeal turns into a scream as the ride jolts them all into movement. Frank's low laughter rings out through the ride's creaking, noisy gears.

The Caterpillar ride moves on a continuous circular track that bobs the rider up and down along small dips. Eva has to admit it's actually a nice one to ease into as their first ride tonight. She closes her eyes, the breeze from their movements blowing on her face and hair, drying the beads of fretful sweat from the earlier clash. This is her favorite part, as the ride starts and her tension melts away because now she has to relinquish control to it for the duration. There's also a relief in it, finally getting started on the night's plans.

No matter what the night throws at them, be it overzealous

security guards or rule-stickler ride operators, she's going to keep pushing the group through them. Javi would never let anything keep him from having the best night ever and neither will she.

The ride thunders around her, wheels clattering on the track, fast-paced carnival music blaring through the seat's tinny speakers. Definitely a ride for babies, but Greg is lifting his arms and screaming like he's skydiving. The one somewhat-exciting moment on this ride, though, is when the half-circle roof raises itself over the riders to turn it into a dark ride. The cover has a musty smell, like too many sweaty bodies have sat under it. The screeching and laughing always intensifies when the ride gets to that stage. CJ howls like a wolf, Hyun yelps like a hyena, and Greg laughs maniacally.

Javi's shout of choice was the loudest and longest "Weeepaa!" a frequent exclamation of excitement for Puerto Ricans. Their mom always uses it to cheer them on at special events.

Eva closes her eyes and tries to imagine hearing him over the commotion, his deep voice turning high-pitched at each dip in the track. She grips her messenger bag tightly, while her other hand holds onto the safety bar. Her head bobs and her body slides more and more to the side as the ride goes on. She wishes in vain that the movements of the ride will loosen the weight in her chest. It's silly to think this would be anything like riding with Javi, but she can't help but hope for it anyway.

The yelling dies down and gives way to laughter, both from their group and the other riders. It's the kind of laughter that comes from relief after a fright or high emotion. Eva does her best to ignore Clare's distinct laugh as it rings out over everyone else's. It's the kind of laugh that's all dorky, raspy inhales. Her own laughter bubbles up in her chest, but she tamps it down. Damn Clare's infectious laugh.

At last the ride slows down, jostling Eva. The roof pulls back, bringing them into the darker sunlight of twilight. Rumblings, music, and screams from other rides flood her senses again.

Ahead, Bless leans in towards Clare to whisper something in her ear, and they both laugh. A troublesome pang of jealousy grips Eva's chest, and she huffs at the ride as if it's somehow to blame.

The cars stop and everyone climbs out.

"Hair clip's fine, *Kevin*!" Hyun yells Kevin's name in the most nasally voice.

Eva pushes the safety harness harder than she needs to open it and climb out. She wobbles on her feet, readjusting to solid ground, when a strong hand grabs and steadies her.

Eva looks up at Clare, then quickly takes a step away, pulling out of her grip. It's so annoying how she's always right there when Eva needs her.

Clare sighs and shrugs, shaking her head. If she's thinking what's wrong with Eva, she'd also like to know.

"That was awkward," Frank mutters as he passes Eva, and all her frustration flashes through her like a prism and concentrates onto him. She purses her lips together, flattens them into a line, and aims the most intense middle finger she can produce at him.

Frank's lips twitch into the idea of a smile, and he returns the finger flip. Close by, CJ hoots, steps in between them and mimes stealing each of their raised middle fingers.

"Bless, I got something for ya," CJ calls out, pretending her middle fingers are something heavy she's carrying over to her.

"No, no. I don't like those." Bless waves her hand, batting the offered fingers away.

"Don't drop them, they're still good!" Hyun jumps in and mimes catching the dropped finger flips. He turns to Kevin and flips multiple birds in his direction.

Kevin sips the last of the lemonade loudly, but does not miss a beat in holding his cap out as if to catch each one. He nods a thank you and puts the hat back on.

Eva's chest feels a little lighter as she walks with her friends down the exit stairs, exchanging middle fingers with each other while giggling goofily. Javi would've laughed so hard at all this.

They gather just past the last step, most of them stopping to look back at Eva.

Greg and Clare get a few paces ahead, only to realize the group is not following. They turn back in confusion.

A question seems to bounce between Bless, Hyun, and CJ as they glance at each other, then at Eva's messenger bag.

Oh. Right.

Eva's eyes grow wide and she shakes her head just the slightest bit, hoping those who know get her message without tipping off those who don't: *no spreading ashes at this one.*

It's Greg's ride; he doesn't count.

Minuscule nods all around confirm they understood.

Eva feels eyes boring into her, and of course it's Clare, her brow furrowed like when she's trying to solve a puzzle. How is she supposed to tell her she brought Javi's ashes to the county fair in his water bottle?

"Are we going to the next ride then?" Greg asks, bouncing a bit as he walks back to the group.

"Yeah, what's next?" CJ asks.

"Hyun's ride," Bless responds, the only person who seems to be keeping track.

"Actually, my thing is eating spicy nachos!" Hyun responds. "Javi and I would compete to see who could finish their whole plate without quitting." He smiles wickedly. "Or throwing up."

"Aww, it's too early to stop for food," Greg whines petulantly. "Come on, the spin cups are right here!"

"Greg, we have a plan," Eva says with as much authority as she can muster, hands wringing the bag strap.

"We should go with what's closest, though. That makes the most sense," Greg argues, huffy. He looks so childish, Eva once again can't believe he's sixteen, a whole two years older than her.

"We're doing the nachos," Eva says more firmly.

"I don't understand why this—"

Finally, Frank steps in front of Greg. "Bro, you are so dense."

"What?" Greg asks, indignant. "What am I missing here?"

"Frank, no," Eva says quietly.

Frank rolls his shoulders as if working through the tension in them. "Javi. He's not here, right?"

Greg shakes his head, slow and unsure. Panic rises in Eva's chest. She doesn't know what Frank's going to say. He didn't even *want* to be here. He could give it all away and they'll get kicked out and she'll never get to do something right by Javi. Mom will enshrine him at home, and he'll be stuck there forever when he should be outside. Somewhere fun and bright and colorful where he loved to be.

Her hands ball into tight fists at her sides, but she can't step in just yet. She's too aware of how exposed they are as people walk by. A family exits the caterpillar ride, trying to step around them. They're too close. The mom asks her small son if he's feeling okay.

"And we're here to do things like we used to do with him." Frank's frustrated tone makes Greg take a couple of steps back.

"But we can still go on other rides, no?"

"Greg! We are—" Eva steps in between Greg and Frank just as the kid nearby turns in their direction and projectile vomits onto her.

Eva's frozen in place, brain stalling as she processes what's just happened. The smell hits her first, sour and putrid. Almost worse, it's followed closely by the sensation of warm, chunky liquid seeping through her shirt and onto her skin. Eva could scream but she's afraid to open her mouth and breathe more in.

"Oh, *gross*. I can't!" Hyun groans between retches.

"Oh my gosh! I'm so, so sorry." The mom says in shock. She doesn't pull the kid away in time and he lets out one more spurt of corn at Eva's feet.

"Control your hellspawn, lady!" CJ yells in Eva's defense.

"Napkins!" Clare is the first to spring into action. She pulls them out of her backpack and hands some to CJ. They wipe at Eva's jacket, getting the bigger chunks off.

"Do you have an exorcist?" Frank says unhelpfully.

"I think that's chili too," Hyun mutters, his voice stoppered as he breathes through his mouth.

The mom steps in to help, wiping at Eva's arms and hair.

Eva stays still, unable to move because the slightest shift makes her feel the vomit all the more. She's trying not to panic. She can't cause a scene. Attention is bad as Palchuck could come around that corner at any minute.

A tug at Eva's shoulder guides her eyes down. The mom wipes at a large, gross wet patch on the canvas of her messenger bag.

Dangerously close to Javi's ashes.

And something in Eva bursts, like torrential water through a failing dam.

She whips around to the kid and yells in his face. "Look what you did, you little shit!"

The kid squeals in fear, and his dad holds him close. The dad frowns indignantly, coming to his son's defense. "Hey, he didn't do it on purpose!"

Eva's fury refocuses on the dad. "You idiot! You pump your kid full of sugar, shake him up, and let him puke it out wherever? There's other people here! Think about someone but yourselves for once!"

The mom and dad gape at her, too flustered to react.

"Look at my bag! Look at it!" Eva holds it up, motioning to the wet spot.

"It'll come out!" The mom finally manages. "It's canvas. Throw it in the wash when you get home."

But Eva's too far gone to stop herself. "It's ruined! It could get to the stuff inside! It's going to stink all night! You're terrible parents!"

Clare takes hold of her and covers her mouth with a napkin.

They jostle as Eva fights her grip, practically kicking off the ground to get loose.

"Eva," Clare rasps against her ear in harsh warning. The shock of her breath over her skin stills Eva long enough to look where Clare motions.

Through the crowd, Eva locks eyes with Palchuck. The gruff older woman adjusts her security guard belt, eyes narrowing as if she's deciding whether she should interfere.

Eva's brain finally catches up. She's causing a scene. Drawing suspicion will only get them in trouble, exactly what she should be avoiding. Her jaw works, hands tight.

"Sorry," she mutters, doing her best to settle her breathing and let the spots in her vision dissipate.

The parents gather their sniffling child, all the while glaring at the gaggle of unruly teens.

The group falls into a strained silence.

"We're all good," Bless calls out to Palchuck, her meek voice barely audible.

Palchuck nods suspiciously. She points at her eyes, then points to the group with that *I'm watching you* gesture. At least she walks away.

Eva releases a harsh breath, squirms in her sneakers, and jabs a nail into her thumb's cuticle.

"What the hell, Eva?" Clare asks quietly, her eyes taking Eva in as if seeing a rude stranger she doesn't recognize.

Eva purses her lips into a line and bites into them, tensing every muscle. She has to hold it all in or she'll explode again.

CJ places a careful hand on Eva's arm. She leans forward and tilts her head, catching Eva's gaze. The gentle concern in her friend's face allows Eva to breathe, to unclench her fists.

"If we get you cleaned up, you'll feel better, yeah?" CJ asks with the softest voice.

Eva nods, glaring at the ground, ears hot and forehead sore with furious embarrassment.

"Everyone, we'll meet you at the usual spicy nachos stand, okay?" CJ says to the group.

They nod, though they all wait around, unsure who should lead the way.

"I still have my uniform shirt," Clare offers.

Eva feels like the absolute worst. She wants to ask Clare not to help, but her throat is all closed up. She has to choose between breathing or talking.

Without saying anything at all, Eva allows herself to be led away.

CHAPTER 6

6:02 p.m.

CJ AND CLARE BRING Eva to one of the regular stalled restrooms in one of the large marketplace buildings. Eva's grateful. She wouldn't have survived having to use a porta-potty sink for cleanup after all that. It's a big plus to have sinks with taps instead of having to pump the water out with your foot. And, most crucially, it offers far more privacy.

"Coming through!" CJ says as she pulls Eva past the line of women waiting for the toilet stalls. "Not cutting, just need to use the sink." The women grimace and cover their noses. Eva wishes the ground would open up and swallow her whole.

The three girls huddle at the very narrow bathroom counter. Clare's too close to Eva again, but it can't be helped in this space.

"Okay, what do you want me to—" CJ stops suddenly, then turns away and gags. "Ugh, sorry. I can't keep it together with the smell."

"CJ . . ." Eva pleads, lips quivering. She's not going to cry, not now, not over this. She may have lost her temper, but she's not going to cry in this bathroom.

"Right, sorry." CJ pulls the collar of her hoodie up over her nose and ties the strings around her head to keep it in place.

"Let me take—" Clare reaches for the messenger bag, but Eva jerks it away as if by instinct. She bangs her elbow on the wall and earns herself two frustrated looks.

"What is it with you and the bag?" Clare asks, exasperation clear in her voice. "Do you want help cleaning it or not?"

Eva glances at CJ, hoping for some help. She can't let go of the bag, not while Javi's inside. She brought him, and she has to carry him.

"Clare, could you go get more napkins?" CJ asks, her demeanor serious as she motions to the empty paper towel dispenser.

Clare lets out a huff, clearly aware she's being sent away. "Watch my stuff," she says as she drops her backpack by CJ's feet and heads back out of the bathroom. It's a little less stifling without her.

"Hey," CJ says. Her voice is so kind and understanding, like a mother trying to soothe an inconsolable child. It makes Eva want to cry again. "You'll have to give me the bag or give me your shirt if you want me to wash one of them.

Eva needs to take a deep inhale to steady herself, but she'd rather not breathe in her own smell right now. She nods, and lets her bag strap fall to her waist so she can place it on the sink. Without glancing around, not wanting to know if anyone's watching, she pulls the bomber jacket off, then her T-shirt. At least her sports bra offers some coverage while she's undressed from the waist up.

"Okay," CJ says, a calm hesitation in her voice as she takes the shirt and drops it into the sink. She rolls the sleeves of her hoodie up to her elbows, revealing a fine-point Sharpie drawing on her right arm, her tattoo practice she calls it. Whenever an old design fades, she draws the new image over it, which is why it currently looks like a realistic skull with a faded rose pattern underneath.

"So," CJ says, careful to avoid wetting too far up her arms even as she pumps a generous amount of hand soap onto the shirt. "Clare doesn't know what we're *really* here to do, does she?"

Eva swallows. "No," she admits through gritted teeth. Someone was bound to figure it out.

"Did you actually ever invite her tonight?" Even the way CJ asks this question carries the tone of someone older and wiser trying to guide Eva to an important lesson. She's only a few months older than Eva, but she'll never let her forget it.

Eva shakes her head no. She carefully takes each item out of her bag and places them onto the sink's beige laminate wood countertop. She gently runs Javi's water bottle under the tap to wash off some of the sick that got through the bag. It wobbles as she stands it on the counter, the large dent having distorted its base too much to remain stable. In front of the mirror it's always in her field of vision.

Eva scrubs harshly at the puke on her empty canvas bag.

"I thought it was weird you texted us all separately instead of in the group chat, but I didn't want to say anything." CJ's voice is quiet but clear. They don't look at each other as they take turns rubbing soapy fabric, rinsing, then repeating. Eva feels CJ's next statement coming by the way CJ sort of braces for it. "For like a year she was all you could talk about, and then you both finally—"

"I don't want—"

"You don't want to talk about it, I know." CJ finally looks at Eva, leaning in, a wet hand placed on top of hers. "And I haven't pushed you to. But there's a lot I don't understand, and the way you blow up sometimes . . ."

Eva turns away from her, wrings her bag out harder than she needs to. She already depends so much on CJ so how can she ask her to take on even more? To admit the dark thoughts she keeps secret. How she can't stop herself from blaming Clare for Javi's death because that's at least easier than blaming herself. To give those thoughts voice would be like exposing a deep, oozing gash to someone. You don't want to see them turn away in horror.

"Whatever happened between you and Clare after Javi's funeral . . ." CJ's tone is placid again. "She was Javi's best friend. It was wrong, not telling her we were coming tonight."

Eva shivers as the cold air combats the hot embarrassment that climbs up her skin. Being delicately reprimanded by her best friend while shirtless and stinky in a crowded county fair bathroom is not how she wanted to spend any of her time tonight. Or ever.

"It's complicated," Eva says, voice low.

"It always is," CJ responds, not missing a beat, like she's already been thinking it. "It sucks, but I know you know I'm right."

"I blew up at her after Javi's funeral," Eva blurts out. "Said some . . . terrible stuff to her. And with everything that happened right before . . ." She finally meets CJ's eyes, and the patience and understanding Eva finds there constricts her chest, almost stopping her from admitting the rest. But CJ's cleaning a strange kid's upchucked corn and chili from her shirt, so she owes CJ *something* at least. "I thought she wouldn't want to talk to me ever again."

CJ nods, with that look like she's about to give Eva one more push. A level of compassion that twists up Eva's chest. "You still should've told her. Let *her* make the decision if she didn't want to come."

She can't admit it, but that's what Eva feared the most about inviting Clare. Seeing her in person again felt too difficult to bear. And yet she didn't want to find out that Clare didn't want to see her every bit as much. That she also hated Eva enough to turn down spending tonight with the group for Javi's proper goodbye. It felt better not knowing.

Eva sighs, relenting. "You're right."

"I'm always right," CJ says with a cocky smile and a gentle

bump against her, lightening the mood somewhat. That's her superpower. She feeds you the bad and finds a way to make it easier to swallow.

"I just—" Eva stops when she sees Clare's reflection in the mirror step in behind her.

Clare's already large blue eyes widen when she sees Eva in her bra, then quickly dart away as she holds up a large bundle of napkins.

"Thanks," CJ says, taking about a third of the stack. She pauses just long enough to give Eva a pointed, eyebrow-raised look, with a slight head-tilt to Clare. "I'm going outside to wring your shirt out." There's something underneath her words that Eva's not quite catching.

"Here." CJ hands Clare the bomber jacket and leaves.

And that's how Eva ends up shirtless in a bathroom next to the first girl she's ever liked. Who kinda makes her hate herself, and who probably actually hates her, but who for some reason hasn't left her side yet, so . . .

Yeah. Complicated.

Clare gets right to work. That's always how she's been. Even in a tough situation, give Clare a task and she focuses all her efforts on completing it. They clean in silence for a few moments.

Eva sniffs the bag and smells only the generic hand soap. A good sign. She'll have to use it wet, but the canvas is sturdy at least. She sets it aside and gives her own chest and shoulders a quick wipe-down, grateful for the napkins.

Eva is so focused on her work she almost doesn't hear Clare's soft voice beside her. "He stopped talking to me first, you know."

The right thing would be for Eva to acknowledge that she knows that, to allow herself to finally talk about it. It had all been so messed up and tangled right before he died, they were all struggling to figure out what to do.

Say something.

Say. Something.

"Excuse me," someone says as they take up the other open sink. The space around Clare and Eva shrinks as they press closer together, side against side.

Their eyes meet in the mirror. Clare's gaze flashes to Eva's chest before she clears her throat and stares down at the jacket more intently. Eva's almost worried her jacket might end up threadbare by the end of all this. The slight dark red in Clare's cheeks sends a pang of awfulness through Eva's stomach.

"I'll get my work shirt out," Clare says, struggling in the tight space to angle down and access her backpack.

"I'm not an employee. Will I get in trouble if I wear it?" Eva blurts out, realizing at the way Clare stares up at her in confusion that it's a silly thing to worry about, especially with everything else going on tonight.

"Fine," Clare sighs, giving in. She turns her back to Eva and pulls the bottom hem of her shirt up her torso.

Eva lets out a nervous "eep" and turns her back to Clare. *Both* of them shirtless in a county fair bathroom was *definitely* not in her plans for tonight. A few scattered giggles come from the line of women waiting for the toilets.

"Here." Clare's T-shirt drapes over Eva's shoulder, and she's immediately flooded with the smells of cherry blossom lotion, fried corn dogs, and sweat. It's mortifying how her stomach twists and her ears burn as she pulls the shirt on. She has to remind herself this is better than having no shirt at all. It's so soft.

Holding her breath, Eva can't help wanting to turn back to look at Clare. Relief and an embarrassing feeling of missing out war in her chest as she sees Clare close the last button on her ugly multicolored work shirt. Despite how pretty Clare looks, Eva is glad she got the cartoon rock T-shirt.

There's too much going on inside her. She shakes her shoulders, pushing the emotions out all the way down to her hands, fingers flicking at an imaginary guitar pick. She's gotta tell Clare the plan for tonight. She can't stay quiet again. *Come on, this one's easier.*

"Right, okay." Eva nods, breathes out. Breathes back in. "Clare, you know we're here for Javi."

Clare blinks, eyebrows up in confusion. "Yeah."

"Well . . ." Eva gathers every last bit of courage she can muster. She can let Clare in, even just a little. She moves in closer, but Clare leans away and that reaction chips off a piece of Eva's heart. She manages to hold it together and continue. "We're here . . . *with* Javi."

Intense eyes squint into a frown as Clare gives her that sharp, scrutinizing look. A chill runs through Eva's skin.

"I don't— what?" Clare stutters, shaking her head. "You mean, like . . . in spirit?"

Eva tilts her head, motioning to the dinged water bottle on the counter. Clare's eyes flick between her and Javi's colorful metal container.

Clare's brows lift and eyes widen, posture straightening as, to Eva's relief, realization sets in. "Oh . . ." she whispers, not taking her eyes off the water bottle. "With Javi's . . ."

Eva shushes her and wrings out her bag over the sink, then quickly stuffs all her things back inside.

"How did your mom ever allow . . ."

"I didn't tell her, but I think she's already guessed. Or she's close to it." Eva's so focused on placing everything in the bag exactly as it was that she almost doesn't hear the sniffle that comes from next to her. She looks up in time to see Clare wipe at her eyes.

"Your jacket," Clare says as she hands the garment back to Eva, heavy from the water. The cool, damp fabric gives Eva goosebumps as she ties it around her waist.

They're silent as they finish up and leave the bathroom.

CJ stands outside the entrance, clearly waiting for them to have their time. She holds up a small plastic shopping bag when she sees them. "Your shirt's in here, damp but clean." She hands it to Eva. The wink she gives them confirms she orchestrated their time alone just now. As if she'd been at all subtle.

Doing what she does best, CJ gives her trademark, lopsided smile.

"Hey, it's not the county fair if you don't get someone else's vomit on you, right?" she laughs, halfway between forced and genuine. "Let's get back to the group."

CJ leads the way through the crowd with Eva in the middle and Clare behind her. It was strategic positioning on Eva's part. Her pounding heart needs a break from having to look at Clare and remembering the glimpse of torso as she pulled her shirt up.

The spicy nachos stand—aptly named "Nacho Average Nachos"—sits grouped among other food stalls that stand in clear challenge to the eater: Godzilla Turkey Legs, Pucker Up Pops, and the like. Each have their palette of bright, intense colors, vibrant reds and greens to make you think of something hellishly spicy or painfully sour.

On Hyun's first trip to the fair, food was all he had eyes for. Deep-fried butter, fried frog's legs, ramen tacos, donut-fried chicken sandwich. But when he saw the spicy nachos, he wouldn't stop daring everyone to try them with him. Unable to resist a challenge, Javi enthusiastically agreed, which surprised Eva. Puerto Ricans aren't known for their spicy food tolerance.

But that's who Javi was, a bit like a dog, easily excited by anything as long as you said it in a high-pitched and animated voice. He always wanted to know more, what you liked about it, what he needed to know to join in. It was as if he enjoyed the very act of liking things, and *what* you liked was actually secondary.

Eva breathes a sigh of relief when she sees their group surrounding a small table in the already crowded eating area.

"Hey! You're just in time!" Hyun says as soon as he notices them. "You ready for Mount Nachuvious?"

Taking up every inch of available surface on the table are an assortment of milk cartons, water bottles, and seven heaping baskets reminiscent of middle school volcano science projects. Instead of the usual yellow melted cheese, these nachos are fully coated in alarmingly dark red flakes, mysterious bright yellow sauces, and generous slices of dark colored peppers. The radioactive, acidic smells coming from the food make Eva cough and her eyes water. It's as if the food provides its own warning: *eat at your own peril.*

"I feel threatened." CJ can't seem to look away from the nachos.

Eva is not looking forward to this, especially as she doubts there'll be yet another shirt she could change into if there's a repeat of earlier.

"What are the rules?" Greg asks as he pinches his nose closed and pulls one of the baskets closer. They each pick a basket and settle in their spot.

Hyun counts out each rule on his fingers. "Eat the nachos as fast as you can. If you drink anything, you're out. First to finish or last one standing wins." He raises a fourth finger, then stops to think. "And that's all. Any questions?"

"How sick do you usually get the day after?" Clare asks, looking a little pale.

"Oh, you'll wish you had died. Now . . ." Hyun claps his hands and rubs them together. "Let's see who will survive Mount Nachuvious!"

"Nobody lives forever, right?" Frank mutters, head hung low as he glares at his basket of nachos.

Eva rolls her eyes. *Could he for once keep his asshole thoughts to himself?*

"Someone need a hug?" Bless jokingly chides Frank, elbowing him.

"Nope." Frank hunches deeper in his seat. "Let's eat the damn nachos or whatever."

Hyun falters, smile dimming. He stutters, takes a deep breath, and his big smile is back in place. "Uh, you heard the angry man. Eat!"

Hyun, CJ, and Greg dig in with exaggerated enthusiasm. Bless daintily tucks a napkin like a bib into her dress collar and starts on her own basket. Clare pinches her nose and shoves a chip in her mouth as if eating faster will make it easier.

Eva can't help the thought that this proves she brought everyone here just to torture them. At least she's being fair and doing it to herself too. She can't think too much about how that'll affect the group in the future if this is all she can bring them together for.

Eva goes right for a chip with a stack of peppers on top. Instantly her eyes water as her mouth explodes into hellfire that crawls both down her throat and up to her nose.

Frank stares at his pile a bit longer, then tentatively takes a half bite of nacho, only to spit it back out and rub his tongue with a napkin. "Nope," he says as he opens a milk carton and takes a big drink.

"Out!" Hyun yells with his mouth full and immediately chokes. Eva smacks his back a few times before he waves her away, laughing even with his nose already leaking.

"You okay?" She matches his smile.

"Yeah!" His voice is a little raspy as he shoves the next mouthful in. "Hurtf fo 'ood."

Just before she turns back to her food, Eva's eyes meet Clare's again. It's a short, disarming moment. The fire in her mouth and Clare's red face and tear-filled eyes are enough to distract her from every bad feeling that floods her whenever they look at each other. Do they just have amazing timing that they keep looking at each other at the exact same time, or is Clare watching her constantly? Could it mean she doesn't hate her, or is it the opposite, that she *super* hates her?

Stop that. Eat the nightmare nachos for your brother.

Eva tries to swallow her next bite without chewing too much, but it does nothing to lessen the pain. Despite the increasing discomfort, the entire group is into it, laughing, groaning, coughing, commentating ("This is like hot magma," CJ says. "And it'll be the same on the way out!" Greg responds,) and cheering each other on.

Eva realizes this is the biggest group that's ever participated in the spicy nachos challenge. There's a sudden sting in her eyes, though whether that's the emotions or the nachos she's not sure.

She doesn't wait to find out and would rather hide it, so she grabs for a milk carton.

Hyun gives her a look, asking *"Are you okay?"* And as soon as she nods yes, he gives her a wink, then clenches his hand into a fist with a short punch gesture. Like a baseball ref declaring her out of the running.

She nods, raising her hands in surrender, mostly glad it's over for her.

Even through the pain, the tears and snot rolling down his face, Hyun laughs like he's having the best time ever, and he could almost convince Eva that she is also. Maybe that's why Javi would put himself through all this. Doing something *with* someone brings you closer together. That made it worth doing, even through the torture of the spicy food.

Eva takes stock of the group as she finishes her drink. Greg seems to be out as Frank helps him clean out his eyes (he must've rubbed them with his hands, rookie mistake). Hyun laughs, then covers his mouth as if trying desperately to hold it all in, which makes Clare guffaw and bow out altogether. They both tap out.

Hyun sits back and Eva catches his eye. A quiet smile passes between them, funny in that they're both kind of gross-looking, covered as they are in snot and spicy dust. She can't help smiling even as her lips sting and her sinuses scream. Javi would've had a blast seeing everyone step out of their comfort zone together. He would've loved this. A perfect choice after all.

"Bless! CJ! Bless! CJ!" The chanting brings Eva back to the group. Amazingly, the two are the only ones left eating the nachos from hell. Eva hoots and claps, cheering them both on, and even some strangers sitting by their group join in. But a glance at their nacho trays instantly reveals there's no real contest here: CJ still has a quarter of hers left as Bless scoops up her last chip.

A loud cheer rings out as Bless holds up her empty paper tray like a trophy. The napkin bib hanging from her dress collar is coated in cheese and nacho dust.

"Sorry," she says with an apologetic look at Hyun.

"No, no, I'm glad you won. I think you're the first person ever to actually finish the basket!" That gets a round of laughter from the group.

The celebration lasts for only a few seconds before everyone quiets into small, pathetic groans as their focus returns to easing their spice-induced pain. Frank brings a few more water bottles and milk cartons for everyone, which surprises Eva. Oddly thoughtful.

"So what are we doing next?" Greg asks, blowing his nose into a napkin.

Wiping her hands, it dawns on Eva that it's time for the next step of the ritual. She won't be able to delay it a second time. Now she *really* wishes Greg wasn't here. This would be hard even without him, and, as is, she's utterly unprepared to deal with it.

"CJ," Eva says suddenly, startling her best friend. "Didn't you say you wanted, um, some Oreos?" She makes her eyes intense, hoping to convey what she needs from her.

"Oh yeah!" CJ nods slowly, as if locking onto her same wavelength. She claps a hand on Greg's shoulder and turns him around to face away from the group. "I *desperately* need something sweet after all this. Can you get me some deep-fried Oreos?"

Greg frowns at her in annoyance. "Why do you keep asking me to get you stuff?"

"Well, why don't you get yourself some, too?" CJ's amazing at misdirection, and she seals it by handing him a large bill. He's reluctant for a moment, then shrugs and walks off to the food stalls.

CJ waits until he's out of earshot. "Phew, okay. Now we can do the next part."

"Hang on, does Greg not know what we're doing?" Bless asks, shoulders stiff and eyes wide with growing panic.

"He wasn't really *supposed* to be here," Hyun answers, hands clasped together uneasily.

"Feels like you should've told him once you knew he was coming, though," Clare says with an accusatory look at Eva.

"Well, we didn't, so we're handling it, okay?" CJ says, defensive.

"What if he reports us when he finds out?" Bless's voice is rapidly approaching the kind of pitch only dogs can hear. "We could get in so much trouble. We could get arrested!"

Frank rubs a stiff but supportive hand on Bless's back. "We're not going to get arrested; this is a misdemeanor. *Maybe* light jail time, but more likely we'll just get fined and banned from the fair for life."

"Oh, is that all?" Bless responds with an exasperated, angry huff. It's never a good sign when she turns to sarcasm. But it's understandable—with security already suspicious, the thought is scary for all of them.

"Alright, alright," Eva steps in, holding her hands up, hoping to quiet the anxious rumblings. "We don't have a lot of time. Maybe we should, *you know*, get to it before he comes back?"

The group nods, even if some do so begrudgingly. Eva

tries to ignore the glare she gets from Bless, feeling smaller the more her eyes bore into her skull. She'll apologize later. She'll apologize for a lot.

"Ready?" Hyun asks. He holds a hand out to Eva and waits.

She hesitates. She's been preparing for this night for days, carefully planning and imagining how it would go. The idea is clear: each one gets to do something special they used to do with Javi, then say a few beautiful words, and scatter his ashes nearby. She thought she'd made peace with the idea of giving away parts of him, but facing the reality of it now, she finds herself struggling.

The mood was right moments ago, but now it all feels wrong. This spot is wrong; it's just dirt. There's trash on the ground and people all around them who don't even know Javi, don't know how great a brother he was. They don't know how he would give her half his tostones because they're her favorite, or how he scraped his arm catching her when she fell off her bike. They get to go on living their lives without realizing the void he left behind in hers. They're ruining this.

No. Eva snaps out of her spiral with a shake of her head. *She's* ruining this, freezing again with indecision. A few breaths in and out don't help her feel any better this time, but she can't afford to delay again.

"Alright, yeah," Eva says, forcing it out before anyone else can ask her if she's okay. It's almost mechanical, the way she has to move. These are not her arms opening the bag, not her hands grabbing the water bottle. She holds it out to Hyun a little too forcefully. He almost fumbles it, and the nachos threaten to make a reappearance up her throat.

Breathe. Calm. Breathe. Feel the electricity, guide it down the arms.

Hyun clears his throat as he carefully opens the bottle.

It looks wrong without the lid on.

Eva bites her lip. She runs a nail over the edge of the guitar pick then snaps it twice.

"Um, Javi," Hyun starts, voice unusually quiet as the group closes in around him, hiding him from view to any outsiders. "You were an amazing guy, and we all loved you. And that's why we're all here, I guess, 'cause we miss you. I remember the first pun you ever told me." He turns to the rest of the group. "Why were dinosaurs so big?"

"Because Jurassic times call for Jurassic measures," Clare finishes without hesitation.

Hyun nods, laughing, and all Eva can focus on is his hand holding the open sticker-covered water bottle and how there shouldn't be puns and laughter right now. It should be a solemn, emotional moment. These aren't the right words.

Hyun crouches low to the ground. "We love you, man." He tips the water bottle and the ashes spill out.

Eva balls her hands into fists to keep herself from stopping him.

A sudden gust of wind blows past them and picks up the ashes, blowing them past their legs as they step away to avoid them.

Eva's eyes widen and follow the ashy breeze as it weaves towards a young couple sitting at a table nearby. They grab hold of all their napkins as the wind passes them, carrying the ashes to their table. Blowing right onto their fresh basket of blazing red nachos.

"No," Clare breathes out.

"Maybe it blew past them and didn't get in their food?" Hyun asks meekly without conviction.

Eva's never seen Bless move so fast. One moment she's next to her, and the next she's at the couple's table knocking the basket of food out of their hands.

"What the hell?" the woman exclaims.

"So sorry," Bless says, voice quiet and squeaky. "I saw . . . there was . . ."

"We're very sorry," Clare says. Somehow she's already over there too. A blink, and so is the rest of the group, all rushing to help Bless.

Eva's lucky that Hyun hands her the water bottle and lid before he joins them. She makes sure to close it.

"There was this really scary bug, and it was flying—" CJ's voice penetrates Eva's mind like a wake-up call. "And this falcon swooped in and—*crunch*—ate it. The falcon ate the bug, not us. Which was gross, but hey, me when I see some cotton candy, right? So it wrestles this big bug, I mean eats it—" She's weaving one of her ridiculous lies. It's not that she's good at lying, per se. It's that she'll tell a story so confusing it lulls people into accepting it just to get out of the conversation.

They're here for Javi. She brought him here so they could put him somewhere special, somewhere he loved. Though he probably would've had a good laugh at someone almost eating his ashes too.

She wipes at her damp eyes, hands shaking, unable to look away from her friends all doing their best to clean up a mess that feels like her fault. Her brother's ashes are in those nachos and someone almost ate him and now they're on the ground and will likely go into the garbage along with other trash no one wants anymore. She leans on the wall behind her to steady herself, breathing as deeply as she can.

"Whoa, what happened?" Greg says as he joins the group at the couple's table, carrying a plate of deep-fried Oreos dusted with powdered sugar.

Clare takes the Oreos and offers them to the couple, apologizing profusely. The couple accepts them, though they seem much more interested in getting the group to leave them alone.

Soon, the group is back over where Eva stayed.

"I'm not getting more Oreos after that, CJ," Greg says, irritated. "You can get them yourself if you want."

"It's okay," CJ says to him with a nod to Eva. Handled.

"What was all that about anyway?" Greg asks.

CJ doesn't miss a beat. "This really big bug flew out, and—"

"Stop, stop, we're not doing this all night," Frank says suddenly. His deep, penetrating voice freezes everyone in place. He steps up to Greg with all of his high school senior authority. "Greg, we're here to say goodbye to Javi, so we're—"

"Don't—" CJ warns, but he ignores her.

"We're spreading his ashes around the fair." Frank's voice is clear and direct, though quiet enough for their group alone to hear. "That's what we were doing when the wind blew the ashes into those people's food, and then Bless had to stop them from eating it so she knocked their food to the ground."

Everyone has a different reaction to what he's said—a gasp, a flinch, or a glare.

"You're . . ." Greg starts, eyes twitching to each of them as he processes.

"Why are you such a jerk?" CJ squares up against Frank.

"You were really going to try to hide this from him all night?" Frank doesn't back off, wholly unfazed by CJ's intensity.

"We would've told him eventually!"

"*Eventually*. Great idea, brilliant plan."

"Better than blurting it all out like that! You ever heard of tact?" CJ looks like she's ready to shove Frank. Knowing CJ, it's probably due to her embarrassment at being called out.

Clare steps between them, prying them apart. "Stop, both of you." Her eyes catch Eva's, and she can't help feelling the stab of accusation in her glare again. Eva looks down at her sneakers instead, digging the toes into the dirt.

"Greg, you can leave if you'd rather not be a part of this," Clare says, a soft understanding to her voice.

Greg blinks, frowns, thinks through it. "Well, I already paid for my ticket. I don't want to leave."

"You can go on your own if you prefer not to be involved,"

Eva suggests. More than she wants to get rid of him, in this moment she feels bad for getting him caught up in all this.

Greg pauses long enough that everyone starts to shift uncomfortably.

"Naw, I don't want to be by myself," he says quietly. Again, he doesn't seem his sixteen years of age, somehow younger and smaller. Eva feels a twinge of guilt over having wished he weren't here.

A collective, soothing breath passes through the group, some of the tension floating away at Greg's acceptance. This should make things a little easier, Eva hopes, even as she tamps down the bit of guilt over lying to Greg.

Slowly all their attention shifts to her.

"Um, my turn, right?" Eva says, receiving nods as answers. "Bumper cars next."

They all quietly head in the direction of the ride.

"If they had eaten the ashy nachos . . ." Hyun speaks barely loud enough to be heard. "Would that have counted as cannibalism?"

CJ smacks him on the shoulders while Frank stifles a snort.

CHAPTER 7

6:31 p.m.

THE BUMPER CARS ARE farther into the Fun Zone, and the trek there takes them several minutes. Hyun continues his attempts to lighten the mood with jokes and puns, each one yielding diminishing returns. Weaving through the crowds as a large group does nothing to improve everyone's mood. Bless in particular keeps anxiously glancing around, which seems to add to everyone's nerves.

Eva hates this. The mood is all wrong. She should be feeling better, lighter. This should be getting *easier*, not harder. Why is nothing going according to plan?

She zips up her bomber jacket, a bit of the cold seeping in through the still-damp fabric. *It'll be okay*, she thinks with a decisive nod. There's plenty of time to fix this, to steer the ship in the right direction. She just needs to be clearer about how things should go. Tonight can still be the special night it's supposed to be.

"Here we are!" Eva says with forced enthusiasm as they arrive at the bumper cars. It's a large, flat, oval-shaped enclosed area with a rubber floor, like a skating rink but with colorful buggies whizzing and whirring across. The outside of the ride is decorated with maniacally smiling children riding cartoon-faced buggies. A black light accentuates the neon colors. The frenetic, upbeat music adds to the madness as riders laugh in glee and crash small rubber lined cars into each other. That chaos makes it a popular ride, so the waiting line is pretty full even at this time of night.

Loud shrieks pull Eva's focus. The Big Drop looms a short distance from them, the top of the tallest ride at the fair reaching far past the palm trees. Its current group of riders has been sent hurtling straight down from hundreds of feet in the air. Eva winces through a shiver. Every single year Javi would try to convince her to ride the Big Drop, but she's never gotten over her fear of heights. She likes the bumper cars, close to the ground but still fun. Despite his disappointment, he was always excited to ride something with her, any ride at all. He'd often add his own unhinged song to the rides as he chased her in his buggy.

A different sound startles Eva from her reminiscing. She hears a loud grumble beside her and turns to its source.

CJ hugs her stomach, an apologetic look on her face. "I think those nachos are plotting revenge."

"Oh no, are you gonna be okay?" Eva asks, growing more concerned with every disconcerting sound that comes from CJ's guts.

"Actually—" Hyun starts, only for his stomach to interrupt him with a similar growl.

"My eyes are still burning, honestly," Greg says, and sure enough, when Eva looks up at him, they're bloodshot and watery.

She studies the sad state of the group, trying to think of a solution. There's still a long wait ahead of them before they'll get their turn on the bumper cars. "I'm feeling alright. How about I hold the place in line, and everyone who needs to go to the bathroom can go?"

"Great!" Hyun doesn't wait for a group consensus before his long legs skip over the metal stanchions.

"I didn't get to use the toilet the last time we went, so . . ." Clare sidesteps through the line after Hyun.

"Just gonna get a tour of every bathroom this year, huh?" Frank says as he and the rest of the group walk away.

Eva takes a deep, calming breath, needing this moment alone. It's not like the fair is any less quiet without her friends (and Greg), but not having to manage the group offers its own level of peace. She has a moment to herself to prepare her reaction when it comes time to spread Javi's ashes. Soon she'll have to let more of him go, after this ride and the next. More and more as the night goes on. Leaving little pieces of him behind that could become memories, a part of somewhere special. Still, a part of her wants to hang on and keep as much of him as she can. Is that what her mom was feeling, wanting to keep him home?

"I hated that, you know."

Eva startles, turning to see Bless. Oh god. She didn't notice her stay behind; she's so *quiet*. Eva's neck and ears warm in embarrassment as if she'd been caught doing something shameful.

"You don't have to go to the bathroom?" Eva asks, doing her best to sound questioning rather than accusatory.

"Guts of steel." Bless shrugs, a little of that shyness sneaking back in and accentuating the lisp in her s's. "My family eats worse than that for breakfast."

Eva doesn't respond right away, allowing Bless the space to lead the conversation. She can smell it in the air, that she's about to be scolded.

"That wasn't fair for you to lie and hide your omissions from the group." Bless tucks her long black braids behind her ear, a sign of nerves despite her direct words. "I wouldn't have agreed to be a part of that."

Eva swallows the lump in her throat. Being scolded by adults—that much, she's used to. But getting it from another teenager, even an older one, sparks an even hotter shame, and a stronger determination to defy it. To reject the accusation. She crosses her arms. "Well, you didn't *have* to knock those people's food out of their hands."

"Yes, I did, and I'm not talking about that," Bless says as she steps closer to Eva, keeping her voice low so no one catches their conversation. "I'm talking about lying to Greg."

Eva wants to roll her eyes, but she has a feeling that this conversation would be made harder. Bless and her whole good Christian girl thing. You didn't have to believe for her to make you feel bad.

"It's not like I planned it," Eva says.

"Planned or not, you made me a part of your lie. And everyone else who didn't know."

Eva keeps her stiff scowl. "Look, I panicked. I made the best choice I could think of."

"We're all in this together, right? I know you and I aren't as close, and things might be different next year and all that. But you still need to take our feelings into account. I already had to compromise my morals, you know, coming here to do something illegal."

"Semi-illegal."

"Illegal is still a word in it. We're all taking a risk, and, yeah, we made that choice." The next time the line moves, Bless steps a little closer to Eva. "But I can't stand being made a party to someone's lie."

Embarrassment heats Eva's cheeks, even though she knows Bless is right.

"I'm sorry," Eva says, meaning it as much as one can while knowing she wouldn't change what she did.

Bless's eyes are serious, seeming to measure her. "Anything else you've lied about?"

Eva's jaw works, as if reluctant to let out her next words. "I never actually invited Clare tonight." That's all she'll share. She doesn't have to elaborate on the *why*.

Thankfully, Bless doesn't prod. She only hums pensively, twisting the hems of her long cardigan sleeves around her fingers. "I don't know everything that's going on between you two, so I won't speak to it. But thank you for admitting it."

Eva blinks, realizing that Clare must not have told anyone about their fight at Javi's funeral. About how shitty a person Eva really is.

"You've never talked to me like that before," Eva says, hoping to add some levity.

"We've never really talked before, period." Bless' frown shrinks as she smiles slightly. "I have a lot to say when I think something's wrong. Javi knew that. That's why we first became friends."

Eva's eyebrows raise in surprise as her lips quirk into a smile. "Did you ever call Javi out like that?"

"Oh yeah, all the time," Bless replies with a small laugh, posture relaxing as she walks next to Eva when the line moves again. "Didn't he tell you how we met?"

"He said you helped him with his calculus homework."

"He tried to cheat off me during a quiz first." Bless's shoulders shake with laughter at Eva's wide eyes, and she lightly taps Eva's chin with a finger, as if picking her jaw up off the ground for her.

"Javi cheated?"

"I said he *tried*. I didn't let him. And then I said I'd tutor him if he promised to never cheat again."

"Wow. He never told me all that."

"He was embarrassed, I bet. He had that good boy image. And he felt so bad." Bless lets out a fond laugh. "Probably why he agreed to help out at my church's fundraisers."

Eva grows quiet, processing this new information. It doesn't fit with the idea of the Javi she knew. But Bless wouldn't really have a reason to lie about something like this. Eva's hand rests over the bump of the large water bottle in her bag.

If this is a clearer picture of Javi, what else is she missing? What else did he share with others but not with her?

The group returns at that moment, each one stepping past others in line to meet back up with Eva and Bless. They look revitalized, weaving into the crowd with higher spirits and joining in with idle chatter. Frank offers a bundle of cotton candy to Bless.

"Your prize for winning the nacho contest," Frank says, tone flat even as he waves it in the air in celebration.

"Oo, thank you!" Bless says, taking it eagerly.

"Can I have—?" Greg barely finishes the question before the rest of the group shouts a resounding "No!"

Amid the rekindled jovial spirit, Eva watches Clare out of the corner of her eye. She wants to ask why she hasn't told anyone about what happened, why she hasn't pulled back the mask of how terrible Eva can be. They wouldn't want to talk to her ever again, and she'd get what she deserves. Eva feels her heart thump as Clare notices her watching and meets her eyes. For a moment, Eva worries Clare can read her mind. It wouldn't surprise her. If anyone could, it would be Clare.

As always, Eva's the first to look away.

More settled now, they wait in line patiently, moving along with the flow, sharing little jokes, commiserating about their aching stomachs. They're a few groups away when the music suddenly stops. Everyone looks around in confusion when a monotone voice comes on over the loudspeakers.

"Due to mechanical issues, the bumper cars ride is now temporarily closed."

Eva looks for the announcer.

"You're welcome to wait in the line while our technicians figure out what's wrong, but, uh, good luck with that."

"Oh my god," Hyun groans next to Eva.

She follows his gaze and sees, at the operator station, Kevin speaking into the announcement microphone.

"Sorry, I guess," Kevin says, voice as flat as ever. "Please enjoy any of the other marvelous rides the fair has to offer."

"Do they make clones or is it just one guy running this whole fair?" CJ lifts her arms in frustration.

"What the hell, Kevin?" Hyun cups his hands around his mouth, calling out loudly. "We've been waiting here like forty minutes!"

Kevin sees their group and tilts his head with an eyebrow raised. He speaks into the microphone and motions to the group with a two-finger salute. "The ride broke down to mess with those kids specifically."

"You're the worst!" Hyun yells back.

"That guy's hilarious." Frank's laughter is somehow genuine.

Eva can't help shooting Frank a glare. Is he trying to rile her up again by having the opposite reaction to everyone else?

Other patrons grumble around them, some leaving right away, others hovering in line. Little kids whine as parents try to placate them.

Their group idles, unsure whether to leave or take their chances waiting. Eva glances at her phone screen, careful to angle it so Clare can't see her lock screen image. It's 6:49 p.m. already. They have just over four hours before the fair closes and leaves until next year, and this could be a big time sink.

Nearby, frightened gasps ring out as another batch of riders are slowly brought up to the full height of the Big Drop. Eva observes the contraption: a ring of seats that leave the rider's arms and legs exposed and flailing, moving up a huge neon-lit pillar to stop about two-hundred feet in the air. The ride pauses, many of the riders wriggling and squealing already. The thought crosses her mind that they could get in line for The Big Drop ride. It's right there and she never got to ride it with Javi. Will never get to, now . . .

Then the riders scream their heads off as they drop straight down. Eva shudders, a cold chill spreading through her. *Nope nope nope. Never mind.*

Eva tries to look anywhere but at the ride, her eyes of course landing on Clare, who isn't even trying to hide her laugh at Eva's expense. She even looks like she's holding back some particularly incisive bit of ribbing.

The worst was when she and Javi would gang up against Eva, both teasing her to join them in something out of her comfort zone. As much as Eva misses that normalcy, she feels it would break her right now. This time, thankfully, Clare doesn't say anything, and the moment passes.

"Are we waiting, then?" CJ asks. It takes a moment for Eva to realize she's talking to her.

"We could go out of order." Clare suggests. "Go to whoever's next and then keep checking for when the bumper cars open up again?"

"Or is there a different ride you want to do, Eva?" Greg suggests.

They're waiting for Eva's answer, looking at her with anxious eyes, making her shift uneasily in place. She has to decide for everyone?

"Or, does waiting in the ride's line count?" Hyun says, his voice a little desperate. "We were *almost* there. Could that be enough?"

Eva frowns. "Of course not."

"What if the bumper cars don't come back all night?" Bless asks. "Wouldn't it be safer to do the ceremony now, so you don't miss your chance?"

"I mean, I guess that makes sense . . ." Eva mumbles, unsure, feeling pressured by all the suggestions. If she takes her opportunity now, she could say her words to Javi like she's been practicing, and maybe that will show everyone how they should do theirs, so they don't make the same mistake Hyun did. What he said was nice and all, but it didn't *resonate*. They should all be taking this seriously. It's to honor Javi, after all.

"Your call, Eva," CJ says, nudging her. She offers a smile, attentive, the kind that lets Eva know she'll have her back no matter what she chooses. It eases her worries slightly, as CJ usually does.

"Y-yeah, I guess . . . let's do it," Eva says, a nod to strengthen her resolve.

The group steps out of line and moves to the side, close to a cluster of trash cans by the ride's exit gate. They have to start picking better spots for this, but at least most patrons in line have left by now, and the ride operators are too focused on fixing it to notice the group.

A reverent silence falls around Eva as she opens her bag and carefully reaches in. All eyes are on the dented, chaotically stickered water bottle. This feels a bit better—she could do this with the proper attention and recognition. She slowly unscrews the cap with trembling hands and holds the bottle out, careful not to tilt or spill any until she's ready.

"Javi, you are—were . . ." Eva starts, gathering her words, embarrassed at slipping up already. "You were the best brother, and—"

"Hey!" The booming voice cuts through the ceremonious air, startling everyone. Eva jolts and the tiniest bit of ashes shake out of the water bottle. She stares at the spill, eyes wide, trying to calm her nerves and steady her breath.

The group turns to see Palchuck marching toward them like a tank ready for battle. Unstoppable and frightening.

Eva freezes, open water bottle still held up.

"Palchuck!" CJ takes a clear step forward, trying to engage Palchuck in conversation in an attempt to stop her before she gets too close to the group. "What's up?"

"We've received some *complaints*," Palchuck says with her gruff, authoritative voice.

"Oh, well, don't worry about it too much. I'm sure you're doing the best job you can. But what does that have to do with us?"

Palchuck's stern expression deepens, accentuating her wrinkled forehead. Then she sighs in exasperation, already tired of all this. "We heard from a family who got into a screaming match with a group of seven teenagers, and a couple who had their food knocked right out of their hands, also by a group of, fancy that, seven teenagers."

Bless lets out a small "eep," and Frank takes a casual half step in front of her.

"That doesn't sound like us, does it? There's plenty of other groups of seven teenagers at the fair," CJ says, feigning confusion. "In fact, do you even verify if these people know how to count?" She turns to the group, giving everyone a "*come on, back me up*" look.

Eva wants to join in, act casual, but she's paralyzed with anxiety and indecision. Should she stay as she is? Close the water bottle and put it away? Would that draw attention? Is it better to hope Palchuck doesn't see it? Shit, she's already breathing weird.

Palchuck sighs harshly, placing her hands on her chunky belt. "I know you're all . . ." She frowns, looking for the word. Her eyes grow a bit softer. "Going through something. But don't think just because of that I'm going to let you get away with bad behavior this year." She points at each of them. "Trouble is trouble, and you lot bring it everywhere."

CJ shrugs, shoulders coming up much higher than they should. "Us? No, we're cool. We're hanging. No trouble here."

Palchuck purses her lips, patience clearly expired. "Please, be considerate of others. Don't mess with people. That's all I ask."

Eva almost feels relief as Palchuck turns away, only to have the feeling snatched away as the bulldog of a security officer does a double take.

Then Palchuck's eyes focus right at Eva and the water bottle in her outstretched hand. "Why are you all huddled back here?"

"We were taking a breather. Talking about what ride to do next is all!" Hyun says quickly. He makes an attempt at CJ's convincing nonchalance, but it comes out much too fast and shrill.

Eva's still frozen. *Do something dammit. Move!*

"It's important to stay hydrated," Eva says, speech slow and a bit flat.

This does nothing to assuage Palchuck's suspicion. She takes a step forward—oh god, any closer and she could look inside the bottle.

Eva's body acts before her brain can think through reason. She brings the open water bottle to her lips, and tips it back just slightly as if to take a sip. She holds her breath—can't let herself inhale or exhale.

Pulled by gravity and the tipping motion, the ashes inside the water bottle inch closer to her lips. Eva stiffens, trying very hard not to externally show how much she's freaking out.

This is way harder with everyone staring.

Focus. Focus. Slow. Nothing's wrong. You're a normal person drinking normal water.

Eva works her throat to pretend a swallow, lips clamped shut against the bottle's metal opening.

Then she rights the water bottle and replaces the cap, wiping at her lips as if she has taken a real drink.

"Refreshing." Eva forces it out, sounding like she's in a tacky soda commercial.

"Okay . . ." Palchuck says, her frown more puzzled than suspicious now. "You didn't have to maintain eye contact the whole time."

Acting natural doesn't seem to be a part of Eva's abilities. All she can do is stand still with the water bottle and hope Palchuck leaves.

"What do you have in that?"

Eva can only watch as Palchuck's large hand reaches for Javi's water bottle. Her beefy hand seems to move in slow motion, chunky watch rattling like an alarm. Her round sausage fingers are about to brush against the water bottle.

"We love pixie sticks," Greg blurts out, stepping next to Eva. "We mix all the flavors together and enjoy them throughout the night."

Palchuck's face contorts into a look of pure disgust, and she recoils. "And you *share* it?"

CJ steps in also. "Palchuck, ma'am, while we honestly love our chats, we wouldn't want to keep you from your very important duties. I'm sure you've got other people to annoy– I mean, assist."

"I know you're up to something," Palchuck shoots back, voice serious. She looks at each of the teens in turn, gaze lingering on Eva as she slowly twists the lid back onto the water bottle. Thankfully, she's already turning away from them. "I'm watching you."

With that, Palchuck leaves the group to their tense silence.

Once she's out of earshot, Hyun is the first to breathe out, the gasp turning into a laugh. CJ joins in. Then the entire group dissolves into giggles as they release their collective stress.

"You didn't—" Clare asks.

"Almost!" Eva answers, her laugh coming out a bit manic.

"Would *that* have counted as canniba—" Hyun begins, but CJ smacks him before he can finish.

"Wowee!" Greg says, with a celebratory fist pump.

"I really, really hated that," Bless says, fingers massaging at her temples, shoulders shaking along with her giggles.

"We have *got* to be more careful," CJ says. "Someone has to keep watch."

"Eva." Clare's voice pulls her attention. Suddenly she's much too close for comfort, her tone soft while everyone else chatters around them. "I think we should wait until the bumper cars are back up and running, yeah?" There's concern in her gaze, and Eva doesn't want to look too deep into it.

Eva pushes down the instinct to argue and nods instead. A quick glance at the bumper cars confirms the ride's still down, with no solution in sight. "Yeah, I'll wait."

The anxious laughter around them dies down as they all focus on tonight's purpose.

"Frank next?" Eva asks and the group nods.

All except Frank, who shrugs.

"Whatever," he says, and walks off without waiting for anyone.

CHAPTER 8

7:15 p.m.

FRANK ISN'T A FAST walker, but despite the roundness of his torso he has a surprisingly long gait. He walks on without glancing back to make sure they're able to keep up with him. Eva's still tense from their interaction with Palchuck, which irritates her due to his lack of concern for everyone else. They're a big group weaving through a dense, suffocating crowd. If he's leading the way, he should at least make sure he hasn't lost anyone.

Eva grips her messenger bag strap tightly, wringing the rough texture against her palms and hoping that focusing on it will calm her nerves. That was too close. They've only done one ride and eaten some nachos and Palchuck almost caught them already. They're going to have to be so much more careful now that she's received complaints and noticed Eva acting really freaking weird with the water bottle. Any small step out of line might get them noticed, and—

Hyun bumps her hip, shaking her out of her thoughts. He smiles down at her, wide and silly. Eva winces, knowing that smile means he's about to try something big to cheer her up.

She's keyed up, doesn't feel ready for it.

"Here we go, here we go!" Hyun chants as the group follows Frank, extending his last cry as he cups his hands around his mouth. "Here! We! Gooo!" Though begrudging, Eva can't help but crack a smile at his silliness even as she glances around in case Palchuck is near.

"I didn't quite hear you. Are we going?" Frank mutters, hands shoved into his pockets, thick eyebrows low on his forehead in his signature scowl.

Hyun grins at him, crouches, then jumps and yells even louder, "LESGO!" His spectacle is made all the worse when CJ joins the chorus, yelling and bounce-dancing around both boys, blond, messy bun whipping every which way.

"Okay, you're going overboard," Eva says, but she's smiling even as she nods apologetically at the nearby patrons.

"Remember, we're not the only ones here," Bless says quietly, voice squeaking from behind the rest. Eva appreciates that at least *someone* in their group cares about going unnoticed. They shouldn't be attracting attention like this, even if it is improving the mood.

"You're going *down*, my man!" Hyun taunts, prodding and pushing at Frank's shoulders. "I've been practicing!"

Despite everything—Javi's death and the fracture it caused in their group—Hyun always manages to stay upbeat and positive. Eva finds it admirable, even if a part of her is jealous that he can do that while she struggles to feel anything but guilt or anger.

Eva's lost in her thoughts when Hyun jostles Frank into her and sends her stumbling.

Strong hands grab her shoulders and keep her from falling. She turns to see Clare next to her, one arm practically wrapped around her.

Clare smiles thinly, then lets her hands drop. Eva tries not to mourn their absence.

"He's lying, of course; he hasn't practiced anything," CJ says, reaching up to drape her arm across Hyun's shoulders to wrangle him in. "But you have to admire his confidence."

"I do not," Frank says unenthusiastically.

They walk up to the skee-ball Horse Racing carnival game, crowding around the three players already there. The stall has a brightly colored blue frame with cartoon racehorses painted along the sides and top. Eight flat horse and jockey figures line up on a wavy track that goes from right to left. The current players sit at short skee-ball stalls, each labeled with a number corresponding to a horse.

"That's right, folks!" the animated worker calls out loudly, charming the small crowd in her black polo shirt as her twin braids bounce with her exaggerated movements. "Move your horse along the track by getting your ball into the numbered holes, the higher the number the faster your horse moves! First one to the end of the track wins a grand prize, easy as that! My name is Trisha, talk to me if you want to be part of the next race!"

Their group of seven is hard to miss as they mill about the stall. She turns to them. "Are you all ready to test your skills at the next race?"

Eva leans across the railing toward Trisha and speaks loudly to be heard over the noise and music. "Yes, but could we please wait so we can sit all eight—" She catches herself, feels her throat close up for a moment, and has to swallow through the lump. She pushes through and finishes the question, voice quieter, "—sorry, seven of us?"

Trisha counts them. "Sure, just wait for this race to finish and I'll get your group seated." She catches the eye of another person walking by. "Hey, you want to be the eighth player? Get a full bracket?"

"Actually!" CJ calls out, waving the passerby away. She pulls out a five-dollar bill and holds it up to Trisha. "We want it to be our only our group playing the next race." CJ wiggles her eyebrows as if she's offering a tantalizing bribe.

Trisha looks at CJ, then at the offered bill. "Sure, kid," she says as she takes the money. Despite Trisha's lack of enthusiasm, CJ pumps her arm like she's won them a big victory.

Eva turns to her, concerned. "You didn't have to do that. You're kinda throwing a lot of money around tonight—"

"Hey, it's okay," CJ answers with a smile. "This is for you and Javi. It should be just us anyway. What if some weirdo skee-ball horse racing expert comes in and kicks our asses? That would totally suck."

Eva looks at her friend with an appreciative smile. Even when she's at her worst, somehow CJ knows how to be the best. "It would, yeah."

Returning the smile with a knowing wink, CJ calls out to the group: "We're the next race!"

Waiting for their turn is the hard part. Hyun and CJ stretch, Greg tries to imitate them but instantly hurts himself, and Clare has to intervene to help him. Bless comments on Frank's bad posture, but he ignores them all to sink deeper into his hoodie.

It's not too much longer before one of the players wins and Trisha hands them a prize: a Squishmallow the size of a large dog. They approach the seats, and Trisha scans each of their ticket cards. Hyun and CJ muscle and jab at each other, both fighting for the number four spot. Everyone else takes up their numbers randomly, with Eva settling into number seven. She carefully, almost ceremoniously, places her messenger bag on the empty number eight spot.

As the group settles, someone calls out to Trisha from the back of the booth. Nerves and confusion swirl in Eva as she watches her step away from the game.

Eva's anxiety increases as Kevin—*oh no, not him*—walks through the back curtain wall, tucking a black polo into his baggy cargo pants.

Kevin says something to Trisha who shrugs, nods, then

points to the group. He takes her microphone and card scanner, then steps up to take Trisha's previous spot in the stall.

"Everyone ready for an incredible race?" he asks in his deadpan tone. He seems absolutely unsurprised to see them all seated and ready to play.

Eva frowns. Is it paranoid if she's starting to suspect he's out to get them somehow? But why?

"We have one more seat if anyone wants to join—" Kevin starts, but CJ stands up quickly to interrupt him.

"Hey hey!" she yells, trying to drown him out. "I paid five extra bucks to keep that seat open."

Kevin looks at her, eyes half-lidded in his yawning uninterest. He checks the card scan machine. "I count here enough scans for seven players."

"I gave it to the other operator!"

Kevin makes a halfhearted show of glancing around. "Well, it's just me here now."

"This is bullshit!" CJ fumes. "You absolute, annoying little—" Hyun stands up to his full six-foot height, bristling in solidarity.

He hypes her up with his own, "Mess him up, CJ."

A small chorus of "No, don't mess him up" comes from Clare, Greg, and Bless.

Another kid approaches the open seat.

Kevin turns to the newcomer, ignoring their complaints. "You playing?"

"No!" This time Eva jumps in, placing a hand on her bag before anyone can touch it. The kid looks at the scene in confusion, then steps away, hands raised in a clear *I'm not getting involved in this* motion. Eva's chest tightens, but she manages to breathe better the farther away the kid gets.

"Kevin, CJ already paid to keep that seat open," Clare speaks up, using her best rational adult voice.

"I count seven card scans and no five-dollar bills in my hand."

"Can you call Trisha back?" Clare asks through gritted teeth.

“That asshole took my five dollars!” CJ is so livid her voice comes out a squeal, like a teakettle boiling over.

Kevin stares at Clare with his eyebrows slightly raised. He has the smallest smirk on his lips. Eva is sure he’ll get the crap kicked out of him someday. Maybe soon, maybe by them if she’s lucky. But not right now while they still need him to operate this game.

Maybe the easiest thing would be to give in and stop arguing. If someone else joins, whatever. Nothing’s gone as planned anyway, so why would this?

Clare sighs. “Anyone have anything to give him?” she asks as she turns to the rest of them.

“Hey, don’t look at me,” Hyun says, raising his hands up. “I sacrificed my lemonade last time.”

“I’m a bit hungry after that lemonade, actually,” Kevin says, his voice aggravatingly monotone as he smacks his lips. “Something sweet and moist would really hit the spot.”

CJ and Hyun shoot him a murderous glare. Even Bless looks at him, completely grossed out.

Everyone lays out the contents of their pockets and bags on the booth stall: various loose pieces of gum, some change, a pocket Bible, a couple of rocks (“Shut up,” Frank says. “They’re cool rocks”), and various flavors of lip balm.

“Should we . . .” Eva says, thinking aloud as she looks through everything. “Go buy something?”

Greg sighs loudly, then pulls out a Ziploc bag from the pocket of his cargo pants. “I have a PB&J.”

He holds the sandwich out to Kevin, who thinks about it, then nods. Greg tosses it at him, and Kevin has to juggle to keep from dropping it.

Eva’s nails flick at her guitar pick. This is costing them so much time.

Kevin is unperturbed as he opens the sandwich and eats half of it in two bites.

The rest of them pick up their loose belongings.

"I'll take a rock, too," Kevin says through his mouthful.

"What? Why?" Frank asks, frowning in bafflement.

Kevin shrugs. "It's cool."

Frank presses his lips into a line as he gathers all of his precious rocks.

"Give him a rock, Frank," Hyun hisses through his teeth. "We all have to make sacrifices."

With a grunt Frank slams one beige-and-brown speckled rock back on the game counter and Kevin takes it. He looks at it with one eye closed, as if inspecting a precious jewel.

"I hope you choke on that sandwich," Frank mutters.

Kevin stops, makes a gagging sound, clutches his chest.

Hyun's eyes grow wide in momentary panic, glancing between Kevin and Frank. "Are you a witch? Are those cursed?"

But then Kevin stops, gives Frank a two-finger salute as he chews and resets the horse track.

CJ leans over to Eva and whispers, "Do you also get a *he does that 'cause he likes you* kinda vibe from Kevin and Frank?"

"Oh, *please* no, that's just wrong," Eva mutters as her phone buzzes and she instinctively looks at the screen.

The little hairs on the back of Eva's neck stand on end. It's a message from her mom. A voice mail this time.

She swallows, her anxious thoughts warring, telling her to delete it—no, to listen to it right away. The phone won't transcribe a preview of the voice mail, meaning it's probably in Spanish. She'll keep obsessing over it if she doesn't check. She holds the phone to her ear, and Mayra's voice roars through the recording: "¿¡Donde *carajo* están las cenizas de Javi?! Si te las llevaste al puto county fair ese—"

Eva deletes the voice mail. Her chest is heavy, constricting, that unstoppable wave of pressure bearing down on her. She lets one hand free to flex, open and close, releasing the energy through the movements of her fingers. She practically bends the guitar pick from pressing into it with her thumb. Well, at least now she knows for sure her mom's realized Javi's ashes are gone.

Don't freak out. She does some quick math timing. It would still take her mom at least an hour to get all the way out here, and then she'd have to park, walk to the entrance, go through security . . . All the more reason to focus on getting this night done right in the time they have.

"Okay!" Kevin calls out flatly, spraying out bits of PB&J with the words. Gross. "Get ready to race."

Each teen sits back at their chosen skee-ball track. Despite the unforeseen obstacle, they exchange smiles, a sense of excitement growing among them.

"Giddyup," Kevin says as he presses a button. A bell rings out loudly, and upbeat western music with hoofbeats and horse neighs plays. A single skee-ball plops out of each of their stations.

As soon as the race starts, CJ and Hyun shove and get in each other's way as much as they actually play. Clare and Bless opt for the more slow and focused approach, aiming carefully for those higher numbers. It occurs to Eva they should've given Greg some quick tips and tricks about skee-ball, given how lost he looks until he realizes what everyone else is doing.

Eva notices Frank toward the end of the row and frowns. He's hunched in his seat, rolling his skee-ball between his hands, leaning back as he watches the board of racing horses. Maybe this is some kind of odd strategy of his, or he's waiting for a moment to jump in and smoke everyone. Or maybe he's being his usual Frank self, stubbornly refusing to do anything he's told to do. Eva tries to focus on her game, but can't keep herself from glancing back at him from time to time. At no point does he make any attempt to play the game, even when everyone's horses reach the midpoint of the track.

"Frank," she calls out to him, missing her next throw. "You playing?

"Sure."

Annoying. He's so annoying.

He's been complaining all night, moping about not wanting to be here. What is even the point if he's going to keep ruining the night for her? And for everyone else, of course. This is supposed to be a special night. A goodbye, a memorial. Something beautiful they can all think back on after this tragedy. Who knows when they'll all be able to spend time together like this again.

"You're gonna lose," Eva says, a tense attempt at a competitive prod.

Frank's shrug makes her angrier.

"Watch out, Eva, you're not doing much better!" Hyun says, reaching as close to the higher numbers as he can before rolling his ball.

Eva ignores Hyun, pointedly looking past the group between them to stare at Frank. "You're not going to play? Really?"

Frank returns her glare. "I already said I don't want to be here." He places the ball down and leans back to cross his arms.

"Then why don't you leave?" Eva grits out. Oh no, she's doing it again. Unable to keep her words in. This is for Javi, not her. He'd want Frank here.

Stop that, stop, stop.

"I'd *like* to! You've got us all trapped here," Frank says, his mouth in a disgusted sneer.

"What? I haven't trapped anyone!"

"Well, if we didn't come tonight, *we're* the assholes, right?" Frank turns in his seat to face her. "Trying to re-create something without him is not going to be like it was, and you need to accept that!" His words seem rehearsed, like he's been holding them in for a while.

"Re-create—I'm trying to give us all a moment to say goodbye to him!"

"We already said goodbye. That's what the funeral was for!"

Eva frowns, stands to face Frank head on and yell at him over the heads of their friends. "Some of us needed more. Some of us wanted to do it how Javi would've wanted!"

"He's dead, Eva! He doesn't want *anything.*"

A gasp ripples through the group. The cartoony western music and sound effects continue, but no one's playing now.

"Hey, chill out," Hyun says, standing to place a hand on Frank.

But Frank doesn't stop. "You just want to wallow so you have to drag the rest of us down with you. Sad little sister needs someone to pat her on the shoulder and notice how sad she is. You want to make sure everyone knows you miss him the most, yeah? Well, you've proved it. You won the Sadness Contest. Congratulations!"

"Stop!" CJ yells in Frank's face, pushing his shoulders back. "Don't talk to her like that!"

"Don't push him!" Bless says, voice quiet but firm.

Eva breathes hard, hands clutching at the strap of her bag over her heart. Frank's words jab her like needles.

"Settle, settle," Kevin's monotone voice sounds through the chaos. "There's no fighting in fake horse racing." He sounds like someone who's not surprised a fight would break out. Is it the game or is it their group? Or both?

"You're such an asshole!" Eva yells, towering over Frank only because he's still sitting.

"So are you. Should we start a club?"

"We're doing this for Javi, to remember him and all that he means to us."

"Meant. *Meant* to us. And *are* you?"

"We are!" Eva can't stop from stomping her feet, and waving her fists. Every word from Frank's mouth feels like a gut punch. It's easy to sharpen and direct every negative feeling from tonight right at him. The worry and disappointment at their goodbye speeches. The shocking revelation from Bless that Javi tried to cheat off her.

Frank's the reason it's all been going wrong.

Eva slams a hand down, fully pressing into his space. "You'd rather forget who he was to you?"

"Sometimes!" Frank yells and stands up, then stops, eyes growing wide at his own admission. He stumbles a half-step back. Eva stills from his silent and shocked expression, his answer finally registering.

The rest of the group glances around, stunned.

Frank's confession hangs between them, as if no one is sure what to do about it. Then Frank shakes his head and kicks at the ground. Eva sees his face twist as he turns away from them, the display of ugly vulnerability tucked away quickly.

"Frank—" Eva says.

"Shut up," Frank interrupts. He sits back in his chair, sinks further into his hoodie. "Let's finish the stupid race." He rolls the ball up the skee-ball track and easily sinks it into the highest value hole.

No one else sits back down. They all watch him play by himself, throwing the ball with inhuman precision and sinking it into the high-value numbers. His hands tremble between throws, and he pulls his hoodie up as if trying to wrap himself back up in his strong outer shell.

Bless places a hand on his shoulder. Eva expects him to flinch away, but instead he stops and leans back into her touch. He breathes hard, sniffles a couple of times, wipes his face.

"We're not playing anymore then?" he asks, voice shaking as he turns to the group.

They all hover in place, some shrugging feebly. It doesn't feel right.

"Let's just do it." Frank stands and walks off.

"H-hey," Kevin calls after him, his stutter a bit surprising. "The race isn't done."

The glare Bless shoots at Kevin jolts and silences him.

The group hesitates a moment, exchanging glances, then follow Frank.

He actually picks a good spot, up against the back fence wall between the stalls. It's tucked away, not an area many would casually venture into and not close to trash or bathrooms.

Without a word, he holds a hand out towards Eva, asking for the ashes. His tense jawline and deeply furrowed brow make her all the more reluctant to give him anything.

"I thought you said this was all stupid and you didn't want to do it?" she asks.

Frank exhales roughly. "You want me to do it or not?"

Unsure, Eva reaches into her bag and carefully takes the water bottle out. She doesn't want to hand him the bottle and risk him spilling it all at once out of spite. She doesn't honestly think that he would, but she'll always worry about the worst-case scenario. To be safe, she uses the lid as a cup to pour some ashes into, then carefully hands over the cup to Frank.

Frank looks down at the cup of gray dust, silent, lips thin. He wipes at his nose and eyes with his sleeve, then nods, cementing a decision. He holds the cup up like giving a toast.

"Javi." Frank's voice is ragged, as if saying the words out loud pains him. "You're dead so you're not going to actually hear any of this." Bless clears her throat in warning, but he ignores her. "And now I'm supposed to pretend to talk to you so. . ."

Eva glares at the ground. *Dammit.* It's going to be wrong again. She digs the guitar pick under her nail so hard she has to hold back a flinch of pain.

"You were a really good point guard, and sometimes even a good friend." Frank's deep monotone feels like nails on a chalkboard.

Buzz. Eva pulls her phone out of her pocket to silence it, but sees the screen. A call made it through. It's her mom. Her chest seizes up, the tightness of every muscle revolting against this moment, against Frank and all his anger that's supposed to be just hers. Like all she risked will have been for nothing.

He continues. "You kinda sucked at making arroz con salchichas, though, so it's a good thing I'll never have to eat one of your—"

"That's enough," Eva says, voice rough. "Stop– stop saying that. What's wrong with you?"

Frank glares at her, the heat of his gaze burning holes through her. His hand shakes as it tightens around the cup. He starts to tip it, and Eva panics.

"You're doing it wrong!" She grabs his wrist. Some ashes spill and billow out from the rough movement. "Take it back and say something else, something better!"

"You're gonna get it all over you if you don't let go," Frank threatens.

"Not 'it'—him! It's him!"

"But it's *not* him anymore." His mocking laughter is a punch and squeeze to her chest.

They struggle, pulling and pushing, trying to gain sole control of the cup.

"Hey, careful!" Bless steps in and grabs the open water bottle. Eva lets it go without much thought, all her focus on Frank and his stunt.

Clare tries to intervene. "Let's take a step back, okay?"

"Do it right!" Eva yells at Frank.

"I am!"

"No, you're not! How dare you talk about him like that?!"

Strong, gentle arms wrap around Eva's waist, smelling of cherry blossom hand moisturizer. But Eva refuses to back down.

"I'm being honest!" Frank growls at her.

"You can be honest without being a jerk! Like, how about thanking him for bringing us together, or everything he did for everyone!"

He pulls away suddenly, spilling ashes that balloon delicately in the air like a gray cloud before dissipating into the breeze. They slip past her fingers, leave her knuckles dusty and dry.

Eva tries to grab Frank, but Clare's strong arms keep her away.

The rest of the group takes a step back from them.

"Fine. You want me to thank him? I'll thank him." Frank drags his furious scowl from Eva to the cup in his hand. "Thank you, Javi, for finally kissing me just before you went and fucking died."

What?

Eva stops fighting, tries to process.

What did he just say?

"Shit," Hyun says, a shocked breathing out of words.

Frank tips the cup.

A sudden bright light shines onto his hand as the gray ashes drop, the finer granules puffing out around their feet.

"Hey!" A deep female voice calls out.

Eva turns, eyes adjusting to the brightness.

Palchuck stomps across the walkway, shoulders squared and flashlight in hand. "What was that? What did you drop?"

A cold shiver runs up Eva's spine; a small animal caught in a hunter's sights.

She saw everything.

Palchuck's long, running strides will reach them in no time at all.

"SCATTER!!!" CJ yells.

Chaos erupts as everyone runs in different directions.

Everyone except Eva. Her legs won't move.

She tries to see where everyone's going but can't keep track.

She's going to collapse; she's going to crumble.

Clare hauls Eva farther into the small alley between the stalls.

As Eva watches their friends disappear, she realizes her messenger bag is much lighter than it's been all night.

She doesn't have Javi.

CHAPTER 9

five weeks ago

MORNINGS WHEN EVA HAD nothing planned were her favorite. Mayra had already left for some early errands, so there was no one to stop Eva from putting too many spoonfuls of sugar in her Special K cereal. She'd sat down to watch a documentary about an obscure marathon in Tennessee that most people don't even finish when Javi yelled a quick "goodbye" on his way out the door.

"Where are you—" is all she managed to say through her mouthful before he disappeared.

She frowned, processing what she saw. Had Javi been wearing a shirt with sleeves? But it was summertime. Suns out, guns out time, as he called it. He never wore sleeves. And had he straightened his hair?

Weird.

Anyways. With the whole day and house to herself, Eva finished the documentary, then spent the next few hours in her room working on her scale transitions and fingerpicking.

Then she heard the front door open and close loudly.

She held her guitar strings quiet and listened to the

thumping footsteps running through the house. Javi came into view barely long enough for her to see him run into his room and slam his door closed.

Weird, again. Eva's brow furrowed at the unusual behavior. He usually came into her room to chat after getting home. It was as much a part of his routine as taking his shoes off and putting them away.

Javi only ever shut himself in his room when something was wrong.

Eva, wanting to be sensitive, waited a few more minutes before walking up to Javi's door.

Their house wasn't fancy: old, well-worn carpet in the hallway and bedrooms with flat, unfancy doors. Still, inexpensive came with the perk of Mom allowing them to decorate their own doors however they wanted. Eva couldn't commit to anything, but Javi's door was covered with stickers. He had snarky bumper stickers, random local businesses, and energy drink brands. Her favorites were stickers of every National Parks he'd visited. Some parks even had multiple stickers, each one marking the number of times he'd been. Joshua Tree had the most stickers.

"Javi?" She knocked on his door, but he didn't answer. It was so quiet she wondered if she'd actually seen him run in there.

This was all too odd. Eva was the moody one, not Javi. He was known for his golden smile and booming chest-laugh. He was the one who usually knocked on her door until she let him in so he could drag her from her bad mood and into the brightness of the day.

She knocked softly again, unsure but not wanting to leave if Javi needed her.

This time a muffled, shaky voice answered from inside. "Come in."

Eva let out a relieved breath before turning the doorknob.

Javi was curled on his unmade bed staring at the wall, bed sheets cocooning around him. His room was the kind of messy of someone who never sat still: clothes and sporting equipment strewn about, half-finished projects on every surface, desk, dresser, window sill. Incomplete Lego sets scattered around the room with the instructions laid on top of them because they were taking too long to complete and he would get back to them later anyway.

"What happened?" Eva's voice didn't sound soft enough to her. Too much worry had crept in.

Javi sniffled into his pillow.

Eva decided to wait. He'd at least let her in, which was a good sign. She pushed a pile of pillows off the corner of the bed and sat. She was always good at waiting quietly.

"I went to Clare's." Javi's voice was muffled.

That fact in itself wasn't odd to Eva. They were both constantly at each other's places.

Eva waited.

"I told her . . ." His voice was so small, like he wanted to crush it into his pillow. Eva's mind raced with that bit of information, attempting to guess where he was going with this and dreading that she already knew.

She placed a gentle hand on his shoulder to encourage him, but also to stabilize herself.

"I told Clare that I like her." He said it so slowly, like it took all his energy and focus.

A lump formed in Eva's throat. That's why he'd dressed that way and done his hair. He'd chosen today to confess his feelings for Clare. She should've paid more attention, and then maybe she wouldn't feel so blindsided.

So she could prepare herself for how their group dynamic would change.

Obviously, it hadn't gone well. Her heart twisted for him, seeing him like this. Yet she couldn't help her desperate need to know every detail of what happened. Not for his sake but for hers.

"What did she say?"

Javi huffed so loud and long it turned into a groan. He shrugged a few times, then forcefully sat up. His hair stuck out, draping over his ears and eyes. He hadn't scheduled his haircut yet.

"She doesn't feel the same way," he croaked out. "About me."

New feelings pushed out Eva's jealousy and worry. First confusion, then anger and indignation on Javi's behalf.

How could Clare not like Javi back? Javi was the best person Eva had ever known, and that was even with all his teasing and pranks. He was thoughtful and funny, and everyone liked him. How could Clare not return his feelings? How could she say no? They'd spent almost every day together since they met. They shared almost every hobby, got into rock climbing at the same time even.

"She said she loves me, but not *that way.*" Javi's voice pulled her from her spiraling thoughts.

Eva hated seeing Javi like this. She wanted to help, to make him stop crying. "Well, that's a good thing. She still wants to be friends, right?"

Javi groaned and shoved his pillow over his head.

"Sorry." Eva apologized, not sure why.

Did this mean their friendship was over? Would she have to stop hanging out with Clare, too? A part of her wanted to in solidarity with Javi. That bigger, ugly part of her wondered if she'd have Clare all to herself now.

Ugh, no, she was being the worst sister ever.

In truth, she didn't want anything to change. They couldn't avoid Clare forever. They'd see her around eventually, likely at school. Different grades, but not like she was completely avoidable. Unless Clare moved away. Would she move over this? New fears circled around her thoughts at possibly losing Clare forever. Why did Javi have to go and say anything? Eva had feelings for Clare, and she wasn't going around telling anyone but CJ about them.

"This is the wooooorst," Javi grumbled under his pillow.

"It's not!" Eva's optimism felt overdone even to her. "You've been friends for years. You don't throw it away like this. Aren't you going rock climbing together tomorrow? I doubt she'd skip out on that since it's, like, both your favorite thing."

"I don't want to see her right now. I doubt she wants to see me." He sniffled and rubbed at his nose again.

Eva had to stop thinking about herself and needed to think about Javi instead. He'd done something brave and admitted his feelings to the girl he liked. He'd put himself out there, and this was probably the worst outcome he'd expected. Despite all her feelings for Clare and the conflicting churn of relief and sadness at all this, Eva was still angry on Javi's behalf.

How could someone, even someone as amazing as Clare, reject him? How dare she break his heart like this?

"Did she say why?"

"I kind of stopped listening after she told me she didn't like me back."

"So she didn't give any reason at all?"

Javi pulled the pillow off his face, messing up his hair even more. "She said she already likes someone else."

The kindling of anger that had begun to heat up Eva's chest flared up instantly. A new kind of roaring jealousy fueled it. She'd never even thought there could be someone *else*.

Clare spent any time she wasn't at school, work, or home with the Vargas kids. How would she have time to hang with someone else, let alone grow to like him?

It had to be someone from Clare's work, maybe that weirdly handsome new dishwasher guy who never shut up about his sneaker collection. Oooh. Eva always thought he had the most punchable face. Is that what Clare was into? Wow, there's no accounting for bad taste.

Without another word, Eva stood.

"Where are you going?" Javi's big, watery eyes followed her to his door.

"She was at her house, yeah?"

"Eva, what are you thinking?

"Don't worry about it," Eva said, leaving Javi's room.

Eva was furious. She'd had enough time to think about everything during her bike ride to Clare's house and she wasn't angry, cross, or miffed. She was absolutely, unquestionably furious. She'd thought through scenarios of what she'd say or do. She was ready, practically bouncing on her toes like a boxer prepared for the fight of their career, led by the forward momentum of her righteous fury.

And she was bringing all of it to Clare.

She barreled through the side gate and into Clare's house's backyard. The gate slammed loudly against the side of the house, momentarily startling Eva out of her rampage. She hoped that wouldn't upset Clare's dad.

Ugh, focus. She stamped her feet a few times, restarting her fury. She was hot under her bomber jacket and pulled it off roughly.

Clare sat right where Eva had expected her to be: under the small lemon tree where they often spent summer days.

The gate noise had obviously announced her presence, and Clare was already looking back at her in confusion. There was no turning back now.

Eva wrung her jacket between her hands and stomped across the yard to Clare.

"You rejected him?" The accusation burst out of Eva's mouth in a flurry. She gave Clare a moment to respond, give some kind of explanation or apology.

Instead, Clare blinked up at her with her stupidly pretty

blue eyes. They now looked almost golden in the setting sun. The blotchy redness around them did nothing to diminish their shine. She'd clearly been crying.

"W—what?" Clare asked with a small sniffle.

Eva balled her hands into fists, clinging onto her righteous rage. "Javi!"

"Oh." Clare hugged her knees to her chest. "Is he okay?"

"Is he *okay*?" Eva mocked.

"Yeah, is he okay?" Annoyance crept into Clare's tone and she frowned.

Eva tilted her head in accusation, resting her hands on her hips. She realized too late it was the same pose her mother used when she was angry. She tossed her jacket at Clare's feet.

"*Is* he okay?" Eva exaggerated her words to get her meaning across.

Clare's frown deepened into a scowl, and Eva's umbrage waned slightly.

"Why are you repeating what I say like that?" The irritation in Clare's voice was clearer now. She wiped her palm across her cheek, smudging the mascara streaks running down her face.

"I—I was . . ." Eva stammered, the fight draining from her at the puffy redness around Clare's upset eyes.

No, she needed to stay strong. Clare broke Javi's heart, and Eva was angry about that. She was on her brother's side, and so she would resist the upsetting urge to sit next to Clare and wrap her arms around her in comfort. Clare rejected Eva's amazing, kind brother. For someone else, worst of all.

"You broke him!" Eva surprised herself with how high-pitched her voice came out.

"Broke him?" Clare leant forward, challenging.

"You broke his heart!"

"He's the one who had to go and make things awkward." Clare stood, picking up Eva's bomber jacket and tossing it at her chest, which Eva fumbled. She towered over Eva, puffy hair adding to her stature.

Eva tried not to let it intimidate her into backing down. "He told you how he felt and you—you were supposed to—"

Clare's eyes narrowed, and she took a slow step closer to Eva. "I was supposed to what?"

"He's your best friend." Eva shrank back, words shaking in reaction to the heat of Clare's anger aimed back at her. She didn't back down, though. "And you reached into his chest, ripped out his heart, and stomped on it."

Clare's breaths came out harder as her outrage grew to match Eva's. She rested a hand on her hip, lifting the other and letting it fall and smack against her side in exasperation. "Is that what he told you?"

"He's too nice to say that's what you did, but I know him." Eva's voice quieted, remembering Javi upset and crying. "You really hurt him."

Clare took another firm step closer to her, but Eva refused to give up any more ground.

"He hurt me too," Clare was so close Eva felt her breath on her own cheeks. "And I can't believe he would send you to argue for his, what, his honor?"

"He didn't send me!" Eva was too riled up, her jacket felt like a furnace in her hands. "I came by myself on his behalf." She threw the jacket away.

Clare managed to catch it by the sleeve, as if some sporting instinct took over and she couldn't let it fall to the grass.

"Eva." Clare sighed, fingers rubbing at her temples. An attempt at calming down, though the anger roiling under the surface was palpable. "What did Javi tell you?"

Eva swallowed, preparing herself. "He said he told you how he feels and you said you didn't feel the same. Which is ridiculous; you do everything together! You've been friends for years! You should—"

"I like someone else," Clare interrupted, bomber jacket

bunched in her hands, and Eva swallowed her words. "Did he tell you I said that?"

The words felt like a shove. They deflated the rest of Eva's outrage, replaced again by worry and that growing, inconvenient jealousy.

"Yeah, but that doesn't make any sense. Like who else are you hanging out with? You're always at our place or we're at yours." Eva had to ask. "Is it that new guy from the restaurant?"

"That guy sucks." Clare's immediate response further knocked over Eva's carefully constructed reasoning.

"Well, then," Eva stammered, struggled to reignite her indignation, a lighter that keeps flicking but won't spark. "Who?"

Clare huffed but there was amusement along with exasperation. She hugged herself and turned away, pulling her shoulders up as if fighting a cold breeze despite the warm afternoon.

She liked someone.

Clare liked someone and it wasn't Javi and it wasn't dishwasher guy.

"Who is it then?" Eva repeated in her quietest tone, looking down at her shoes. She wasn't sure she wanted to actually know, but mostly not sure she could live with the uncertainty.

The answer could very well destroy her.

They were silent for several moments. Enough time passed where Eva couldn't keep looking away.

So she glanced up.

Clare looked at her with the guiltiest expression Eva had ever seen. Her cheeks were even redder now, tears gathered at the corners of her long lashes. She looked scared, but Eva couldn't imagine of what.

Nothing was connecting for Eva. "Who—?"

Clare stepped into Eva's space, hands awkwardly pressing the jacket between them, and kissed her.

Everything stopped all at once.

The smell of cherry blossoms fully encircled Eva as Clare pressed soft, tentative lips against hers. Her skin was warm from the sun, lips a little chapped from biting them. The jacket between them bunched awkwardly, but neither one of them seemed to mind working around it. Eva was thankful for the rough, thick fabric. It felt grounding somehow, like she might float away without it.

So this was what it was like to kiss Clare Morris.

Clare pressed more firmly into the kiss, and her height made Eva tilt her head back. Clare moved a hand to Eva's shoulder, and the contact melted her from the outside in like chocolate in a warm palm.

If anyone was going to claim her first kiss, Eva was glad it had been Clare. It was the kind of kiss that could make her forget how this would further break her brother's heart.

They pulled apart and Eva kept her eyes closed, trying to commit the sound their lips made into permanent memory.

"Did that answer your question?" Clare's voice was shaky and quiet, barely above a whisper.

Eva nodded, eyes still closed.

"You gonna open your eyes?" Clare asked.

Eva shook her head no, and Clare's laughter was like chimes dancing in a soft breeze.

"Why not?" Clare's voice sounded closer again.

"What if I wake up?"

"From what?"

"This dream."

"I could pinch you."

"Okay."

Instead, Clare's thumb touched the corner of Eva's mouth before it brushed across her cheek. Eva managed to open her eyes.

Clare's smile grew like a sunflower, bright and encircled by the warm setting sunlight. That single dimple on Clare's left cheek was the most beautiful thing Eva had ever seen.

"Me?" It was a pathetic question, but Eva needed to make sure. Needed certainty.

Clare's nod was answer enough, setting her heart thudding in her chest.

And that was all Eva needed to become the worst sister in the world.

She wrapped her jacket around Clare's shoulders and pulled her brother's crush closer so she could give Clare her second kiss.

CHAPTER 10

7:31 p.m.

JAVI'S GONE.

His water bottle is gone.

Eva doesn't even remember who has it. And it's missing its lid. She's pretty sure Frank still had it when they all separated.

Frank. She's going to punch him the next time she sees him. This is his fault. His stupid mood and his angry dramatics. He was probably lying about kissing Javi to get a rise out of her. Javi never told her he liked boys. And if he did . . . Frank? Really?

She shivers and gags at the intrusive mental image of them making out. Clare carrying her with her arms wrapped tight around her stomach is definitely making it worse.

"Urp, let me down," Eva says with a warning, lips tense and closed.

"If I do, can you keep up?" Clare takes a very sharp turn just then, and Eva's vision jitters. Best to close her eyes, cover her mouth, and trust that Clare knows what she's doing.

She immediately loses that trust when Eva finds herself shoved into a very small, cramped space. They sound like a falling stack of books as Clare forces both of them into a two-person photo booth and presses in just enough to close the curtain.

"What the h—?"

Clare's hand covers Eva's mouth and shushes her firmly. They stay still and quiet, listening, trying without success to calm their ragged breaths after their escape. Are those running footsteps coming towards them? Will Palchuck pull back the curtain any moment now? She couldn't be faster than Clare, even carrying Eva.

"I think we lost her," Clare whispers, her breaths brushing at Eva's bangs as she turns.

Their eyes meet, and she's so close Eva can count her freckles and the flecks of brown in her dark blue eyes. She's suddenly very aware of how small this space is. Their chests still heave, and their sweat makes the space humid while their breathing makes the air stuffy. Eva's half on the seat, half off, short legs spread and knees bumping against the photo-taking console. Clare stands between Eva's thighs, knee on the seat to keep herself from falling too far forward.

Almost like she noticed at the same time, Clare clears her throat, murmurs a "sorry," and gives Eva the space to sit up. Their knees brush as they adjust, Clare lifting her legs one at a time to let Eva swivel her knees forward. Eva's bigger, rounder thighs take up most of the seat.

Clare's eyes dart around, as if unsure what to do.

"You can sit," Eva says quietly, squeezing as much of herself against the wall as she can.

They adjust enough to share the seat, but can't avoid their legs pressing together. Only a month ago this would've been Eva's dream scenario, trapped in a small space with Clare. Today, it's practically suffocating.

The photo booth's screen flashes as it takes a picture. It must be in demo mode as the screen displays a sample picture of the both of them. Clare's face isn't visible yet. The camera caught her as she was turning to sit. But Eva's brows are furrowed into the deepest frown, face red all the way down to her neck. She hadn't realized how deep her frown could go. She's grateful when the demo mode deletes it and moves on to an animated little bird showing you how to pose for your pictures.

The curtain doesn't reach all the way to the ground, but it's hot enough for them to feel like they're in a fully enclosed room. Eva is trapped both by Clare's presence and the threat that Palchuck might be right outside looking for them. She doesn't have enough space to reach for her guitar pick. Her fingers press against her pocket instead, looking for the hard plastic shape through the fabric. She fights off some of the oncoming anxiety by tracing the outline of the guitar pick with her thumb and pointer fingers. It's something.

"We'll give it a few minutes, and then I'll check, okay?" Clare's kindness twists a sickness into Eva's stomach. She nods, looks at the smiling, dancing bird as it holds up a camera, ready to take another demo picture of them.

It's quieter in here, the regular sounds of the fairgrounds muffled by the thick fabric of the curtain. And yet Eva's all the more aware of each noise, every loud stomping run that passes them. Her skin's on edge, whether by nerves or worry, or this unbearable closeness to Clare.

How could it all go so wrong so quickly? Not that anything has really gone right. She even tripped and fell before she made it into the park. She planned this whole evening and then she couldn't go through with it. She should've let Frank say whatever he was going to say and get it over with. It's not going to be the perfect goodbye night she had pictured. Nothing she ever does is perfect anyway.

All they have to do is wait it out. First, stay hidden and don't get caught. Second, get the group back together. Hope someone has Javi's ashes and is keeping him safe. Third, punch Frank's lights out. The humorous thought doesn't keep her growing worry at bay.

"Javi . . ." is all Eva can croak out, glancing at Clare, hoping she understands what she means to ask.

"I think Bless has him."

Eva releases her breath all at once as partial relief sets in. That's good. If his ashes had to be with someone else, she's glad he's with Bless. She can trust her to keep him safe. One worry somewhat abated, now time to move onto others.

"Did you see if Palchuck caught anyone?"

Clare shakes her head. "I'm not sure. Everyone ran in different directions."

They're all separated now, six friends (and Greg) scattered around a congested, busy maze of a fair with bad cell service. Hopefully they all escaped Palchuck and can find their way to each other again without using up too much more of their limited time. Hopefully no one's just alone and they paired up the way Eva and Clare are.

Oh.

Right.

She's alone with Clare.

Despite the growing mustiness of their breaths sticking to this small space, a shiver runs down Eva's back as their situation settles over her. The bigger group helped her avoid too much one-on-one time with Clare. Now that it's the two of them, there's nothing to put between them. The adrenaline from their run has now fully dissipated and been replaced by the discomfort and tension that have permeated them since Javi's funeral.

The rising tide of anxiety in Eva's chest makes her want to run again. She can't be alone with Clare. She'll say her mean thoughts out loud, push her away again. Her nervous energy bottles up, making her hairs stand on end. She wants to bounce her knee, but if she does she'll rub her thigh against Clare's. *Calm down, don't freak out.* This isn't life or death, just a one-on-one conversation with her . . . With her brother's best friend and the girl they both had a crush on.

The beautiful girl who somehow picked her instead of him and ruined everything.

Eva adjusts, ignoring the brush of their limbs so she can pull her cell phone out. Her mom's missed calls blare at her along with the time: 7:40 p.m.

"You could've picked a new picture," Clare mutters next to her, voice so close Eva jolts slightly. She's leaning into her space a bit, eyes on Eva's phone, on the lockscreen picture of her, Javi, and Clare, except she cropped Clare out as much as she could.

Cheeks and ears running hot, Eva knows it was a childish thing to do. It fixes nothing, addresses nothing. But in her moment of pettiness it made her feel a little bit better when she needed whatever she could get. She never meant for Clare to see it.

Clearing her throat in embarrassment and having nothing to say, Eva carefully dismisses her mother's missed calls without tapping to call her back. Who knows if it would even go through. Cell phone signal always suffers the busier the fair gets. Still, she needs to hope. She types out a quick "*is everyone alright?*" text anyway and watches as it hangs and her few bars struggle to send the message. They'll find each other. They have to.

Flash! The photobooth screen slowly develops the new demo picture it just took. It's the two of them, Eva slouched and glaring into her phone as if it has insulted her. Next to her, Clare has her shoulders pinched together as her wide shoulders fit into the booth. Her face is turned, looking at Eva with her lips pouted and eyebrows together in a concerned frown. Eva's throat stings at the realization that this is now Clare's usual expression when she looks at her.

It silences her thoughts, the sick feeling in her stomach that Clare is probably better off having never met her. Everyone is.

Eva glances back at Clare. She wants to say something. As always, she isn't sure what. *Thank you for carrying me even though I'm a dead weight* doesn't seem appropriate, but neither does anything else. Saying "*please don't touch me again*" might break both of them.

"Hey . . ." Clare says quietly, and Eva can only stare at her shoes, pretending to still be busy with her phone. "Can we—"

"I texted everyone, and hopefully it goes out," Eva says as she squeezes her phone between her hands. She has to stand up, to go. She tries to push herself up, with no plan how she's going to get around Clare, but she has to go. "If we're careful, we can—"

"Wait." Clare's hand reaches out. With the sudden movement, it catches Eva in the throat.

"*Hugnh!*" The hit knocks Eva's breath out.

Clare flinches and looks immediately contrite. "Sorry, I didn't mean . . . I thought I heard running."

Eva falls back onto the seat, crumpled up against the plastic wall as she struggles to regain the ability to speak.

Clare makes an unrecognizable sound. Eva can feel Clare's shoulders hitching and shaking next to her. Was that a sob? Is she crying?

No. She's laughing.

Flash! On the screen she can see Clare's head thrown back, hair pillowing around her face, mouth open and bright teeth on display as she laughs. Her own face looks at her with a deep, confused frown. Clare cackles even louder when she sees it.

"Sorry, sorry," Clare says, wiping at her eyes with the collar of her shirt. "That sound you made when I—." A giggle fit stops her words. "When I hit you." She covers her mouth, trying to stifle the uncontrollable laughter. Then imitates a jolt and surprised face and makes the same *hngugh* sound Eva made moments ago.

"It wasn't *that* funny." Eva tries very hard not to smile. Clare's laughter was always contagious.

"This whole night has been against you, hasn't it?" Clare wipes more tears from her eyes. "You got puked on. Some kid keeps asking us for food. Someone almost *ate* Javi. Twice! And you were one of them!"

Eva bursts out laughing finally, then quickly covers her mouth to minimize the noise. "Karma's seriously coming for me." They can't control it now, their manic laughter multiplying—that sort of slouch to your knees, hang onto the wall, onto each other kind of laugh. The way that laughing too hard makes you lose all ability to hold yourself up properly. It's a little drunk, a little unhinged. Like so much tension finally boiling over and releasing.

"Palchuck's like a bulldog that can hunt," Eva says. She tries so hard not to love Clare's squeal of laughter.

"She is!"

"You think she's been following us all night?"

"Probably! She's been everywhere."

"You think she figured out what Frank was dropping?" The question, the mention of Frank, causes their laughter to fade, a reminder of what tonight is. That someone now knows what they're really here to do and could potentially stop them. That Eva no longer has Javi and they don't know where their friends are.

Everything about tonight has been so bizarre.

"Did you know . . ." Eva finds herself asking. Clare's silence makes her nervous for the answer. "About Javi and Frank?"

"I knew Frank liked Javi for years." Clare says it like she shouldn't be sharing someone else's story.

"How'd you know?"

Clare shrugs. "A feeling. He glared at me a lot, seemed kinda jealous that Javi and I were so close."

"Really?"

"That's why I stayed away when they had games. But that's just what I gathered. I didn't know about anything else."

"Oh."

One more thing she didn't know about her brother. Didn't he like Clare? Was kissing Frank about something else? It seems like such a cruel thing to do, if so. Nothing at all like the kind of thing the Javi she knew would do. Or the kind of thing she used to think Javi wouldn't do. And when would it have even happened? Was Frank even telling the truth?

Eva clears her throat, straightens. "We should get going."

Clare nods, clenching her jaw like when she's trying to hide her real feelings. She doesn't move, doesn't seem ready to leave yet. The mood's shifted and Eva feels a chilly, heavy weight in the pit of her stomach.

Clare turns to face Eva and their knees knock together.

"He was your brother, but he was also my best friend." Clare's voice is quiet. Eva flinches and cowers at that word: *was*. She can't run, not with the way she's pinned. The way Clare's eyes bore into her, sticking her in place, a twisting shiver climbing up her nerves.

"The worst thing . . ." Clare's breath shakes, as if continuing a conversation she's been having with herself for a long while ". . . was losing both of you at the same time. You didn't have to do that on top of . . ." Her voice breaks, quieter. "*He* stopped talking to me and *he* decided to go climbing without telling me."

"I'm not—" Eva starts, but her throat seizes almost immediately. "I'm so—"

"Shit." Clare's voice is so small as she pulls the collar of her shirt up and buries her face inside it, shoulders heaving and sobbing breaths coming quickly. "I hate that you didn't tell me you were doing this tonight." Her voice is muffled under neon striped fabric. "I'm not ready."

Eva leans her head against the back wall, her bangs the only thing that can hide her. Her pants pocket must be starting to fray where she's been scratching at her guitar pick.

She's not going to survive this, not if it's just her and Clare. Not if she keeps making the same mistakes over and over.

Her jaw hurts from gritting her teeth, a vise grip that seems the only thing keeping her words in place. She has to breathe through it, push to get out what she wants to say. What she knows can at least be the beginning to fixing any of this.

"I'm sorry," she grits quietly through her teeth, like she's dragging the words out of herself, pulling them painfully and cutting up her insides on their way out.

Clare looks at her, incredulous, lets out a scoff. "Mean it the next time you say it."

Eva grunts, turning her face away. She deserves that, which doesn't hurt any less.

Minutes crawl by, and all they can do is breathe enough to make it through.

"We have to get everyone back together." Clare's the first to break the silence.

Eva looks at her phone, sees the notification that her message didn't send. "I don't think anyone would think to look for us in a photo booth."

Clare nods and it almost feels like defeat.

Slowly, doing their best to touch the least amount necessary, they exit the booth. Eva glances at her phone. More missed calls from her mom.

Clare looks over her shoulder. "What is it? Someone get through?"

Eva hesitates, then scrolls through her notifications of missed calls, voice mails, and texts. The looming weight of Mayra's anger washes over them, both clearly too aware of what might be coming for them. As much as Eva fears Palchuck, she fears her own mother even more.

"She's probably on her way here already."

"How does your mom always know? Like what made her check the ashes?"

"I probably bumped a framed photo and didn't angle it back just right. Or maybe spilled some. Who knows. It's one of her mom superpowers."

"Scary," Clare says with a shiver.

Eva sighs, resignation already seeping into her muscles. Was sitting here and waiting for her inevitable doom to catch up with her a viable option?

A loudspeaker calls out some announcements nearby. The words come into focus in time for Eva to hear, "—and the bumper cars are up and running again, so if you don't want to miss that ride, make your way to—"

Eva and Clare look at each other, the same idea coming to them at once.

"Signal's crap," Eva says, tempering her excitement.

"Text it anyway and we'll have to hope they hear that announcement if the text doesn't send," Clare says. "I hope everyone else is alright."

Eva nods as they make their way back into the crowd toward the Fun Zone and the bumper cars.

CHAPTER 11

7:31 p.m.

Hyun

HYUN *REALLY* HATES RUNNING. He's meant to be pretty, not sporty. His idea of exercise is the multiple trips he has to take from the fridge to the couch in order to bring all his snacks and drinks with him because he can't carry them all in one go. He should buy a tray.

Worse than running would be getting caught and being the reason he or his friends get in trouble. And then for sure his parents would find out he didn't go to bed, but instead snuck out to the county fair without their permission. When he had asked them if he could go, they'd said they needed his help at a client's house early tomorrow morning. Hyun really had no choice but to sneak out to CJ's. So he keeps running and dodging through the crowd as fast as his long legs can carry him. Ugh, and now he's sweating. This is going to make his hair flat.

He has to keep moving. Even with the thumping music and his heartbeat pounding in his ears, he can hear someone running behind him. He hasn't heard if they're shouting, can't tell who it is, but he's not going to slow down enough to find out. He's got to lose them, whoever they are.

The garden center is up ahead and is as good a place as any to try to hide. There are often rows of trees and tall bushes, as well as carts of potted plants that could provide cover. He usually purposefully stays away from the fair's garden center, like he assumes most people do, so it could be a good place to lay low. Who goes to a place with roller coasters and sugary fried foods and decides to go look at plants? Likely the only people in there are those passing through, using it as a path from one actually fun thing to the other.

He weaves into a small maze of plants, taking sharp turns then doubling back into a corner, pressing his back against a tall shrub wall. He closes his mouth to breathe more quietly, but breathes just as loudly through his nose. His pursuer will hopefully keep running, rather than stop to look behind them as they pass the corner.

Loud, tired-sounding steps slow down as someone comes into view, gasping for breath. It's not an adult at all, not even a security guard. Hyun would recognize that ugly haircut and unfortunate T-shirt anywhere.

"Greg?" Hyun steps out of his hiding place and startles Greg enough he falls back against a small tree.

"H-how y-you run so f-fast?" Greg's face is so red he looks like he might pass out.

"Sit down and catch your breath." Hyun grabs his arm and pulls him into his tucked-away corner. "Was anyone following you?"

Greg shakes his head no, shutting his eyes tight, gulping in air.

"Your face looks like a tomato, good camouflage in here." Hyun smiles, proud at the burst of laughter he gets out of Greg even with that dumb joke.

"Stop. I still can't breathe."

Hidden and with no one chasing them, Hyun pulls out his phone. No messages from anyone yet. Then again he has absolutely zero bars back here. All his parents' money to get him the nicest phone they can afford, and what good is it if it loses signal at pivotal moments? But damn if it doesn't take great pictures.

Hyun grunts in frustration as he puts his phone away. "My cell isn't getting service. Does yours have a signal?"

"I don't have a cell phone."

Hyun turns to Greg slowly, eyes wide in surprise. "What?"

"I'm not allowed."

"Aren't you older than me?"

"My parents don't believe in cell phones."

Hyun faces Greg fully, as if paying better attention will somehow make it make sense. "*What?*"

"Hey, you have a cell phone and it's not helping us right now, is it?"

Hyun shushes him. Not that anyone's around, but better to be safe. Right, he can't get upset. He sets the tone. Keep it happy and light. Help everyone else get through this. He shakes his shoulders, breathes out, and pulls the corners of his mouth up into a smile.

"It'll be okay, yeah?" Hyun nods rapidly for emphasis. "We're not lost. We just don't know where we are or where anyone else is."

"Isn't that the definition of being lost—"

"We'll bump into someone I'm sure. CJ's ride was next. I know hers would be the rotor ride. Ninety percent sure. Or maybe some people will be at the bumper cars since we had to skip that one?"

"So which one should we go to? Or what if they go somewhere else?"

Hyun glances at his phone. Still no signal. Annoying! This is why he hangs out with CJ and Eva. CJ does the heavy lifting and Eva all the overthinking. They might have to check both rides or go back and forth between them and hope to bump into someone. Dammit, he's going to have to do more running.

Loud rustling nearby jolts Hyun out of his thoughts. At first, he thinks someone's about to burst through the foliage and tackle them. Then he realizes Greg is pushing one of the small potted trees out of its spot.

"What are you doing?" Hyun glances around, making sure no one's noticed them. This kid gets weirder and weirder each year. How is he related to CJ?

"This oak's not getting enough sun right here." Greg grunts as he pushes the pot to a sunnier spot.

"I don't think we're supposed to manhandle the plants, Greg."

"Then they should've done a better job at placing this blue oak in the right spot."

"That's a canyon live oak."

Hyun jolts at the way Greg pops up suddenly, eyes intense on him, then squinting. "You know the difference?"

Ugh, no. Hyun doesn't want to answer, doesn't want to reveal this nerdy information he never meant to learn. But he loves being right, and he knows he is. He bites his lip, trying to stop himself. And loses. "They're similar, but a blue oak's leaves are bluish-green, waxy, and thick, and a canyon live oak's leaves are dark green and oblong, with smooth edges usually."

Greg glances at the tree, then back at Hyun. Then back at the tree.

"Wait, so are you really color-blind?" Hyun blurts out.

"What? No! I didn't look all that closely." Greg ducks and checks the base, finding a small identifying tag. After a short pause to read it, he springs back up. "You're right, it's a canyon live oak."

Hyun bites his lip and does a little fist pump in celebration. Then raises his chin, haughty. "Alright, we should go—"

"Just a sec." Greg walks to the next tree in the shade. "I don't want to see these trees wilt because someone doesn't know what they're doing." He continues shifting the trees around.

Hyun huffs. "Well, if it'll get us going faster." Both boys push and space out the small potted trees so they are less in a line and more spread out, maximizing their access to the sun spots coming in through the garden area stall walls.

Curiosity gets the better of Hyun. "How do *you* know what a blue oak looks like?"

"We lived in a commune for a couple years, near San Diego. They were really into naming and identifying the trees."

Hyun plops another tree down. "Commune? What about school?"

"Homeschooled."

"Are you in a cult?"

"That one wasn't. My parents like to go from hippie group to hippie group. It's usually people who want to do their own thing, off grid. But one time, yeah, almost ended up in a cult. Fortunately, my parents knew when it was *too* weird and left."

"Ee-yikes."

"And you?"

With a shrug, Hyun grabs a nearby hose, sets it to a soft spray to water the base of each tree. "Not as interesting as you. My parents have a gardening and landscaping business, and they make me help a lot."

"You don't like it?"

"They worked and sacrificed a lot to build it up. They're worried about it continuing after they're gone. My sister didn't want to take on the business, so it's kinda up to me now."

Greg shrugs. "Can't say *I'd* pick my life if I had the choice."

Hyun doesn't know how to respond to that, so he says nothing.

It doesn't take them long to finish rearranging the trees. The few people that walk by say nothing about their game of musical potted trees. Now each one has a better chance of getting as much sun as needed.

They stand back and to admire their handiwork.

"Rotor ride then?" Greg asks as he wraps up the hose after Hyun turns it off.

As they walk, their silence is surprisingly comfortable. Hyun's never given himself the chance to get to really know Greg. He's merely the weird cousin who visits once a year and takes up some of CJ's plans so she can't spend her whole summer with Hyun and Eva. Now Greg's insistence at spending time with them makes sense if that's not something he's able to do because of his parents. And that's probably why he wears outdated, hand-me-down clothes. He's always been in the periphery of their group, a part of it sometimes but usually forgotten when he wasn't there in person.

"So . . ." Hyun can't help himself with so many questions rolling in his brain. "Why'd you stay tonight even after you found out what we were *actually* here to do?"

Greg sighs, shoulders hunching up as if he's embarrassed before he even responds. "I don't ever get to do stuff like this, go to the fair with a group of friends. Closest I ever got to it was a singing and meditation circle for teens."

"Yikes—uh, I mean. Could be nice?"

"Trust me, I know it's pathetic." Greg laughs, lolling his head to the side. "I sat there eating a whole jar of olives to look as sad as possible so CJ would let me tag along."

That gets a burst of laughter out of Hyun. They side-step into one of the smaller alleys of the fair, keeping the booths to their backs so they can keep a lookout.

Greg shrugs. "I didn't know Javi all that well. He was a nice guy, though, the few times I hung out with everyone. I guess I wish I'd known him better, too. I wish I had a group of friends like this one. You're all so enmeshed, like *really* together. I don't think I have anyone who would care so much about me they'd risk jail time."

Hyun presses a hand to his chest, looking at Greg like he's the sweetest, smallest animal that's done the cutest saddest thing.

"Don't look at me like that."

"That's so sweet, though." Hyun waves at his eyes, holding back the prickle of tears that threaten to mess up his makeup.

"I only want to be normal! Like in the TV shows."

"You get cable in the communes?"

"I sneak out when I can. There's a lot you can do from a library computer even if I get to stuff kinda late. Only way I was able to figure out how to get my driver's license."

"Getting that government-issued ID, such a rebel!" Hyun raises his hand for a high five. Greg attempts to return it but half-misses.

"Oof, tragic." Hyun takes a step back, raises his hand again. "Watch my elbow this time."

Greg blinks with such innocence Hyun almost wants to scruff his hair. He watches as Greg raises a tentative hand, keeps eye contact with Hyun's elbow.

"Three, two, one—"Their proper high-five makes a satisfying *smack* sound.

"Whoa." Greg stares at his hand as if they've performed some special kind of magic. Hyun can't help beaming, even knowing how simple and basic that trick is.

"How do you do that?" Greg asks, still staring at his hand.

Hyun shrugs, "I dunno really."

"No, I mean, like you're the funny guy of the group. Always joking around, happy and positive. You make everyone laugh, always at the center. I wish I could be like that."

Hyun slows. Someone bumps his shoulder, walking faster as they move around him.

Greg's a few steps ahead when he finally notices that Hyun is not keeping up. It's not that Hyun's unaware that's how he behaves, but he's never had someone say it out loud. It makes a lump form in his throat, the pressure of it all.

Greg walks back to his side. "Did I say something?"

Hyun shakes his head no, steps aside to get out of the way

of people walking past. He tries to distract himself by looking at the small potted plants in the stall nearby.

"Javi's funeral was rough." Hyun idly traces the leaves of a fern. "Their mom was wailing, pulling at her hair. And Eva looked really bad. She looked like she was ready to break apart, and I felt that too, but seeing her made me glue myself together for her, you know? He wasn't my brother, or even my best friend. He was my friend, so I thought I could do that for Eva. It didn't have to mean as much to me. But I miss him too."

Greg looks back at Hyun with pity, like Hyun's just shared the saddest thought. In a way, Hyun doesn't like that directed at him. In another way, it feels nice for someone to acknowledge his feelings and how all this has affected him.

Greg drops his hand on Hyun's shoulder and gives him a little squeeze. "Even if you weren't close, you're allowed to miss him. I knew him even less and I miss him. It's weird . . . this'll sound stupid, but it's weird to think he was alive . . . and now he's just gone."

Hyun twists the hem of his long sleeve around his fingers. "He was always so nice, like he'd save snacks for me 'cause he knew I liked them, or he'd tell me about new hair products he heard about. He was a pretty good guy, and he's gone now."

Greg nods. "Javi always asked me where I'd been, like I was some old friend who happened to bump into him. CJ's hello is more of a punch to the shoulder, you know. It was nice that he seemed genuinely glad to see me."

Hyun sniffles, dries his eyes with the collar of his cardigan. "I think it's easier for me to joke around, you know? I want to make it better for everyone else."

"You definitely made things better for those trees back there."

Hyun laughs and gives a soft shove to Greg's shoulder, carefully dabbing his eye again. "Dammit, now my face is gonna be all splotchy. I didn't bring my foundation with me. Help me stop crying. You be the funny guy now."

"Knock knock."

"I said be *funny*."

"I didn't grow up with TV. I have a very limited joke repertoire."

"Okay, then shock me or something."

"Greg's not my real name."

That stops Hyun in his tracks for sure. He stares at Greg— not Greg?— wide-eyed. "What's your real name then?"

"Don't laugh."

"I can't promise that. Tell me your real name."

Greg hesitates, pursing his lips as if he has to force it out. "My real name is Green Clover."

"Green . . ." Hyun's whole world has been turned upside down. "Why do we call you Greg then? Oh my god, does CJ not know your real name? She's the worst cousin."

"No, she knows my real name. I asked her to call me Greg around you guys. I dunno, I want to be normal when I'm here. I'm already the kid who doesn't have a cell phone and never eats sugar. I didn't want to be Green on top of being the guy who knows too much about plants."

"Well, you have stiff competition on that last one."

They share a laugh and the tension eases. Now Hyun's kinda glad Greg chased after him.

They arrive at the rotor ride.

"You see anyone?" Greg asks, looking around.

"Not yet."

The loudspeaker near them whines as a voice comes on. "Last pig race of the day is starting in five minutes, and the bumper carts are up and running again, so if you don't want to miss that ride, make your way to—"

Greg and Hyun exchange a look, nod, and rush off farther into the Fun Zone.

Hyun holds his fingers crossed tightly.

CHAPTER 12

7:31 p.m.

CJ

IF THERE'S ONE THING CJ's good at, it's getting into trouble. Fortunately, she's also pretty good at getting herself out of trouble, be it talking, groveling, or even cutting and running when that's her last option. When your parents don't really pay attention to what you do, you figure out your own way around situations.

Even if she's not worried about herself right now, she's worried about her friends. She can't let them get in trouble. Not with what tonight's supposed to mean, and especially with what Palchuck might do to them given her years-long vendetta. But herself? She doesn't have anything important to lose.

The first thing she does is look around, try to take in where everyone's going as they run in different directions. Clare pulls Eva away. Good, she's probably the only one she trusts alone with Eva. Hyun ran off with Greg close behind. Well, at least they got away. She probably doesn't have to worry about Bless and Frank. They're attached at the hip anyway, and Bless always knows what to do. If she stays here, Palchuck will grab her and not chase after anyone else. She'll protect everyone and make sure she's the only one to get in trouble.

CJ turns to face Palchuck, ready to attract the full force of the security officer's authority. The movement puts her right in Bless's path as she attempts to run away while tightly clutching Javi's open water bottle to herself.

Hard metal hits CJ in the chest, and she clamps her hands down hard over Bless's, hoping to keep her from dropping the water bottle and spilling. It's a sort of tug of war with no winners as they both stumble onto the ground in a heap of joined limbs. Both clutch at the bottle as tightly as they can, which only adds to the awkwardness as they can't catch their balance well enough to get back up. Dammit, this is CJ's favorite hoodie. She was not expecting to roll around in the dirt tonight.

"Come on, Bless!" Frank yells from behind them. He's sitting on top of a fence, legs at either side, water bottle lid still clutched in his hand. Bless looks about ready to crumble as she turns back to see Palchuck looming over them.

Shit, they're both caught. This won't mean much for CJ's future, but Bless is going to USC. Could a misdemeanor charge from county fair security ruin her chances? Would they rescind her acceptance? CJ feels mean thinking it, but maybe Bless would be less insufferable if they did.

"Hey!" There's a loud thud as Frank lands back on the ground. He squares off in Palchuck's direction, taller even if not as scary as the military tank of a woman. "You want to know what was in this cup, yeah?" His voice is taunting, way different from his usual affectless monotone. He runs past Bless and CJ tangled in each other on the floor. He fakes left, then right, Palchuck way too slow to keep up as he bonks her on the head with the cup.

"You'll have to catch me!" He whirls past her, basketball skills on full display as he runs off into the crowd.

Palchuck seems almost dizzy as she turns after him, meaty hand on her chunky security guard belt. She shoots one look behind her at Bless and CJ. "Don't go anywhere!" Her voice booms, deep and angry as she hustles after Frank, calling into her radio for backup.

Wow. CJ would've never guessed he could move like that.

Lost in the confusion, it takes her a moment to realize she's still lying on the dirt, tangled up with Bless.

A few passersby stare at them, confused. They pull apart, and she lets Bless win the water bottle tug-of-war.

"You're not going to do what she says, are you?" CJ asks, never sure how much of a kiss-ass rule-follower Bless is.

"Hell no!" Bless is up before CJ can regain mastery of her legs. She stumbles upright, following a few paces behind the older girl as they move in the opposite direction of where Frank and Palchuck went.

"Aren't you worried about Frank?"

"He'll be okay; he can outrun anything."

"Really?" CJ glances behind her as if she expects to see him still. "But he's so, I dunno, top heavy."

She almost misses the glare Bless shoots at her. CJ feels the chill of embarrassment, knowing she's said the wrong thing. For some reason it makes her need to explain. "I mean because his legs are skinny, but he's—"

"Let's focus on getting away." Bless's tone is sharp. She doesn't turn to look at CJ this time.

They move past the game booths and rides of the Fun Zone, entering a wider pathway lined with food stalls. She knows Palchuck is chasing Frank, but the back of her mind worries the security guard might pop out at them from nowhere. She'd rather find a less exposed place for them to lie low, rather than stay out in the open like this.

Down both sides of the walkway are more food stalls. To one side they'd get to the grandstand where they have the animal races, and the other way takes them to the shopping and product display buildings.

Bless holds the water bottle tight, hand completely sealed

over its opening. Thinking as fast as she can, wanting to at least get out of sight, CJ jogs towards the tall teal-and-cream building with a large banner outside reading "Home Arts."

"In here," CJ says, opening the door to let Bless in.

The inside of the building is actually a nice respite from the fairgrounds. It's quieter and less crowded with working air conditioning. When their friend group comes to the fair, they rarely do anything other than games, rides, and food. This building feels like something completely new, something she didn't even know was part of the fair. It's mostly crafts like quilts, decoupage, and flower arranging. She wants to take a closer look, having had no idea this was here.

"Whoa, where are we?" Bless asks, though it feels more an exclamation of wonder than an actual question.

"We should probably keep moving," CJ says, stepping farther into the building. "We could get out on the other side as long as we get farther from where Palchuck went."

Bless nods, but looks a little overwhelmed with everything around them.

"Want me to take a turn with it?" CJ asks, motioning to the brightly stickered water bottle in Bless' hands.

"No, I got him." Her fingertips are white with how tightly she's holding it.

Calling it "him" makes CJ cringe, but she's not going to say anything about it. She wouldn't say it to Eva and will definitely not get into it with Bless either. They usually go months between seeing each other and she prefers it that way.

"Let's go." CJ leads them past the hanging quilts, a kaleidoscope of color and pattern. The artists' patience and skills are properly on display. They're almost at the end of the row, heading to the other exit of this building, when a security guard steps into view.

They both freeze. He hasn't seen them yet, but might if he turns more in their direction. Maybe he doesn't know Palchuck is looking for them? Do they want to take that chance?

His radio beeps with static, and CJ can't help her nervous reaction as she pushes Bless down the partition between sections, moving through the cloth section to decor. Bless squeals and fumbles the water bottle at the sudden direction change. They both clasp hands on it, making sure not to drop it.

They breathe hard through the worry, Bless now shooting an actual glare at CJ. "Don't push me like that. This thing's open."

"Sorry," CJ mumbles, rolling her eyes at being scolded again. She looks around. There aren't any security guards in this area. There are fewer people in here, which is probably why. Best to stay tucked away here until they can make sure the coast is clear.

This section has rows and rows of tables that seem cluttered with too many decorations. Each one is set as if for the fanciest two-person meals, with napkins, plates, cutlery, and glasses all matching in style. Some are constructed with general themes in mind, like America or farming, while some have very specific themes, like The Addams Family. It's all a little ridiculous, and yet CJ finds herself thinking what kind of table setting she would put together for something like this.

"Oh wow," Bless says behind her and CJ snaps her head up, expecting to see security making a beeline for them. Instead, Bless motions to a piece of paper in front of a table that's all in purple. "They were dinged points 'cause they forgot to include forks."

CJ blinks, processing that.

She looks at the table next to her. "This one says the dessert doesn't match the theme."

Bless lets out a single laugh through her nose, then works up to an actual shoulder-shaking laugh. Despite fighting it, CJ finds herself chuckling too.

They walk past a few table settings, calling out the judges' commentary for each one.

"The wine glasses should be six inches from the cutlery."

"Forgot the placemat!"

"The flower centerpiece covers the wallpaper design too much!"

It's a strange distraction, and yet a much-needed release. A reminder that things out there that seem silly to you, other people can care about deeply.

"Tablecloth isn't the same length on all sides." Bless leans over the railing, resting on her elbows, hands still holding the water bottle.

"Careful," CJ says, shushing them through her own laughter. "They're gonna hear us. There's like no one else here."

"We gotta get out of here before I really lose it."

"Want me to take a turn?" CJ holds her hands out.

"No, I got it," Bless says as if CJ's offering something inconsequential.

"Aren't your arms getting tired?"

Bless shrugs. "My palm's already covered in ashes. No sense getting yours covered, too."

"You know!" They startle when a nasally, uppity voice speaks from the next row over. "It's really rude to make fun of people's hard work."

They both look wide-eyed at a heavy-set man, hands resting on his hips, dressed in a loud Hawaiian button-up shirt and shorts. His colors match a luau-themed table behind him. His glower and red face give CJ the idea he had been waiting for his moment to confront them.

"We're not making fun," CJ says honestly. She didn't think that's what she was doing.

"You've been laughing since you walked in here."

"We're enjoying the work."

"Shh, CJ, stop." Bless steps next to CJ and bumps her arm.

The man brings his arms up and crosses them over his chest. "So disrespectful. People put a lot of time and thought into their art."

"We weren't making fun." CJ steps closer to him, a defiant tone overtaking her indignation. Bless elbows her in the arm but she ignores it. "And if we were, you have to admit that some of these are pretty silly."

The colorful man scoffs. "What do you even do other than make fun of people's passions?"

CJ bristles.

Her voice is loud enough to echo off the tall expo hall ceiling. "You don't know anything about me, asshole." She glances down at the judges' sheet by his table. "No wonder yours lost, didn't even get honorable mention. Colors went a little too wild, huh?"

The man blubbers, about to retort.

"Hey!" A deep male voice calls out to the both of them. The security guard from before.

CJ and Bless freeze, eyes wide.

"No drinking in here." He points at the water bottle between them.

"Sorry," Bless breathes out, still in shock.

"It's just water!" CJ says quickly, her heated argument still fizzing inside her chest.

"Take it outside." He points out the door.

The colorful man purses his lips and nods as if he had anything to do with getting them out of the area. CJ's glad her hands aren't occupied, and she flips him the bird as Bless shoulders her out of the building.

They quickly find a tucked-away section behind a large planter and water feature. CJ leans against the wall, breathing hard as if they'd been running again. She rubs at her forehead, trying to shake off the lingering adrenaline making her want to go back inside and yell at that annoying guy some more.

"Why do you do that?" Bless's voice is almost too soft to be heard over the blasting music, the sound of rides, and people talking and laughing. She carefully sets the water bottle down on the wide lip of the nearby planter.

"Do what?" CJ's response is too quick and gruff. She swallows and closes her eyes, letting out a breath. Her voice is softer but still forced. "Why do I do what?"

"Act a fool." Bless doesn't look at CJ when she says it. Her hand has a fine layer of ash on the palm, shaped in a perfect circle from holding it over the water bottle opening. Bless hesitates, almost wipes it on her dress, almost wipes her hands against each other, then stops altogether and holds her hands away from herself.

"I don't act like a fool," CJ says, pushing herself away from the wall to stand up straight. "I'm willing to say the shit no one else wants to say. He was being a jerk and deserved it."

"What about the lady at the ticket counter? Was she being a jerk?"

CJ pauses, looks at Bless, incredulous. She's never been alone with Bless before, but she had never gotten the impression Bless ever did anything other than cower silently. "I didn't hear you complaining about getting a discount on the tickets."

Bless's serious expression cracks into a smile. "That was pretty cool, yeah."

CJ exhales again, long and slow, trying without much success to let her tension go. "I use these bargaining powers for everyone's benefit."

Bless shrugs. "I guess it's not a bad way to use who you are."

CJ's jaw tightens, diving back into the anger from just moments ago. That didn't feel like a compliment. "What do you mean?"

"I mean that there's a reason you're not afraid to act out." Bless shrugs, awkwardly holding her ash covered hand away from herself. "You can afford to get into trouble."

CJ's cheeks grow hot so quickly her ears ring. "Say what you want to say. Don't bring something up then dance around it."

Bless finally looks at her, and almost seems unsure whether CJ is joking or not. She lets a breath out, covering the bottle's opening and picking it up. "Forget it, keep ignoring it."

"Please, tell me, what can I afford? I'd love to hear from you, Miss Early Admission into USC, who can *afford* to go to USC. Dad's a minister with a nice big house."

"What does that have to do with it?"

"You have everything, don't you? You don't *have* to care about saving three dollars on park tickets. *I do.* Every single bit of money I brought tonight is counted."

Bless stands up straighter than she has all night. She's still not taller than CJ, but with the intensity in her eyes, she feels taller. Her voice stays quiet and calm, each word enunciated and purposeful even through her lisp. "Because if I tried to do what you do, talk to people like that, I'd probably get kicked out of the park. Maybe worse. Just because I grew up in a nice house doesn't change that fact."

CJ swallows, embarrassment cooling the heat in her chest. How did they get into this conversation? She's never thought about the color of their skin when she thought about what Bless had that she didn't.

But then maybe that was the point. She didn't have to think about that specific aspect. Sometimes she does run her mouth without thinking, gets poked so she retaliates. No one likes being called out, especially by someone who barely knows you. She knows when she's gotten something wrong. Still, she's unsure what to say.

"Are you upset I got into USC?" Bless says that like she had it locked and loaded.

CJ does something rare: she gives herself a moment to think before speaking. Then CJ nods.

"I don't know why, though." CJ tugs at her large hoodie's sleeve. "I don't even want to go to USC. Or college in general."

Bless watches her intently, eyebrows raised, like she's waiting for a clearer answer.

CJ continues. "But . . . you have a plan. You know what

you want and how you're going to get there. And a family who clearly wants you to pursue it."

Bless's frown lightens, understanding seeping into her self-righteousness. "You're still a sophomore, right? You have time." Bless's voice is soft and her head lolls to the side. It makes CJ feel like she's a small animal to be pitied. She grits her teeth against the instinct to lash out.

"Can't your parents help?" Bless says, clearly trying to be thoughtful.

The question stings, but it's not Bless's fault. She doesn't know CJ very well.

"They're retired," CJ says finally. "They didn't expect to have a high school-aged kid right now. Don't really check in all that much."

Bless is quiet a few moments. "You're saying you *want* more scrutiny from your parents?"

CJ laughs at her own expense. It's ridiculous, wanting her parents to ask her what she's doing or where she's going or who she's going with. She should love the freedom, the lack of pressure. "The other day I told them, seriously, that I was thinking of becoming a tattoo artist and they didn't even look up from the TV."

"Ouch."

CJ shrugs. "So, if I'm not going to get in trouble for it, I can at least use my big mouth for some good." CJ leans back against the wall, the words coming out like a release, leaving her a little empty. "Who cares about me, right?

The words hang between them. CJ can practically feel her confession pushing them apart. Like she's just done something shameful, and all Bless wants to do is leave.

"What about your friends?" Bless's question comes out quietly.

"They're the ones I want to help the most. Because if I'm at least useful, good for something, they'll still want to be around me."

Confusingly, Bless shakes her head in disapproval. "You don't have to be useful to matter. You also lost a friend."

CJ shrugs. "Javi was cool, but he wasn't my brother. You saw Eva at the funeral. And her mom's not been the most helpful either. It feels like, if I don't cry, if Hyun and me can keep things from getting too heavy or serious, then I'm being a good friend."

Bless doesn't say anything, doesn't nod or shake her head. CJ can't read what she's thinking. She's not even sure she'd want to know.

"You remember the first time Eva brought us along to hang out with all of you?"

Bless shakes her head. "Vaguely."

"When Eva invited Hyun and me to meet her older brother and his friends, I was freaking out. You're two grades above. I saw you in that debate you did against Burbank High. I was, like, these are the other kids Eva hangs out with? This one wins at debates and the other one won't stop glaring at everyone."

"That's Frank's normal face."

"I know. Doesn't make it any less scary. I was, like, what are we doing here? And then Javi came up to us and knew our names already. Eva must've told him about us but he actually remembered, too. He made it okay, actually nice for all of us to hang out together. And now it feels weird, like are we even a group if Javi's not here? Are we just Eva's friends and were you just Javi's friends?"

Bless sighs, then shakes her head, as if to say *I don't know either.*

CJ wasn't expecting an answer. But it's nice to have someone else also not know. Especially a know-it-all like Bless.

With a glance at the water bottle, an idea strikes CJ. She reaches into her pocket and pulls out a crumpled napkin.

"It's clean, don't worry." CJ lays it over the water bottle opening, then pulls her hair tie out, releasing her bun so her hair falls loose down her shoulders. With careful, steady fingers, she wraps the hair tie over the napkin around the opening. A makeshift, temporary lid.

"Smart," Bless says with a nod.

"Eh, that took me way too long to come up with."

"Hey, I didn't think of it at all." Bless's smile is teasing.

"Oh yeah?" CJ allows herself a challenging smile back. "You think they'll give me your spot at USC?"

"Sounds more like a punishment for you, but go ahead and try."

This genuinely makes them both laugh. The mood between them feels lighter, more comfortable. They're not riding off into the sunset together anytime soon, but there's a better understanding at least.

"Should we see if we can find everyone?" Bless asks.

It feels overwhelming to think about trudging back into the large crowds to find their friends.

Bless voices their quiet concern out loud. "How are we even going to find them in all this–"

"CJ!"

"Bless!"

Familiar voices call out to them. They turn to see Clare pulling Eva past a group of people, making their way to them.

"Eva!" CJ runs towards her, carefully maneuvers through the sea of people, and pulls her best friend into a hug. "Palchuck didn't catch you?"

"No! Clare found a hiding place for us."

CJ smiles at Clare with appreciation.

"Hey." Bless joins them, water bottle tucked carefully into her cardigan. She holds it out almost reverently. Eva takes it from her carefully.

"Thank you." Eva's voice is small, like she means so much more than those two words.

CJ's chest constricts with the understanding of her best friend's pain. As much as she misses him, a part of her resents

Javi for going off and dying and leaving Eva like this. But that's a feeling she's not ready to share with anyone.

"Come on," she says, placing her arm's full weight on Eva's shoulder and pulling her close. "Let's find the others."

CHAPTER 13

7:31 p.m.

Frank

FRANK MAY HAVE UNDERESTIMATED Palchuck's physical abilities. He can outrun her relatively easily, but the moment he stops to catch his breath she turns the corner, coming right for him. She's clearly got stamina on his speed. He'd be impressed if he wasn't trying to lose her.

Using himself as bait to pull Palchuck away from their group may not have been the soundest plan, but he had to make a snap decision. He didn't even have time to strategically decide what direction to run in, so he hopes he's not running in the same direction as Hyun. If they're all separated, please let him not end up with Hyun. That guy would make him turn himself in.

He's better off by himself. No one to slow him down or get upset over something he says. He might even be able to take this opportunity to keep on running and go home. They'd probably all be glad he was gone, including himself.

Shit, he's lost track of where he is. He's been hugging corners, doing his best to avoid people, and hoping he can find the exit to the fairgrounds, and now he's not sure at all where he is. He's kicking up a lot of dirt, feels the ground soften under his feet. Oof, a strong, stinging smell of manure hits his nostrils. He must be in the Farm Zone.

Frank's got to stop sometime, has to calm down to control his breathing and not inhale the smells of wet hay and animal droppings. It's a cute area, all in all. Somehow always has muddy patches even when it hasn't rained recently. He usually avoids this area because he doesn't like getting his sneakers dirty. Plus, he's not really interested in learning how cows get milked, or the life cycle of a bee. Not when there's prizes to be won at games involving throwing things. He's good at those.

The soft ground doesn't muffle the hard, thudding steps of someone catching up to him. A quick glance confirms Palchuck's found him again. She must've picked up on his pattern of turns. He has to change his strategy.

He shuts his mouth and breathes through his nose, grunting in frustration as he picks his feet back up and bolts into the large red barn that holds all the farm animal pens. He grunts in frustration, can already feel the dust and mud caking his shoes.

He passes animal pens, each decorated with small farm-themed buildings that make the whole area feel like a little farm city where the animals live. He'll take in the cuteness later. Right now he has to find a place to hide.

Being a big dude usually has its advantages, but not right now. His hiding options are limited and time is running out. Following the theme of not thinking about it too much, he ducks between a pallet of animal feed bags. He scrunches down, making himself into as small a ball as he can, hoping no part of him sticks out. This large, mostly inside space echoes with everyone talking so he can't easily pick out Palchuck's thundering footsteps.

Someone lifts the top bag off of the stack, and Frank falls to his knees. He glances up to see Kevin looking down at him, face uncharacteristically surprised with his eyebrows raised.

Frank brings a dirty, dusty finger to his lips in a shushing motion. He then claps his hands together, pleading, even if the water bottle lid nestled between them ruins the effect.

Stomping nearby distracts Kevin, and Frank ducks down again, practically shoving his head into the dirt.

Thwump. The bag of feed drops back onto the stack, hiding Frank behind it once again. Kevin walks away, and Frank doesn't dare look to see what he's doing. Is he ratting him out or distracting Palchuck? Why would he do that? He seemed to hate their group. Frank places his hands on the ground, ready to spring out from his hiding place if he needs to.

Waiting, Frank finally takes in the sorry state of his sneakers. Dammit. He puts a lot of effort into keeping this pair clean and looking like new. Javi would sometimes borrow them, and it was a big deal because Frank doesn't let most people even touch them. Javi even once gifted him this very fancy cleaning kit as a birthday present. It was way nicer than any of the products Frank could afford so he hasn't used it yet. The thought tightens his chest, and he scrunches his eyes closed to stop the tears.

Fuck him.

Bent down and distracted by his own thoughts, it takes Frank a moment to notice the little pokes of pressure on his back, followed immediately by a high-pitched bleet. He turns his head in time for a little goat snout to lick and nibble his cheek. And then it nibbles his ear and Frank shoves its head away, not hard enough to knock it off. This thing could draw attention to him, but so could moving. Stay still then.

A scuffling close by announces someone walking around the bag of feed.

"Oh, hey! I found you." It's Kevin's voice, but it sounds very weird. High-pitched, excited almost. Frank tries to angle himself so he can look at Kevin.

"Don't move," Kevin's voice goes back to monotone for his command to Frank.

"Why were you talking like that?" Frank says, voice low,

still in hiding mode.

"This is Falafel, yes you are. Yes you are." Kevin's voice is in a register people usually use for babies. "I've been trying to get her to stand still and eat for the last fifteen minutes." Some more shuffling—likely Kevin is looking for something. "If you can stay right there, I'm gonna try to feed her while she's on your back, yes I am."

"Listen, if you're trying to make me look silly, there are less elaborate ways to go about it. I'd say I do a pretty good job by myself."

The little hooves on his back step from side to side, do a little hop. They're surprisingly sharp. Then there's a suckling sound from right above him.

"Oh, good job, girl. Yeah, you're hungry. Just wanted to dirty up a guy's shirt before you ate, huh?"

Frank can't help laughing, still careful not to move too much. "You're really talking to a goat like that?"

"She likes it." That time Kevin's tone is much closer to his usual monotone. "Don't worry. I sent the security woman away to the pig races."

Huh. Okay. Kevin was as likely to help him as he was to turn him in, but he's still surprised at this outcome. "Thanks."

"Sure."

They stay silent for a bit, Frank on his hands and knees, his pants and shoes already ruined. He'll have to hose himself down or his abuela won't let him in the house. Kevin bottle feeds the little goat still balancing and tapping against Frank's spine and shoulder blades.

"So you feed baby goats and you're *not* the biggest asshole?"

Kevin seems completely unfazed, focused intently on his task. "Why am I the biggest asshole?"

"Bro, you've been messing with us all night. Not letting us onto rides, making us give you our food. Don't get me wrong, it's kinda funny to see how the whole group gets all riled up. But why?"

There's a strange, honest-to-goodness half smile on Kevin's mouth now, his barely there mustache making him look so much sillier. It's not a sneer, not making fun of Frank. If anything, Frank would say there's a level of self-deprecation to it. "I really screwed up tonight, huh?"

"Screwed up what?"

Kevin sets the milk bottle down and sits on the stack of animal feed bags. "I've worked at this fair for three years. Your group comes every year, and you always look like you're having so much fun." He glances at Frank, then shrugs. "I thought maybe if I worked all the rides and games you all do, I dunno . . ."

"What, we'd ask you to join us? Then why were you stopping us from riding or making us pay again for a player?"

Kevin's expression drops back down to his more serious look. "I follow the rules. That hair clip looked like bad news, and I didn't have any record of you paying for the extra seat. I couldn't leave it empty if someone wanted to play."

Frank tenses, doesn't move, focusing on the little snout pushing under the hem of his hoodie. "And asking us for food?"

Kevin shrugs, kicks at the dirt, shoulders up as if he's a bit embarrassed. "I overbooked myself, didn't have a chance to eat. You're lucky I wasn't peeing behind the stall. Plus, friends share food, right?"

Frank lets out a sudden guffaw. Finally, the little goat jumps off and hops away. He sits up, stretches his back out with a few pops. "I guess friends do sometimes extort food out of each other."

He hasn't laughed like that in a very long time. It feels weird. Sore. Like working out muscles he hasn't used in a very long time.

"So what was with paying for an extra spot at horse race skee-ball if the seat was supposed to stay empty? And then leaving the whole game partway through anyway?"

Frank looks down at his hands, at his ruined shoes and pants. He's never been good at sharing his feelings. It used to be just his abuela and Bless. Then, at some point, Javi could get him to open up.

Two people, then three people.

Now back to two.

He's always been an old door stuck on its hinges that needs a good shove to open. It was him and Bless since they were kids, yet somehow Javi made it nice to be around such a big group. He both does and doesn't want to be around them, even now.

Lost in thought, Frank pulls the rocks out of his pocket and rubs them together, listening to their little clicking sounds.

Kevin, continuing his work, opens a bag of feed and empties it into a bucket. He'd asked his question but didn't seem like he was going to push Frank to answer. Maybe it didn't matter to him. Kevin doesn't really know him. Somehow that makes it a little easier.

"One of our group died a month ago," Frank says finally.

"Sorry." Kevin slows but keeps working. His divided attention makes this feel like not that big a deal.

"So that was, I dunno, like symbolically saving him a spot to play with us." He scoffs, doodling in the dirt with the toe of his shoe. "I hadn't even wanted to join the friend group, but he really pulls . . . pulled everyone in, you know? We were on the basketball team at school, and he wasn't great at shooting, but he could control the ball and manage the team like a pro. He was always cheerful and encouraging. Could run circles around anyone." Frank's voice grows soft, almost hoping Kevin can't hear him but wanting to say it out loud all the same. "Second week in I had such a crush on him."

He tucks his hands in his hoodie pocket, needing to hide himself from what he's said. If Kevin did or didn't hear him. At least he doesn't ask him to repeat it. He taps his little fidget rocks together. *Tick tick tick.*

Frank leans his head back against the pallet, feed bag crunching under his weight. He'd had a crush on Javi for so long, and then one day he was gone. Some stupid mistake and it was all over before anything started. Before he could ask Javi if the kiss was real or a mistake or something else.

He's angry. Angry he never got to say how he felt. That Javi knew anyway and kissed him and then died. And he could see a lot of his anger in Eva, but wanted to hold it for himself. She should be sad, not angry; she can't have both. Frank knows it's a childish thought, but he can't help himself.

"How come you weren't playing the game even when all your friends were?"

Frank laughs. "It was only half on purpose. I didn't want to play. I didn't even want to come tonight." He pauses, thinks a moment. "The last time we played, Javi won. So if I didn't play then that, I dunno, means he would still be the winner."

Kevin nods, thoughtful, the corners of his lips turning into an understanding smile. It almost looks weird how genuine that expression seems.

Frank continues. "He was a real shithead sometimes, too."

"Everyone's a shithead sometimes."

"Not me, I'm committed to twenty-four-seven shitheadedness."

They both laugh.

Frank's phone buzzes several times, as if his signal's finally let the messages come flooding in. He has a few bars and sees the texts that have all come in at once. Seems like everyone's trying to go to the bumper cars to meet up there. At least he knows where to go.

Frank stands and tries to wipe as much dirt off his clothes as he can, but the damage has been done.

"I could hose you down," Kevin offers.

"Naw, I'll do it at home. I've had worse."

"Alright." Kevin stands there as if waiting for something.

Frank could almost see him wanting to follow him, join their group still.

"Do you need anything else? Water?" Kevin stiffens awkwardly. "Hug?"

Frank frowns a little, processing the weird offer. He almost accepts, then shakes his head. "I'm good."

Kevin nods, turns to get back to work, then hesitates. "Thanks for the rock."

Frank nods and waves as he jogs off, stopping occasionally to kick the mud off his sneakers.

CHAPTER 14

twenty-seven days ago

EVA COULD ONLY HALF process where she was.

Her body was standing in this church next to her mom, wearing a dark dress that was picked out for her, and nodding as people walk by and offered their condolences.

But she wasn't there.

Not really.

The past week had been hell. All she could do was cry and torture herself thinking about what she should've done or said differently. When Javi found out about her and Clare, he had not taken it well. They'd argued, and Javi had said he needed time.

So she gave him time.

She stayed away and barely said good morning the next day. He'd kept his back to her while he mixed his morning protein shake in his giant sticker-covered water bottle. Was he going out for a run? She felt like she shouldn't ask. She wanted to give him space. He left soon after, carrying too big a bag for a simple run.

Eva had been at Clare's that early evening when Mom called her. Mayra was frantic and screaming so loudly it took Eva several questions to understand what she was saying.

He went climbing by himself.

And all Eva could think about was how she didn't say good morning to him.

She didn't tell Clare. She couldn't say anything. Couldn't breathe. Clare asked her what was wrong, but she had to leave. Only realized the next day she'd left her bomber jacket at Clare's.

At home, Mom was distraught. She tried to repeat what the police had said, explaining concepts to Eva that were foreign to them.

The desert heat at Joshua Tree was rough on old nylon.

Webbing failed. Fell nearly eighty feet.

They found him when someone noticed his dented metal water bottle glinting in the sun.

He'd already been dead about an hour.

Clare kept calling her cell, but Eva didn't know if she could talk to anyone ever again..

"So sorry for your loss." The old scratchy voice brought Eva back to herself. One of the old ladies from church who constantly reminded Eva she'd known her since she was crawling around wearing diapers.

Right. She was at church.

At Javi's funeral.

She looked around, as if something were silently calling to her.

CJ and Hyun walked through the door. How did she know they'd arrived?

Their arms surrounded her the next moment, and they swayed side to side with her. She accepted Hyun's blubbering offer to crack her back.

The ceremony was a blur. Scriptures shared out loud that she knew Javi had never read. Old people lamenting a life gone too young. Somehow felt like more for them than for him.

Occasionally glancing at him in the casket was as much as she could take. He looked like a sleeping doll with all the cover-up on his face. His hair was shorter. Someone had given him a haircut while preparing him.

Eva saw Clare sitting in the very back.

They hadn't talked since that day. Eva couldn't. It was all too busy, too tiring, too much.

Eva had been with Clare when Javi died alone.

The air around Eva choked her, and she couldn't breathe in this unfamiliar dress. She had to get out, to run. To leave and not see Clare ever again.

Outside. She needed to be outside.

The grass was too soft so Eva's heels kept sinking into it. She walked as fast as she could though her legs felt heavy. Her head itched from all the bobby pins rubbing against her scalp. Everything scratched and pinched and felt too constricting or too big. Nothing was right. She would burn the whole outfit after the funeral.

"Eva." She heard Clare's voice behind her, far enough away she could ignore it.

No, she couldn't talk to her yet. Maybe never. She would run if she had to, run as far away as she could.

"Eva!" Clare sounded closer this time, harder to ignore. She'd catch up to Eva soon.

Eva wanted to take her shoes off, but not stop walking. She stumbled.

"Why won't you talk to me?"

"Leave me alone!" Eva yelled back, pulling at the straps of her heels. Her fingers didn't remember how to work the clasp. She tore the shoes off, scratching her ankles and soles.

"Eva, please!"

"Go away!" Eva whirled on Clare, too unsteady, and stumbled backward.

Clare caught her by the arm to keep her from falling. Clare was always too good at catching her.

Eva yanked herself free and took a few steps back. She was

too close. Four weeks ago all she wanted was for Clare to be close. Now it swirled her guts and twisted her throat and made her sick. Her skin boiled in anger at the sight of her.

"Why won't you—"

"He's dead because you weren't there!" The words burst out of Eva. She couldn't contain them anymore. Her voice cracked, strained. "You *knew* he was going. You were with me when you were *supposed* to be there with him!"

Clare stared at her wide-eyed, their heavy breaths the only sounds interrupting the silence.

Then Clare's face twisted into a look Eva would never forget. She hated that look, full of hurt, guilt, anger. And somewhere, disgust.

Even more, Eva hated that she caused that look on Clare's beautiful face.

"He said he needed time," Clare blubbered, covering her face with her hands. Her shoulders shook, wracked with sobs.

"You should've—" Eva croaked out but couldn't finish. No. Eva should've known. He had a big bag, and he was wearing his climbing shorts. "You knew he had plans to—" He'd mixed his protein shake.

Eva should've known.

Should've asked if someone was going with him.

"He didn't tell me he was still going." Clare's voice was broken, shaking between her fingers. A small child unable to stop her tears.

Eva couldn't bear it anymore. She couldn't lose her brother and live with what she could've or should've done.

No, it wasn't her fault.

It was Clare's.

Clare should've gone with him, even if they were hurt and angry and not talking. She could've saved him, kept him from falling. He'd be here if she'd returned his feelings and gone with him. If she hadn't kissed her.

“I have to go.” Eva took a step backward, ready to leave Clare forever.

Clare moved to follow, reached out her hand, and Eva’s words burst out of her like a bullet from a gun, right at their tender, crying target.

“*Don’t* follow me.”

Later, when Eva was able to return to the church, she found her bomber jacket neatly folded on the pew closest to Javi’s casket.

CHAPTER 15

8:18 p.m.

EVA FOLLOWS CJ AS they make their way to the bumper cars ride for the second time tonight. The crowd is still thick even at this late hour, but thankfully beginning to thin. Good, this will work in their favor, with everything they still have to get done tonight.

Four rides to go and less than three hours to do them. That's how much time they have left. It took them around four hours to get through the first three, so how are they possibly going to manage the rest in the time they have left? The worry makes Eva sick, that rise of tickling bugs in her skin, in her chest. It presses together, builds pressure at her temples. They wasted so much time already, and then Palchuck had to interfere and make things worse.

They're all still determined, but exhaustion is slowly creeping in. An insecurity is building around them.

Eva's been running on anxiety for too long. Winding herself up to bring herself back down works for only so long before she's frayed her own edges and used up more energy than she has. She holds the water bottle close to her side, tucking it under her arm.

The makeshift temporary lid's napkin sounds like rushing waves when it brushes against her jacket with every hurried step. It could be calming if she let it.

"Almost there, I think," CJ calls from the front.

Eva takes in her friend for what feels like the first time in a month. CJ's hair is down and wild now. It's beautiful even with odd waves from having been tied up in a bun. Her shoulders are straight out and strong as she cuts through the crowd with Clare, herself, and Bless in tow. She's not as bouncy as she's been, jumping in to focus on Eva—isn't hanging at her side and holding her hand.

Behind her, Bless looks straight ahead, silent and stalwart, complete focus on the mission. She protected Javi with her very hands, CJ had said. So odd to think she had his ashes on her palm. Him but not him. What's left, so easily taken by the wind. Bless catches her looking and gives her a raised eyebrow and a jut of her chin, telling Eva to focus forward.

Ahead of her, Clare glances back. Likely to check that they haven't lost each other, and in that moment Eva feels the shift for the first time. No longer anger, brought to an instant boil. It's boiled over, spilled over the edges of her capacity, everything she's been so righteously holding onto. It feels more manageable somehow, what she's left with. She's merely tired, sad now. Like they all are. Like they've all been this entire time.

It's different, the mood between them. Still with an undercurrent of nerves and worry, yet a stronger sense of focus. Ready to finish what they came here to do. They'll do it for Javi and for themselves.

"It's Hyun and Greg!" Clare says, voice surprised and excited.

At the entrance to the bumper cars line Hyun uses the metal dividers to lift himself up a few inches, bringing his already tall frame far above the crowd. He waves at them the moment he sees them.

"Oh my god, I never thought I'd be glad to see Greg," Bless

says, which gets her a shocked look from the other three of them. "What? Even I think he's a bit weird."

The four girls laugh, which cuts right through all their worried thoughts and tensions. They pick up the pace and quickly join the two boys.

"This is amazing!" Greg says once their groups rejoin. His sweetness and enthusiasm cause a pang of guilt in Eva's chest for having laughed at Bless's remark.

"How'd you know we'd come here?" Clare asks.

"I didn't!" Hyun responds, so excited he sounds almost out of breath. "We heard the announcement the bumper cars might be up so we came here on the chance you might, too."

"Anyone see Frank?" Bless asks, looking around.

"Not yet, but we got here seconds before you."

Eva glances around, hoping he might magically be walking over to them now. Should they go looking for him or get in line and hope he also heard the announcement? She's not ready to do this without anyone, not after what they've all had to deal with. They almost lost Javi, lost everyone. Almost got caught, and now security is really on the lookout for them. They're not going to make it through this night unless they all work together. She has to give up her control, of needing things to be exactly like she wants them. She can't dictate everything.

This really is for all of them, not just her. They all lost Javi.

"Yo." A deep voice draws their attention to the bumper cars line, where Frank stands between a couple of families with young kids. They all breathe excited laughs. Eva's happy to see him despite him looking like he rolled around in dirt.

"Oh my god!" CJ exclaims, right over Greg's, "Well I'll be!" The group huddles around him excitedly, a buzzing electricity between them at the remarkable turn of events.

"How'd you beat us to the bumper cars?" Bless asks, smile bright as she smacks his shoulder over the divider.

"I got Eva's text. Told me to be here." Frank shrugs and

holds up his phone.

Huh, as far as Eva's aware, he must've been the only one to get her text. Stranger yet that he would follow her request.

Frank clears his throat, then brings out his other hand from his pocket. He holds the water bottle lid out to Eva.

She takes it, carefully removes the napkin, and replaces the lid.

A "thank you" feels somehow too big and too small for the gesture though Eva gets the feeling Frank doesn't need her to say anything.

Relief cuts through her, and she realizes she'd been half worried he might've taken the opportunity to leave the park. They were all split up, no one to stop him, after all. She breathes out a small laugh, surprised to realize she's glad he's still here.

"This line, though," Clare says from behind Eva, and it's the first time she actually looks at it.

It's longer than any line they've seen tonight. Even with Frank having already been in line, their spot is outside of the regular line dividers. The maniacally smiling cartoon children that decorate the ride seem to taunt how far away they are from actually riding it.

Eva glances at her phone. How much time can they spend waiting? What if they wait too long and can't complete their other rides tonight?

"Guess everyone who missed out earlier heard the bumper cars were running again," Clare mutters, voicing aloud the group's worries.

No, they can't stay here, can't use up their time like this. This is Eva's ride, but it doesn't feel right to waste the rest of their time waiting. Javi would tease her mercilessly when she picked it every year, bet on how many times he'd hit her buggy, counting them out loud only for her to hit his buggy more times. She had meant to ask him if he was letting her win. Now she'd never know.

Screams and wheels grinding jar her out of her thoughts.

The Big Drop nearby must've just dropped its riders. It sends a shiver down her spine and snaps her into a quick decision.

"Let's go to the next one. CJ's," Eva says loudly. "This line's too long. Maybe we can try it again closer to closing, see if the line's shorter then."

"Are you sure, Eva?" Frank asks, his concern surprising Eva. "You might miss your ride if we run out of time."

"I'll be fine, right?" Eva looks at the group as she rubs her guitar pick between her thumb and pointer finger. "This isn't just about me, so we should make sure we get on as many rides as we can."

This earns her blinks and some confused stares. She glances at Clare, who's looking back at her with the faintest curve of a smile on her lips, like she knows what Eva's been thinking.

"Anyone disagree?"

CJ, Greg, and Hyun shake their heads no. Clare shrugs, and Bless raises her eyebrows as if amazed this is Eva's approach now. Frank hasn't looked at her yet.

Eva takes a deep breath and turns to her best friend. "CJ?"

CJ's smile widens. "It's roto ride time!"

Being in the Fun Zone, the roto ride isn't far from the bumper cars. Big neon letters announce its name, "Hurricane Horror." This ride is a large cylinder on top of a rotating base, kind of like a short, wide can with the lid removed. It has cartoon people painted along the outside, all smiling as they're being swept away by what seems like a friendly cartoon hurricane.

The line is much shorter for this ride. They only have to wait for one group before it's their turn to get on. If the rest of the rides go this fast, their chances are much better at making it through everything.

"Man, I love this ride." CJ says to no one in particular.

Realization hits Eva. She doesn't really know why this is CJ's favorite ride. They don't ride it every year, and sometimes Eva doesn't even join. There are a lot of things she hasn't asked CJ, just accepted. She's let CJ do a lot more of the asking and caring. If this is her favorite ride, Eva should know more.

"How come?" Eva asks.

The question surprises CJ for a moment. She thinks as if she hadn't herself put it into words before. "It makes me feel a little sick," she says finally.

"Isn't that a bad thing?" Frank asks from behind Bless. Somehow now he's always listening and tuned in to everyone else in the group. He still hasn't looked at Eva.

"Yeah, but also, I dunno, it makes me a little dizzy, loopy. And heavy. I can barely move. Like a weighted blanket except more like I'm duct-taped to the wall and I'm being held down but also floating. I always want to test how much I can move or lift when I'm in it. Can I lift my arm or my leg? Can I pull myself to the top? Maybe if I can, I'll forget everything else for a moment."

"Yeah, none of that sounds good," Greg jokes, earning him an eye roll from CJ.

"You can wait out of the line then!" She shoves him, but he barely moves.

"Don't test a man who can pick-up a tree," Hyun mutters, and Eva doesn't have time to ask him what that means before they're scanning their ride ticket cards and being ushered into the large cylinder.

The inside is a bright neon orange. A full, circular room with no beginning or end once they shut the door. Each rider spot is designated by a strip of soft padding about the size of a human. There are no handholds or barriers, no seatbelts or harnesses, nothing that you usually expect from a thrill ride.

Eva's fear is in her throat. With all the activity tonight, she already feels like she might throw up.

Too late to turn back.

"Eee, alright here we go!" CJ exclaims, taking her spot. Eva tentatively gets in her spot next to her, and soon they have claimed their section. The other riders seem about their age or older, all much calmer and cooler over the idea of spinning around in what is essentially a large washing machine drum.

Eva ends up sandwiched between CJ and Clare. Coincidence or dumb luck? Or is the universe playing some kind of cruel joke on her?

"I don't like this ride," Clare says quietly to Eva as a shiver runs up her shoulders.

Eva's surprised. "Don't you usually go on taller rides than this one?"

"Yeah, but there's restraints and hand-holds usually. This one's nothing like that." Clare leans her head back on the padding as if she's accepting her fate.

The thought flickers through Eva's mind, unbidden and completely illogical. She shouldn't want to, shouldn't think she could get away with it. But maybe . . .

She thinks back to how many times Clare has touched her tonight, even grabbed her, in order to comfort or save her. She can do the same this time.

Eva moves her hand slowly and holds it out. She lifts her eyes to meet Clare's frowning, questioning gaze.

"You don't have to," Eva says quickly, fighting the instinct to pull her hand back. "But if you need something to hold onto . . ."

Clare bites her lip. She nods and gently takes Eva's hand.

"Okay, riders, please keep all body parts inside the ride and stay within your spot. We don't want anyone—"

The ride announcer's voice fades away as Eva closes her eyes, taking careful breaths, hoping this will be the most thrilling ride of the night.

Bless lets out an "eep" as the ride spins at a slow, manageable pace. At first, the loud, techno-music is more stressful than the ride. As it steadily picks up speed, soon Eva feels herself pushed back, growing more glued against the padding. Her neck strains, and she feels a rush in her head as her gravity changes due to centrifugal force. She has to squeeze Clare's hand to keep them connected.

Eva closes her eyes, letting the motion overtake her, not that she has a choice. It's not the usual excitement of an up-and-down ride, no feeling like you'll fall, not even the sensation you're high up. It's only spinning. Easier to go with it.

A new feeling washes over Eva—maybe letting go could make everything easer. She let go of her strict plan, let go having to do things in a certain order. Maybe she's been getting in her way. And, by proxy, maybe getting in everyone else's way too. She brought the group together tonight, thinking only of what she wanted.

Now it's time for her to make this night truly about all of them. The way it's supposed to be.

Despite the noise and clamor around them, Eva hears a small squeal next to her. She strains to turn her head to the side.

Clare's eyes are shut tight, mouth pressed closed as if she's trying really hard not to throw up. Her shoulders are stiff, free hand splayed and pressed hard against the wall. She's seriously hating this, and Eva's chest stings with guilt. Everyone's been going through their own hell. What one person loves is another one's nightmare. She's really put everyone through it, and not today alone.

Eva squeezes Clare's hand tighter and feels her respond with a tight grasp of her own. They've both always had rough hands and calloused fingertips—Clare from climbing, and Eva from playing guitar. They always felt like they fit, textures that didn't irritate each other because they were so similar.

Clare turns to look at her, and then her eyes grow wide.

Eva clenches her mouth shut to avoid laughing at the absolutely terrified look on Clare's face. Her eyes are comically large, and her mouth is clamped shut like she's trying not to scream. She keeps nodding her head forward.

No, not nodding. Signaling with her chin for Eva to look behind her.

With the ride going full speed, turning her head proves to be a wildly difficult challenge. She expects to see CJ's face, but is met instead with . . . her hips?

CJ's in the process of wriggling up, head fully past the padded backing. She's pretty sporty, but Eva's still surprised to see her able to fight the pull of physics. She can't see the ride operator, but they must not care what anyone does inside the ride. There aren't any seatbelts or harnesses after all.

Eva can't look away, stuck as she is by the ride's motion and by the worry of what her best friend is trying to do. CJ almost has her head all the way to the top opening of the ride. She clutches harder at Clare's hand, needing something concrete and stable to hang onto. And Clare's always been that.

"CJ!" Eva yells, only to realize her voice can't be heard above the ride's loud music and other riders' screams. CJ's too focused on scaling the ride's wall to hear her. Why do they have to make the top open like that?

Keeping a firm grip on Clare, Eva slowly drags her free arm up. Her elbow and wrist fight against the ride's pull, but she manages to grab firmly onto CJ's ankle.

CJ finally looks down at her, attention shifting from her single-minded focus. She looks as surprised at the contact as Eva feels.

Knowing she won't be heard, Eva attempts to communicate with shoulder shrugs and a shake of her head: *what are you doing?*

A laugh bursts out of CJ's mouth, one that seems to have been trapped in her chest for a month. Her shoulders shake and her head drops back onto the ride's wall. Eva drowns in confusion and feels Clare squeeze her hand in sympathetic worry.

Finally, her laughter calming, CJ looks down at her and

mouths: *I'm okay.*

Okay.

Eva lets her ankle go but doesn't look away as CJ shifts and finally reaches the top of the cylinder.

CJ's loose hair whips every which way, like it can't decide where to go. From her angle, all Eva sees is CJ's movements, her chest puffing out, then tensing as it deflates. Her neck muscles go taut, arms flexing.

She's screaming with everything she's got.

Screaming above the music and the noise. Screaming out the ache.

Eva's eyes go to Hyun. He watches CJ with the brightest smile on his face, one more genuine than she's seen from him lately. He's lifted, feet off the ground, laughing and yelling too, something primordial coming out of him. His hair's far more messed up than before, and she could imagine him spending another hour to get it back to his controlled-yet-disheveled state.

Eva wants to laugh and scream too, but she can't yet. There's a stopper in her chest or her throat or somewhere. She can feel something she's not let go of yet. Not in the same way her friends have. She's still holding herself back.

She smiles, though, happy her friends are getting their moment of release. It's what they need right now, even if there's still more to feel, more to grieve.

The ride slows down. Eva's stomach drops back to normal. CJ scuttles down with ease as the force lessens, settling back onto her padding.

She wipes her eyes. Turns to wink at Eva. She's good.

It's not until Eva's feet are firmly on the ground that she feels Clare's hand slip out from her grip.

Luck is on their side after they exit the ride and find a quiet, hidden-away spot. The small seating area by one of the stalls is empty, and although they have to stand near a big trash bin, they're not easily visible.

No guards in sight.

This time it's easier for Eva to hand over Javi's ashes.

CJ smiles as she takes them, eyes still wet around the edges.

Eva's ears still ring, and CJ sounds far away when she speaks.

"Javi." CJ pauses, breaths still coming quickly. She clears her throat, likely strained during the ride. "We miss you."

CJ lowers the lid and drops the ashes.

It's short and sweet, and nothing Eva had been picturing leading up to tonight.

And it couldn't be more perfect.

She was wrong before, thinking that these eulogies had to be something big and poetic and overwrought with emotion. Yes, they can be that, but simple can be good, also meaningful.

Eva wipes at her eyes with her sleeve before accepting the lid back from CJ.

After putting the water bottle away, she grabs onto CJ for a tight hug. Hyun wraps himself around the both of them, pulling Clare with him and further squeezing them together.

Eva smells cherry blossoms again, and also Hyun's woody cologne and CJ's sunscreen.

"Can I . . ." Greg asks, unsure, but CJ grabs him and pulls him in.

Bless wraps an arm around Frank's shoulders.

Only three more rides to go, and they might just get to all of them.

CHAPTER 16

9:01 p.m.

BLESS'S CHOICE IS THE SkyRide. It's similar to a ski lift, floating benches held up by metal frames that run on wires and lift the riders far above the park.

"Does this one even count as a ride?" Greg asks as they get in line.

"Of course it does." CJ snaps at him him, giving him a smack for good measure. "It's called the Sky-*ride*, after all. Doesn't have to be a fast ride to count anyway."

Eva notices Bless give CJ a smile she's never seen the two share before.

The next argument features worries about being spotted since the ride moves so slowly. Ultimately, they agree there's a low chance Palchuck would not be looking for them in the sky. She's probably still digging around behind stalls and in darker hiding spots.

They decide to get on at the ride entry closest to the park entrance, which then drops them off in the middle of the park, just past but still close to the Fun Zone. Then Clare and Eva's rides will be left.

Hyun uses his height to lead the group again. This time Greg's next to him and they're chatting and laughing. Clare, Bless, and CJ make the next row, and Eva wonders what happened when they were all separated to shift the dynamics. There's a comfort amongst them, a new connection and understanding that's brought them together.

Eva swallows the pang of guilt. She knows this closeness doesn't negate how Javi brought them together, nor how important he was to their group. She's wondered this whole time if they'll fall apart without him. It's incongruous, the relief and wrongness of it all.

She's too deep in her own thoughts to notice the one person in their group she doesn't see in front of her: Frank. And she doesn't realize he's keeping pace next to her until she feels a bump on her shoulder, drawing her attention to look up at him.

"Sorry," he mumbles, noticeably not looking at her again.

Eva is too surprised to say anything, so she doesn't. In truth she's a little weirded out he's hanging back to walk with her. He's even taking shorter steps to match her stride. With his long legs he seems like a parent trying to walk next to their slow kid.

In her silence, Frank sniffs and hunches his shoulders. "Um, I shouldn't have said all that."

Ah. Eva gets it now. And it would be easy to accept his non-apology, but Eva never did anything the easy way.

"Is that an apology?" she asks, half a serious question, half a joking prod to see what Frank will say. He might really lose it at her.

Strangely, Frank sighs. His head and shoulders hang lower, jaw muscles tensing, then releasing. "I'm sorry. For saying shit."

"So you're only apologizing for saying it?" Eva gives him a sideways look, her tone fully skeptical.

Frank shrugs with a single laugh. "That's all I'm sorry for. I can't apologize for something I still feel." He scratches his hand through his buzzed hair. "But how and when I said it was wrong, and I really am sorry for that."

Eva's annoyed, but nods in response. Something in her understands that feeling all too well.

"Do you accept my apology?" Frank looks down at her with a raised eyebrow, returning her testiness.

"Yeah, okay." Eva shrugs, keeping it simple. A strange understanding cuts through a months' worth of tension and misunderstanding.

Frank seems relieved. Was that it? Was that all he wants to say?

Eva's question bubbles up inside her.

"You want to ask, don't you?" Frank's disaffected tone veers toward annoyance again.

"I mean, only sort of," Eva says, attempting to hide how much she really does want to ask. "He was my brother so I also kind of don't want to know." She flinches, realizing her past tense.

Frank leans his tall frame toward her. His voice is low, sharing a secret with her. "Yeah. He really kissed me."

Eva's eyes go wide. She doesn't have reason not to believe him, but it's still difficult to trust. So Javi snuck out that night after their argument? There's no way Frank snuck into Javi's room as she would've heard them moving around and talking. The Vargas house makes noise at any kind of movement.

"He never shut up about Clare," Frank says, sharing as if this isn't the weirdest thing they could be talking about. "I think he kinda liked that it bothered me."

Eva's brow furrows and her lips press tight. That's not the Javi she knew. Well, he did do things he knew would annoy her. Like unplugging her headphones while she was listening to music, or taking a bite of the food she'd made for herself when her back was turned. He always laughed when he got a rise out of her, but that's normal sibling stuff. This feels worse somehow. She's not sure she wants to learn more unflattering things about her brother.

"He came over late that night, before his . . . accident." Frank's voice grows quieter when he says "accident." "He was hurt and upset, wanted to talk. So I let him. He wanted to lie on my bed with me while he talked. I let him. And then at one point he leaned over to me and . . . I let him."

Anger flares up in Eva's chest again. Why? Everything was feeling good right now, so why is he telling her this? Why does she hate knowing? Frank's always pissed her off, so that's not new.

Is it that Frank got to have a nice moment with Javi right before? That he went to talk to him because he couldn't talk to her. That Frank maybe got more of a goodbye than she did.

Eva reaches into her pocket to run her finger along the edge of her guitar pick. She can't change the past.

It's not her fault. It wasn't anyone's fault.

"Does that make him . . ." it's the worst question to ask, but it's all she can think of now. "So was he a bad friend?"

Frank shrugs. "Sometimes. Mostly good, though." He finally turns to look down at her from the corner of his eye. "Fair's fair. So was I."

She looks down at her shoes, kicking up bits of dirt, not wanting to answer his question. So she diverts.

"Why did you like him then?"

Frank leans his head back, closes his eyes as if remembering. "He was *so* hot."

"Eeeeew, don't tell me that." She punches his shoulder lightly, but he doesn't even flinch. He's surprisingly solid, built like a lollipop as he is.

"He never forgot me," Frank continues somberly. "Javi had this amazing ability to make you feel included, like you were the one person he most wanted to see. I take care of my grandma, and it's a lot. He used to come over and make us dinner, just to help me out."

"Arroz con salchicas?" Eva's tone is teasing.

"Way too many." Frank actually laughs, like a sudden horn.

Eva catches Bless glancing back with a smile.

"He was getting better at it too," Frank continues.

"He was practicing a lot."

They settle into silence as they come upon the entrance to the SkyRide. Fortunately, the wait looks short.

"So." Frank leans his weight against Eva, veering them off their path slightly. "You and Clare, huh?"

Eva's face grows hot from the question. She glances at Clare in time to see her retie the knot on the front of her uniform button-up shirt. "I don't know. I think I messed that up real bad."

"Hmm."

Their conversation is cut short as they reach the entrance and the group clusters together. Frank shifts ahead in the line to stand closer to Bless. He leans into her side and whispers in her ear. She looks a little shocked, but nods.

"So how are we dividing up seating for this one?" Greg asks the group. "I think we'd fit two or three people per chairlift."

"Eva," Bless says as she moves closer to her. Her glance at Eva's bag makes her anticipate what Bless will ask.

"Would it be alright if I rode with Javi?" Bless asks her question slowly as if she's trying really hard not to scare her.

Eva squeezes the strap of her messenger bag. Now that she has him back, everything has finally started to feel better. She wasn't ready for this. Even if the bag does feel lighter, even if the thought that he's at certain spots of the fairgrounds makes her feel a little sick to think about. Even as she ignores the slightly nagging feeling that maybe she didn't fully know him so maybe she's not quite sure this is what he would've wanted.

Maybe he wouldn't have even known himself.

Bless referred to the ashes as Javi, which Eva appreciates. And this is for her, too.

Worried the wrong words might come out, Eva nods and

removes her messenger bag, handing the whole thing to Bless. She receives an appreciative smile in return as Bless holds the bag close to her chest.

"That makes us eight then, yeah? Kinda?" Hyun chimes in, counting the group for the SkyRide.

The ride operator comes through and scans all their ticket cards.

The Skyride runs in continuous movement. As the benches reach the station, they slowly lower to the ground. Riders have a few moments to hop off and have to keep running forward to avoid the bench they were on hitting the backs of their legs. On the other side of the drop-off, new riders get on by standing in the loading zone, bending their knees. As the bench turns and reaches them, they fall-sit onto it.

"Okay!" Frank calls out loudly, a deep, reverberating authoritative sound punctuated with a clap of his hands. It's a very basketball guy move. "Come on, let's get on." He shoves Hyun and CJ forward, who kinda stumble. But the bench is already swinging around the side for them so they have no choice but to let the bench sweep them up.

Frank is much gentler with Bless as he motions her to the loading zone. She falls onto her bench by herself, Eva's messenger bag clutched tightly against her chest.

"Clare or Eva, either of you wanna—" Greg starts to ask, but he's cut short when Frank grabs him by the collar and hauls him onto the loading zone. The next bench sweeps the two of them away.

It's her turn, and Eva has to move into the pickup zone quickly to catch the next bench before it fully sinks in that she'll be riding the chairlift with Clare.

Alone, again, with Clare.

Her fears are quickly replaced by new worries as she and Clare are slowly swept up by the bench's climb over the park.

Their seat bobs and swings along its route. Eva makes the

mistake of glancing down at her hanging feet and immediately sits back, staring at the sky. God, she hates heights. She hates being any amount of high up. At five feet, she's obviously not meant to see the tops of people's heads.

Eva's eyes water from the cold breeze. This ride moves *way* slower than she remembers. She braces herself as the bench bounces more whenever they pass through the tall poles that support the wire and keep the ride moving. The wind swings them from side to side.

A warm hand presses into Eva's. Her head snaps to look at Clare, surprise and curiosity mixing as she processes the gesture.

Clare meets her eyes, then looks away quickly, clearing her throat. "You're breathing so hard right now." Her freckles shine like specks as her cheeks tinge with pink.

It distracts Eva, her own ears growing hot. Suddenly heights don't matter to her as much.

Somehow, for the second ride in a row, she's holding Clare's hand.

They sit in awkward silence during this long, surprisingly bumpy ride. Eva squeezes Clare's hand tighter every time the bench bobs up and down. Eww, her hand's growing pretty sweaty pretty fast.

Eva looks ahead at Bless sitting alone in her own floating bench. The older girl's shoulders shake and she gesticulates with her hands. She's talking to Eva's bag, and Eva wonders if maybe she should've been letting everyone have their own moment alone with Javi.

The silence between her and Clare feels monumental. They had that argument in the photo booth, and it's so easy to let the group get in the way of them having to interact. Somehow, they still end up right next to each other, like they can't help it. The way the moon can't help orbiting Earth.

Eva breaks the silence first this time.

"I did mean it." She can tell by movement alone that Clare looks at her, but she's not ready to meet her eyes. "When I said I was sorry. Earlier."

This silence feels worse without looking at her. Finally, Eva turns to meet Clare's intense stare.

Seems like that's all Clare was waiting for because she finally responds, "What are you sorry for?"

Leave it to Clare to ask the tough questions, ask for more than Eva's ready to give.

"For . . ." The words are stuck in Eva's chest, her throat closing up as if they're causing an allergic reaction. She knows it's more mental than anything, but that doesn't make it easy. "For yelling at you."

That's not it, that's not enough, and she wants to correct herself before Clare has to. She can't keep putting that on her. "And for blaming you."

Eva keeps glancing away. The eye contact sears the longer she holds it.

Clare waits silently. There's more Eva could say, but how much does Clare want? She thought that summarized it pretty well. Shit, if she wants her to list every little thing—

"Thanks," Clare says finally as if that's all she needs from this.

Eva's mouth drops open in confusion.

"Thanks?" Eva can't help asking.

"Yes. Thank you for apologizing." The corners of Clare's mouth perk up slightly, and she bites her lips, clearly trying to remain serious. Oh, she's enjoying this.

Eva has to fight her own bubbling giddiness at seeing the start of Clare's smile, a glimpse of her single dimple.

"No 'apology accepted' or anything?"

"Hmm . . ." Clare thinks about it. "Gimme a month."

"A month?"

"That's how long it took you to apologize. I should get to

withhold forgiveness for at least that long."

"At *least*?" Eva squeals out, fear of heights and the tension with Clare forgotten by this odd response. "How much longer?"

Clare shrugs, nonchalant. She holds all the cards. "Until I feel ready."

Eva scoffs indignantly, and in a joking huff drops Clare's hand. She takes the opportunity to wipe the sweat off her palm. Clare throws her head back in a laugh. She's enjoying this too much.

The bench bounces and swings as it passes one of the gears, and Eva grabs Clare's hand again, grateful she's allowed.

"Why did you blame me?" This time Clare's voice has lost most of its earlier playfulness. It's Clare's turn not to look at Eva.

Eva takes a deep breath. Their shoulders bump as they both stare forward. "I thought it would be easier than blaming myself."

Clare nods, quietly taking her words in.

"I blame myself, too, if that helps." Clare's thumb brushes against Eva's knuckles.

"It doesn't," Eva says quietly, and it's true. Knowing Clare blames herself makes her ashamed she contributed to it.

A small laugh escapes Clare's lips, the kind that says *wow, we're pathetic*. "I wonder what Javi would think of us now."

Eva fights against the lump in her throat. He isn't around to see them, to know how they're doing without him. She'll never know whether he would've eventually been fine with their relationship or not. She wants to hope he would've come around. He was more complicated than she knew. Could ever know. He was at least loved and admired more than he was disliked.

He was a great brother. She can accept that he was all those things at once.

"He'd probably make fun of us," Eva says, and it feels right.

Clare really laughs this time, and Eva wishes she had been looking at her. "Yeah. He totally would've."

Eva's chest is full of every emotion that cycles through her:

anxiety, appreciation, fear, love. She isn't sure how Clare is here next to her, holding her hand after everything she put them through.

"Clare," Eva says finally, waiting until Clare looks at her. She opens the gates and lets it flow out instead of fighting the tide that was waiting for permission. "I really, really am so . . ." Her voice cracks. ". . . *so* sorry."

Clare nods. She opens her mouth to respond, then closes it. Her eyes never leave Eva's. She's about to try again when they hit a particularly bumpy gear and their bench bounces strongly enough that Eva feels her butt raise off the seat by a centimeter.

Eva squeals and grabs onto Clare with both arms.

Clare laughs and pats at Eva's arms encircling her. "I still can't believe you agreed to get on this ride. You never leave the ground."

"It's for Bless and Javi!"

"And for that, you deserve a reward." Clare laughs when she brushes the gentlest of kisses against Eva's wrist.

Eva's grateful for her fear of heights this time.

Their bench starts to lower. Eva and Clare are the last ones to get off the ride. They keep moving forward through the ride's exit.

Bless wipes at her wet eyes and gratefully returns Eva's bag to her. She feels a small, guilty prick in her chest, realizing while she was with Clare she hadn't been worried at all about Javi's ashes being with someone else. She hadn't even missed the weight of him in her messenger bag. Was that alright to feel?

The group finds another secluded spot for the next eulogy. They're tucked away partly between two electrical trailers that are clearly there to discourage guests from backstage areas.

This time it's easier.

Bless takes the water bottle from Eva, handling it with the most respect anyone's exhibited tonight. Her reverence seems almost comical, given she's holding a dented, stickered water bottle with nature parks and race cars on it. Eva appreciates it all the same.

"No Bible verses," Frank mutters next to Bless, and she elbows him in the side hard enough he groans.

Bless is undeterred as she recites: "For everything there is a season, and a time for every matter under heaven. A time to be born, and a time to die. A time to plant, and a time to pluck up what is planted. A time to kill, and a time to heal, a time to break down, and a time to build up. A time to weep, and a time to laugh; a time to mourn, and a time to dance . . ."

They all listen quietly.

Despite Javi and her not being religious, Eva knows he would've accepted the words in the kind way Bless means them.

Bless finishes her recitation, carefully tips the water bottle over, and lets some of the ashes drift down slowly. She adds one last quote, "Blessed are those who mourn, for they will be comforted."

Even Frank offers a half smile. "At least you picked a good one."

Eva glances at her phone, swipes away the missed calls from her mom. Almost ten o'clock. That chairlift ride is so slow even though it was worth it. "Okay, we only have two more rides and—"

"Gotcha!" A large, beefy hand reaches past Frank and grabs hold of Bless's wrist.

Palchuck pulls Bless back, and the water bottle slips from her grip.

It's almost in slow motion.

Eva's stuck in place watching it all unfold.

Hyun jumps into CJ's arms. Greg covers himself as if he's expecting something to fall on him.

Frank and Clare lunge to catch the water bottle.

Clare's faster; her hand at least touches it. But the bottle bounces awkwardly off her fingers and continues its fall.

Frank pounces forward, but kicks it accidentally and the unsecured lid pops off.

"NO!" The scream out of Eva's throat is haggard and desperate.

The rest of the ashes spill onto the dirt as the water bottle rolls away past their feet.

"Grab everyone," Palchuk snarls as she holds Bless tightly by her arm, hauling CJ by the collar of her hoodie. She must be surprisingly quiet if she managed to sneak up on them.

Eva falls to her knees, eyes stinging, every muscle tense with the panic to do something but unable to do anything at all.

Javi's water bottle is gone, kicked off somewhere. Her hands cup a mound of his ashes and dirt, all of it slipping through her fingers as she looks for something to put them in. She could take a shoe off, she could throw them in her bag, or—

Legs surround her, kicking up dust and dirt and ashes, spreading and mixing them further. More security guards. Bodies scuffling and struggling against each other.

A rough hand pulls Eva up.

Everything slips through her fingers.

"Bring them to the security office." Palchuck's command registers through Eva's shock. "One of your parents is here. Seems she already figured out what you were up to."

Shit shit *shit*.

Her mom.

Other attendees stare as their group is noisily hauled away.

She catches a glimpse of the water bottle against a vendor stall wall.

The cap lies a foot away from it.

Javi's water bottle is completely empty.

CHAPTER 17

five weeks ago

THE SKY WAS FULLY dark by the time Eva made her way home from Clare's. It was later than she had meant to stay out, but since she was now allowed to kiss Clare, how could she stop? Every time she tried to leave they would find themselves pressed up against each other again. Which was the last thing she had expected to happen when she went to confront Clare over rejecting Javi. Not that she would complain.

She glanced at the dark windows as she walked up to their front door. Maybe she would get lucky and her mom and Javi would already be asleep. That would be preferable. She hadn't really thought about what she'd tell him. It was difficult to think about what she'd say when all she had wanted to focus on was Clare and her strong hands.

She opened and closed the front door as quietly as she could and tiptoed her way through the house.

In the dark hallway to her bedroom, a light shone from under Javi's door.

Crap. He was awake.

Avoidance was key tonight. If she could brush her teeth and

get in bed, she wouldn't have to tell him how her visit to Clare went. She would even skip brushing her teeth if she had to.

She was barely breathing, making her way down the hallway towards her room. She regretted leaving her door closed now that she'd make noise by opening it.

"Eva?"

Crap. Running now wouldn't get her out of this.

Javi's door opened and he poked his head out. He'd probably been waiting for her if he heard her outside his door. His eyes were red and tired. "Did you just get in?"

"You're up late." Eva rested a hand on her hip as if she were the one catching him doing something wrong. A distraction she could only hope worked.

"I was worried." And he really looked it with his thick eyebrows practically merging together and his hands in his pockets so his shoulders hitched up. "You were gone for longer than I thought you would be."

Eva had a very short amount of time to decide what she'd do. She could be vague and admit nothing, lie completely, or tell him the truth that what she'd thought was an unrequited crush turned out to be very much requited. She could bolt to her room and close the door before he had a chance to ask any more questions. As usual, uncertainty kept her frozen in place.

"So how'd it go?" Javi asked, taking a few tentative steps toward her.

"It was . . ." Run or truth. Run or truth.

"Yeah?" He moved closer still.

Eva took in a deep, sharp breath.

"Can we sit down?" she blurted out, and the way Javi's eyebrows rose and eyes grew wide, she wondered if he'd already guessed it somehow. Like he could read it right off her face. Could he smell how Clare's fingers had rubbed the scent of cherry blossoms into her hair?

"Sure." He turned and walked into his room.

It was cleaner and more organized than earlier. He must've stress cleaned all afternoon. He motioned her to sit on his bed while he took the computer chair.

"I love what you've done with the place," she said, diverting. She dug her nails into her thumb's cuticle. She wished she had her guitar pick.

"Just tell me what happened. I need to know."

Stop picking. She laced her fingers together, then released them, and rubbed her knuckles against each other.

"Did she tell you who she likes?" Javi leaned forward in his chair, insistent on an answer.

No, she shouldn't lie, not if she and Clare were going to date. Were they dating? Does kissing mean dating? Either way, she couldn't hide it from him forever.

Without looking at him, Eva nodded slowly.

Javi rubbed his hands through his thick hair, messing up his part and making the sides stick out weird.

"Well? Who?" His voice rang loud in the quiet room. She didn't blame him as that had been her a few hours ago.

This was almost physically painful. Eva didn't want to tell him right now, not right away. She was supposed to have a bit more time to figure this out. There was no way this would go well. They'd never been competitive siblings, but Eva had never been able to resist comparing herself to him. And he won most of the time.

Selfishly, she wanted to savor this for herself a little longer.

She really was the worst.

"It's, um . . ." *Me. She likes me me. It's me. I won this time.*

"It's?" His voice felt like a push, bursting from him with accusation.

He'll be upset no matter what. She should just say it.

"Me."

Silence. Heavy and twisting. She didn't look at him for what felt like minutes, though it was probably seconds. When she finally looked, he frowned back at her in confusion. Like she'd said it in a language he didn't speak.

"You? You what?'

Her shoulders fell with the pressure of having to repeat herself. If it didn't go well the first time saying it, it could only get worse from here. "The person Clare likes. It's me."

His scoff made him bounce on the bed, head bobbing. A joke he couldn't even accept.

Eva's affront flared up almost immediately. She stared at him, let the quiet carry the weight of her truth.

The smile on his face was mocking and disbelieving. "You?" His eyes took her in, up and down, as if looking for some answer there.

She nodded, chest puffing. Showing her pride. She'd never seen this side of him, and it prickled. He'd never really lost to her, and now she was seeing how that affected him.

"And you like her, too?" The way he asked suggested he also didn't expect that.

Eva was nodding before she realized. She forgot she hadn't come out to Javi yet. She'd made plans and practiced speeches, but she hadn't gotten far enough to actually tell him. She'd figured it out only this year. Not that she thought he'd reject her, but nothing ever felt one hundred percent sure. Even telling CJ had been hard. It hadn't seemed important before she had a reason to tell her.

Clare was a really good, scary reason.

Javi frowned, blinking hard. His expression kept twisting through different phases, as if every thought evoked a new emotion for him. Was that revulsion? Confusion? Betrayal? Or worse, a combination of all three?

"Talk to me." Eva couldn't keep herself from asking.

"Oh, like you've been talking to me? Because you've shared so much about yourself and your life recently." Crap. He was really upset if he was being sarcastic.

She could be sarcastic, too. "Right, like what did I have to worry about? Clearly, you're having the best reaction I could've hoped for!" He shushed her, which made Eva realize her voice had gotten louder.

"I'm not upset that you're gay." Javi said, then paused. "Bi?"

"Definitely gay," she confirmed, and he nodded.

"But," he said harshly, clearly looking for words that wouldn't settle around the concepts he was trying to pin down. "*Both* you and Clare?"

"Well, I don't know what she identifies as."

Javi shook his hands in front of her like he was wiping her stupid drawing off a dry erase board. "And you caught feelings for each other? When?"

"We hang out all the time."

"But I'm always there."

"So?"

"*So,*" he threw the word back at her. Then he straightened in his chair, almost like a challenge. "I said I liked her first."

Eva frowned. This is not the kind of argument she expected to have. Sure, she didn't think he'd be happy his crush liked her instead, but to say it like that?

"What, did you call dibs?"

"Well, no—" he stammered. "Yeah, yeah, essentially. I told you I liked her and you didn't say anything. Actually, you said you thought she would like me back."

"I didn't *know* she liked girls either, let alone me. This was all as much of a surprise for me as—"

Javi took a deep breath, then let his face drop into his hands. "I'm gonna need some time to process this one."

Eva's heart sank. He had never not been in her corner, had always celebrated every success and discovery of hers. They'd never needed time apart. Not when Dad left and Mom moved them away and they had to start over with just each other.

"Okay," she said anyway.

He nodded without looking at her. She wanted him to say he still loved her, that they'd talk about this later. That he and Clare would still be friends and go climbing together. Maybe Clare and Eva would now spend more time just the two of them, but that didn't mean everything had to change, right? They could still taste his awful attempts at cooking and play Mario Kart together.

Eva didn't remember when she left his room and laid on her bed staring up at the ceiling. Elation and sadness washed over her in equal measure. The rise when she saw Clare's smiling, blushing cheeks. The sink of Javi's dejection and disappointment. Both somehow caused by her. She flicked at the tip of her guitar pick, tapped it against her teeth nervously.

Her cell phone buzzed nearby.

A message from Clare. *How'd it go?*

Eva sighed, blew her bangs out of her face. She responded: *he sd he needs space and time.*

I'm sure it was a surprise for him.

Eva grinned; she could hear Clare's voice.

Clare texted again before Eva could respond. *He hasn't responded to my texts either. Guess he needs space from me too.*

Eva nodded as if they were actually in the same room talking. Their separation right now felt like a weight on her chest. It had been the three of them for what felt like half her life. This wouldn't fully break them apart forever, right?

Her phone buzzed again with another message. *Guess I'm free tomorrow . . .*

Eva smiled, biting her lip to keep herself from squealing.

yeah?

Yeah.

Not sure what to write back, Eva waited too long and Clare messaged again: *But if you have plans that's okay.*

She sat up quickly as if that would help her type faster than ever. *im free!!!*

The wink and kiss emoji Clare sent as a response shoved Eva's heart up her throat.

They would figure it out.

It had always been the three of them. How could it be any other way?

It was going to be okay. She would make sure of it.

CHAPTER 18

10:05 p.m.

JAVI'S GONE.

All of him this time.

Eva can't control her breathing, her chest rising and falling quickly. The collar of her shirt, Clare's shirt, is wet from tears she can't wipe away. Her throat's closing up. She can't take in and release enough air. Spots float in her vision and her head swims.

He's gone.

He's gone.

He's gone.

Spread across meaningful places, by the rotor ride, by the skee-ball horse race game. But also in places he shouldn't be: mixed into the dirt, in someone's discarded nachos. In some garbage can somewhere. This was a bad idea. She should've left him on the mantel in the first place. At least he'd be home. At least she wouldn't have gotten all their friends in trouble.

"Hey, calm down," someone says, an unknown adult voice, gruff and judgmental. She can't calm down even if she wanted to. She doesn't deserve to feel better, not after all she's done. Her heart's going to explode. She's going to die here. Bugs and static vibrate under her skin, writhing and tickling where she can't scratch. Her mom's going to— She deserves to—

"Eva." Clare's voice breaks through the noise rushing through her ears. "I'm right here."

Warm hand in hers. Callouses against callouses. Arm over her shoulders.

"Calm her down." Strange voice, like chalkboard scratching.

"I'm trying to. Give her a moment." Clare said, frustrated, to someone.

Don't fight the current. Let it take her. Feel what's around her. Rough hand. Metal chair. Plastic guitar pick.

Then Clare's counting against her ear. "In, one, two, three, four. Hold, one, two, three, four. Release, one, two, three, four." Repeats. Squeezes her hand. Eva catches the rhythm. Or, rather, it catches her.

She breathes in, holds, breathes out, holds.

The buzzing settles. Her head floats down again.

She breathes in. Holds. Breathes out. Holds.

The room comes into focus. They're in a small, white-walled, rectangular office. Papers and notices up on the walls. Small desks with desktop computers jammed in the corners. They've been here before, in previous years. The county fair security office, built out of a shipping container. Feels fitting they would end up here tonight. It was clearly never meant to hold seven teenagers and several security guards all at once. She's squeezed between Clare and the cold metal wall.

Sound returns in a wave. Everyone's speaking at once, so loudly. Security guards keep barking for basic information. Meanwhile, CJ seems to be trying to convince them they weren't up to anything and they should be released while Hyun keeps telling everyone not to say anything until they get their phone call.

No one's missing. Good. Or is it? Are they all about to get arrested, or have they already been arrested? She should say something, about how it was all her idea and she dragged everyone here and then she couldn't go through with it without first freaking out and almost getting them caught, but then was doing okay only to actually get them caught. It was all her fault. They shouldn't be in here. Oh shit, will Bless get kicked out of USC? Will Hyun's family disown him? Will—

Suddenly Palchuck is there. Was she there the whole time or did she just enter? She walks up to one of the desks and slams down the already dented, colorful water bottle. The loud twang of hard metal against metal rings out and silences the room.

"Alright." Palchuck's voice booms in this too-small room, taking up all the space in the silent vacuum left after everyone quiets down. "I knew when I saw you all walking in you were up to something. Every year you cause me a headache. I should've trusted my gut instead of feeling pity because of your brother." She grimaces at Eva, a disgusted look. "Now I know what you were up to tonight. Anyone want to make this easy and admit it?" She looks at each of them in turn, face serious yet with a smug lilt to the corner of her lips.

CJ's mouth purses even tighter, a show of defiance that she won't be talking.

Is there yelling coming from outside? Or is it the ringing in Eva's ears?

Palchuck's penetrating gaze lands on Bless, who's practically shaking like a leaf. Frank shoulders in as much as he can, putting himself between them. One of the other security guards yells at him to stay in his seat.

Bless presses her back against the wall, trying to get far away from Palchuck.

"We don't have to tell her anything, Bless!" Hyun says loudly, a message to everyone.

"And we weren't doing anything!" CJ smacks her chair in protest. "This is all a huge mistake. If you let us go, we won't tell our parents and we can forget the whole thing–"

"I saw you." Palchuck speaks slowly, undeterred by CJ's empty threats. "I saw what was in this water bottle. I know what you've been running around doing tonight. So make this easier on everyone and confess."

"She's not a real cop." CJ whips her head around, looking at everyone, sending the wordless signal to stay quiet.

"No," Palchuck grits through her teeth. "But they're on their way here. And I could convince them to go easier on you or not. Spreading ashes on private property without permission is a misdemeanor."

Bless lets out an "*eep.*"

Is the shouting from outside the office becoming louder?

Palchuck crouches down to their level. "Come on. Work with me."

"We're minors. You can't talk to us without our parents." Clare adds her voice to the fray, and finally Palchuck looks away from Bless, focusing on her. Palchuck grimaces, enjoying the fear she can smell on all of them and also seeming upset that Clare has a good point.

"Lucky you, one of your parents is already here," Palchuck says as she straightens.

Eva braces, holding her breath, as Palchuck walks to the door. The moment it opens the noise and yelling from outside makes sense.

"Calm down, ma'am!" another guard yells.

Palchuck seems shocked to see the commotion, and she steps out of the office. Her security team follows her, and someone closes the door behind them.

"Okay," CJ immediately gets everyone's attention. "It's past ten o'clock. If we get out of here quickly, we could still make it. We need an escape plan."

Eva listens, her head feeling like it could float away at any moment.

"Anyone have an idea for a distraction?" Hyun offers. "I

could pretend to have a seizure or something."

"That's insensitive," Bless interjects between her panicked breaths.

CJ plows on. "And then what? We go home and they take you to the hospital?"

"Are we still trying to get to the last two rides?" Greg asks, worry pinching his forehead.

"Forget the rides. We need a distraction so we can get the hell out of here," Frank says, voice low and commanding, silencing everyone with his intensity. Then he nods at Hyun. "I'm willing to sacrifice Hyun."

"Hey!" Hyun and CJ say in chorus.

"You're not eighteen. You won't get in as much trouble."

"We're not leaving anyone behind, okay?" Clare looks at Frank with that kind of look your mother gives you when she means *that's final.*

"Think we could make it to the bumper cars at this point?" Greg asks.

"No," Eva says finally with a self-hating, single laugh. Her voice isn't loud, she's not yelling, and yet somehow everyone silences, all eyes on her. "Javi's ashes are gone. What's the point of going on any more rides?"

This silences them. Eva's been the driving force this entire night, gathering them all together, pushing them along when they couldn't agree.

They seem lost now.

Eva sighs. "This was all my idea, my fault. I'll take the fall when they come back, say I convinced you all to come. I made you do it."

"I don't think that's going to keep us from possibly getting arrested or fined," Bless bursts out.

"Two rides." Hyun's voice is muffled with his head in his hands.

Eva groans. They were so close. The surprising thing is

she's not even upset they didn't get to ride the bumper cars. The universe was against them on that one. But Clare. The last ride picked is so often missed, and she really thought they would get to all of them.

"This isn't fair!" Hyun kicks his long feet out in frustration. "We were two rides away! Eva and Clare didn't get to have their moment to say goodbye."

Greg turns to Clare. "What was your ride going to be?"

Clare looks at him with some pity and embarrassment. "Haunted house."

"Damn. I actually love the haunted house," Frank mumbles.

Giggles ripple through them. It reminds Eva of when it felt like things were getting better, not just for her but for everyone. Somehow they'd reached an understanding. Somehow their little group was mending and drawing closer even without Javi there. They still missed him and weren't the same without him.

But they could be something new maybe. Not better, just different. And still together. She realizes she really wants that, and now she fears it won't happen if they get in real trouble because of her.

She has ruined everything.

Eva lifts her head, resting back against the wall. Her eyes glance around the room, unfocused. Then a flash of color. The water bottle on the table. Javi's stupidly large, messily decorated, dented bottle. It really was ridiculous to bring him in that thing and think they could get away with this. But she was willing to do anything for him. They all were. Every single one of them. Even Frank who, despite all his complaints, stayed even when he could've left.

Javi has brought them together yet they can all choose to stay, to find each other, to pull each other back when they need it.

This is for him, and for all of them.

Loud voices from outside the door let her know they're

probably running out of time to come up with a plan.

Then, farther away is a screech of gears pulling a ride up, then down. Loud, scared yelling follows the motion. The Big Drop. The ride Javi had always wanted to ride with her.

And just like that, Eva knows what they need to do.

"We're not done yet," Eva says. They look back at her confused. She can hold them all together. As long as they all want to be here. All seven of her friends.

She continues. "We can still finish this. One more ride. I think it'll all count if we do one last big thing for us, for Javi. Something in his honor. Something he would've really wanted to do with all of us if he knew this was his last fair."

Eva locks eyes with Clare who frowns at first, a little confused. Then her eyes go wide as she does that thing where she knows what you're thinking—or maybe what Eva's thinking.

"The Big Drop?" Clare breathes out all her surprise. "You want to ride The Big Drop?"

"Aren't you scared just looking at that one?" Hyun asks.

"Yes," Eva responds.

"Not even Javi trying to bribe you with freeze-dried candy ever got you to ride it," Clare says. "Are you sure?"

"Yup." The more they question, the more Eva feels certain. "If we only have time for one ride, it has to be that one. That was Javi's ride. It's what he would've wanted to do one last time."

Clare's eyes are wet with tears, cementing that Eva's made the right choice.

"We don't have him anymore . . ." Hyun says quietly with a glance at the water bottle, fearful of ruining this moment.

"We do, though." Bless's voice comes out with so much confidence. "He's always with us." She smiles at Eva.

Eva might not believe it in the same way as Bless means it, but she feels it all the same.

"What's the plan, then?" Frank asks.

The door opens and in walks Palchuck, disgruntled and

frustrated. A short, stout, angry woman follows closely behind.

Eva's mom Mayra stands in front of them, taking each one in with the full weight of her hands on her hips and scowl of judgment. She looks like she ran out of the house quickly, flower-patterned muumuu tucked into some jeans with a chunky cardigan thrown on top. Clothes aside, it's like looking at a mirror image of Eva, but about thirty years from now.

They're *soooo* in for it.

CHAPTER 19

10:20 p.m.

EVA'S GONNA THROW UP.

The small wrinkles in Mayra's forehead, around her eyes and the corners of her mouth deepen as she looks from one teen to the other. Each one squirms uncomfortably as her heated glare lands on them. Without words, she infuses her anger and disappointment into each one of them.

Finally, Mayra's eyes settle on Eva, who's surprised a hole doesn't burn right through her forehead like paper under a magnifying glass. Eva doesn't look away, taking on the full heat of her mother's glare. She deserves it for what she's done.

"I want to speak to my daughter." Mayra looks up at Palchuck, squaring her shoulders again, chest puffing out. Her accent comes through crisp, strong rolled "r's" yet with the melodic Puerto Rican up-and-down intonation.

"We can't—" Palchuck says.

Mayra isn't having any of it. "She's a minor. Most of them are. Have you even contacted their parents?" She rolls her r's with extra precision.

"We're still taking their inform—"

"Until the *actual* police or their parents arrive," Mayra's voice seems to take up every bit of space in the small office. Even Palchuck flinches. "I will talk to my daughter."

Eva's stomach drops. All this time that she was scared of Palchuck she should've been more scared of her mother.

Palchuck swallows, nods, and steps outside.

Mayra sighs, and exhaustion presses her shoulders down. She looks back at Eva but something's softened, cooled the heat from earlier. Almost like she knows Eva's ready to take on the wave of fire, but she doesn't actually want to set her ablaze.

Without her even having to motion, Eva knows to stand and join her.

Not since she was ten has Eva ever been worried her mother might pull her across her lap and spank her. She would deserve it, too. The only reason keeping her mother from actually doing it is probably her fibromyalgia, which makes it worse for her mom.

"Are you okay?" Mayra asks, and Eva has to blink back surprise. That was not the first thing she thought Mayra would ask. Eva nods in response.

"The rest of you?" Mayra glances at the wall of scared teenagers.

The surprised and frightened teens all hesitate but nod as if waiting for something worse to happen.

"Good." Mayra exhales then bellows. "What were you thinking?" They all flinch as Mayra's voice rings out in the aluminum can of a room. "You didn't tell me you were going out, and you didn't tell me what you were doing."

"You would've said no or tried to stop me," Eva says, ready to defend herself.

"¡Claro que sí!" Somehow Mayra keeps getting louder. "You took him from me? From us?" She glares at the water bottle. "Put him in *that?*"

"He loved *that*. He had it with him when he—"

"He belongs at home, like you. And you better get used to it cause you're veeeeery grounded. You're not leaving the house until you're thirty." She looks at the rest of the kids. "And I'm calling all your parents, yes." The way Mayra says "yes" sounds more like "jess."

They groan.

Eva stays focused. "He's . . . he's not . . ." She's not sure how to say this. Especially with how Mayra's eyes are more intense with each stutter.

"We lost him," Eva says finally, looking down at her shoes.

"Lost him?" Mayra asks, glances at the water bottle. "What do you mean?"

"We . . . we dropped his ashes, and . . ." Eva has to force the words out. She's getting a headache from how tightly her forehead scrunches in anxiety. This is one of the worst things she's ever done, and she's known it from the start.

Mayra places a hand over her chest, fingers tightening and bunching the little lace collar of her muumuu. She stumbles back, and fortunately there was a small, crappy office rolling chair for her to fall on. Eva reaches out to grab Mayra and help her stabilize.

"I'm sorry, mami," she says, voice low and small. "I hated seeing him there in that urn. Trapped. He always liked being outside more."

"You could've told me—"

"I did! I told you it didn't feel right. I thought we should do something else." Eva's mouth is dry and her voice cracks. "But I didn't mean to lose him."

Mayra looks at her with such sadness Eva wishes she could make her mom's glare return to volcanic heat.

"So you wanted to bring him here." Mayra looks around the office with disdain. "To this dirty, loud place." She looks at the empty water bottle. "It isn't even here all year; it goes away. What were you going to do, visit your brother in a large empty lot?"

Eva's heart bumps up into her throat. She hadn't really thought about that though how can she admit it? She can't undo it at this point. Hot embarrassment burns through her ears as she wrings her hands.

"Why didn't you talk to me?" Mayra asks with anger and desperation.

"I didn't want to *talk* anymore," Eva blurts out. "You ask me all the time how I'm feeling. You tell me how you're feeling. I didn't want to talk. I wanted to *do* something to make it feel right. Nothing's felt right since he died. He liked fun, he liked this place." She takes a shaky breath. It's a heavy confession that comes to her all at once. "I couldn't sit there staring at him anymore."

Mayra frowns, not comforted by Eva's realization. "And? Do you feel better now?"

Eva gives herself a moment to reflect. She sort of does, sort of doesn't. Although tonight didn't go as she had hoped, it also went better in other ways.

Finally, she nods, certain it's the truth. "I do."

Mayra's eyes widen, her forehead wrinkles deepen, jaw shaking from how tightly she's grinding her teeth together. Her voice comes out low, strained, sounding the opposite of what her words say. Eva can practically hear the piece of her mother she's broken off. "I'm so glad for you."

"I know what I did was selfish," Eva explains. She digs the edge of her guitar pick under her thumbnail. "I know it wasn't right. And now he's gone, but we were both doing it wrong."

Mayra scoffs. "He was my son."

"He was my brother," Eva says quickly. She motions at her friends. "He was their friend. We were a part of his life, and we should get to be a part of his afterlife."

Mayra shakes her head and waves a hand in front of Eva, leaning back as if she's trying to put distance between them.

It's a gesture that begs for time-out, for space. Eva normally grants it, but they don't have the time tonight. Still, she waits for her mom to be ready to speak again.

"Did you . . ." Mayra speaks slowly and softly after a few moments of silence. "Did you have to take *all* of him?" Her look turns accusatory.

Eva swallows. At the time, as she was emptying the urn into Javi's giant water bottle, she hadn't thought of leaving any ashes behind. It was all Javi, and the concept of leaving any part of him at home never even crossed her mind.

With what she's learned and been through tonight, she knows she would do it differently. Knows she has to let her mom have what she needs as much as they all do.

"I'm sorry, mami," Eva says, all she can offer right now. At least she fully means it.

Mayra nods, attempting to put herself back together. Trying to accept something she can't change.

Eva knows she's going to have to earn a lot more than her trust back.

"I wanted him safe." Mayra looks away from Eva as she speaks. "He left the house and he . . . If I could keep him at home, watch over him better." She sniffles and rummages in her large bag until she finds a tissue. "If I'd paid more attention."

Eva tentatively steps closer to Mayra and wraps an arm around her mother's round shoulders. "I know what that feels like."

Mayra looks at the group again as if she'd forgotten they were there. That vein on the side of her forehead is still pronounced, the one that shows up when she really wants to yell at Eva. But the fact that she's holding it in gives Eva the slightest bit of comfort.

Mayra leans forward, resting her head in her hands. "I miss him so much."

Eva hugs her. "Me too."

It's not perfect, but it's a moment of understanding.

Mayra stands straighter though her eyes remain sad and tired. "Did you finish what you were trying to do?"

Eva glances at her friends. They all share her same, disappointed look. She shakes her head no as an answer to Mayra's question. Saying it out loud, admitting to her mistakes and failures, feels insurmountable.

Instead, Eva gathers herself and looks at her mom with intense, pleading eyes. "We need to do one more ride."

The silence between them helps say the rest and Mayra gives one of her scoffs, the kind that says *are you kidding me?*

Mayra squares her shoulders and looks at Eva with determination. "How can I help?"

"We need to get out of here."

Mayra shakes her head no over and over. "You're already in so much trouble."

"We're in *so* much trouble." Hyun chimes in, an odd tremble of panic in his voice. "I don't want to get fined or arrested."

"Likely both at this point!" Greg joins in on Hyun's panic.

CJ tries to soothe them. "Hey, stop, you're freaking out—"

The group bursts into frantic talking, voices mixing and growing as they talk over each other.

Eva can't let their panic crawl up her chest. She has to stay calm and bring them all back. It can't be over. She can't let it be.

This wouldn't be enough for her or for any of them. Not enough for Javi. Eva's not sure if she's made any correct decisions tonight, if she's made things worse for no reason. But there's one thing she does know.

"We have to finish it," Eva's voice rises above the chaos, strong and assertive. She's sure that it's what they need to do. She looks from one to the other. "One more ride."

They all stare at her in silence, in different levels of fear and uncertainty.

Bless stands up, which prompts a small gasp from some of the group. "We're already in trouble." She smiles at Eva. "Why not a little more?"

Hearing this from Bless seems to bolster the group.

"Hell yeah!" Greg yells with a fist pump, only to be immediately shushed by Clare.

Eva realizes she doesn't have to carry them all herself. Javi may have been instrumental, but he wasn't the only thing keeping them together.

Eva glances at Mayra, a tentative, hopeful look on her face.

Mayra's frown softens as confusion settles in. Finally, a smile breaks through. She waves her pointer finger in front of Eva.

"You're going to be so grounded after this." Mayra rearranges the collar of her muumuu, preparing her armor for battle.

With perfect timing, Palchuck opens the door, and Mayra is on. She walks forward with speed and determination. Noticeably shorter than the bulldog of a security guard, Mayra has enough fire and force to bowl the larger woman over.

Mayra's voice booms out. "I can't believe you're keeping our children in these conditions!"

Palchuck stumbles, backing out of the office entrance. "Ms. Va—"

"No, you listen to me!" Mayra barrels forward, forcing Palchuck out of the office. She slams the door to the office closed as she exits. Her deep, loud voice can be heard even from inside. "I will call every single kid's parents. Including pastor Kelly and his wife!"

Okay, it's time. Eva looks at the group and nods, then glances around the room for an escape route. There aren't many windows in this office built out of a used shipping container. The largest window is by the desk. It probably hasn't been opened in a year.

From outside she can hear her mother arguing with Palchuck and her security guards. "You're a power-tripping pendeja. Have you even called the *real* police yet?"

Eva gets everyone's attention. "It's gonna have to be the door."

All eyes look at her with varying levels of certainty and fear.

Carefully, slowly, Eva turns the door handle. It's old and doesn't move smoothly. The worst part is it sticks and squeaks with almost every turn. Eva can only hope that the noise of the rest of the fair combined with her mother's yelling are loud enough to hide the sounds of their escape attempt.

The door opens an inch and Eva's able to see outside.

Somehow her mother's commanded the attention of the entire security team. "¡Mira que voy a seguir gritando hasta que se te caigan las orejas!" Every time they try to place a hand on her she smacks them and whirls away, leading them farther from the office.

Eva smiles appreciatively.

She turns back to the group and looks to each one, taking in the range of expressions. Hyun's eyebrows crease, and he keeps running his hands through his hair, hairclup askew. CJ honestly looks a bit excited at the potential danger. Greg laughs though it's slightltly maniacal, like he's scared and it's all he can do. Bless and Frank nod, lips set in determination.

And, finally, Clare looks at Eva like she's ready to follow her anywhere.

"Okay," Eva says with as much confidence as she can muster, as she grabs her bag and Javi's water bottle. "The Big Drop. Keep an eye on each other. Don't get separated. Ready?"

Their silent nods are answer enough.

She opens the door wider and makes eye contact with Mayra, who is mid-dramatic performance. The moment she sees Eva take a step out of the office she's even louder.

"¡Se me enderezan que los enderezo!" Somehow this group of adults who had managed to pick up seven teens is struggling to control a single middle-aged mom.

There's no time to think about it. Mayra can keep this going for only so long before someone thinks to check on them. At least they can get a head start.

With a firm and quiet "Go," Eva steps out and runs. Six others run behind her.

One more ride. That's all they need to do.

CHAPTER 20

10:46 p.m.

FORTUNATELY, HAVING BEEN BROUGHT to security in previous years, Eva knows where they need to go from here. They're close to the park entrance where they came in, which means they're close to the Fun Zone.

"Stay together!" She yells as she takes off deeper into the Fun Zone. She can't hear the ruckus caused by her mom, but that doesn't mean she's stopped or that they've been noticed. They can't wait to find out either way.

Eva's not the fastest runner of the group, yet somehow she ends up in front, leading them to their destination. It's almost park closing time. The crowds have thinned, most families with small children having left by now. They still have to dodge and weave through people walking toward them trying to get to the exit, but at least they're able to keep up a good pace.

They pass by the caterpillar ride, still running even though hardly anyone rides it. So much has happened since then that it feels like they rode it yesterday.

Eva keeps glancing back, making sure she can still see all her friends. She can't lose anyone now.

They run past the roto ride. Thinking about the spinning and screaming makes her dizzy. It's impressive how much they were able to do tonight, despite everything. Even with the plan changed and some rides missed, everything feels as if it happened the way it was meant to.

If they can get to one more ride, then it will all have been worth it.

"Keep going, Eva!" Clare says from behind her, and Eva realizes she's stuck in her thoughts again. A strong, warm hand grabs hers, and then Clare's running in front of her, keeping her going. It's odd now to think she didn't want Clare here tonight. Or that she ever thought she could continue her life without seeing her again. She was always going to find her way back to Clare.

They pass the bumper cars, which has a small line. She can hear the clangs and whumps of the rubber bumpers smacking against each other and the walls. She turns away, doesn't want to be tempted to change her mind.

The Big Drop is the tallest structure at the fair. The ride's gigantic, rectangular center has a ring of seats around it, three seats per side of the tower for a total of twelve riders at a time. Each seat has its own thick chest harness that pulls down and secures between the rider's thighs, which leaves their legs to hang and swing down freely. Eva shivers at the image of looking down to see her own legs high above the park. Standing almost directly below it, the ride feels even more monstrous now. There's a current group about to ride it, and she watches as the ride's seats climb up the center slowly. Once it reaches the very top, the ride stops. Every single person screams while hanging in the air. Suddenly, as they're all dropped and plummet straight down, the screams are even louder. Eva ignores her faltering heart as she leads her group to the entrance.

"Uh oh, line's kinda long," Hyun says behind her, his worry spiking hers.

He's right. Despite the crowds leaving the park at this hour, this line seems to be a pretty long wait. At this rate, they might not get to the front of the line in time, or Palchuck might even catch up to them.

No, they don't have time to wait.

"CJ, you think you can help us skip the line?" Eva asks.

CJ's response is mostly in her confident, crooked smile, pleased to be entrusted with something this important.

"I got this." CJ leads the charge and enters the ride through the side marked EXIT. Eva ducks her head, trying her best to ignore the shouts from the riders waiting in the appropriate line. She's determined to get this done, but her anxiety and embarrassment sneak in.

"Oh shit." CJ stops so suddenly that Eva and Clare almost run into her.

"What? What is it?" Bless asks, voice loud and panicked.

The skinny ride operator at The Big Drop controls is all too familiar.

Kevin.

"*No,*" Hyun breathes out, as if already accepting their defeat. The rest of them react with varying levels of denial and swears. The ride rumbles down as it drops, and the riders' screams seem to echo their fears and concerns.

"He's not going to let us on," Eva says, defeat in her voice as her shoulders sag. Is this really it? Making it through everything they did only to be stopped by the human equivalent of a bored celery stick.

"It's alright." Frank steps in front of everyone. Somehow, he's calmer and surer than any of them. "We'll be okay."

"How do you know?" Eva asks, unsure whether he's really got some kind of amazing plan or if he's going to approach and hope for the best.

"Trust me." he says, the strangest small smile spreading across his lips. It almost concerns her more than it reassures.

Frank motions for the rest of them to follow him. "Let's go."

Bless is the first after him without hesitation, and the rest follow slowly. Eva looks around, checking for any kind of commotion coming in their direction. All quiet for now at least.

The riders all breathe sighs of relief as The Big Drop's seats lower all the way to solid ground, their moment of terror finally over. Loud clangs ring out as their harnesses release and they're able to slide out of their seats. One person even kneels down and pretends to kiss the ground.

Frank walks toward the ride operator's station. He leans over the railing and calls out. "Kevin! Hey, Kevin!"

After a couple of shouts, Kevin looks over. His expression is as uninterested as it's always been, though his eyebrows quirk up as he recognizes Frank and the rest of them.

Frank cups his hands around his mouth and yells, "Let us on, man!"

He's not even asking, he's telling. Eva holds her breath, ready to turn and run if needed.

Kevin looks at Frank, then to the rest of the group, eyes half-lidded like he's needed a nap for years already.

"We don't have anything to give you this time," CJ says, as if preempting what might be some kind of negotiation. "No food, nothing."

"I'll give you a hug," Frank yells over CJ.

Eva can't believe what she's heard. The entire group, even Bless, all turn to look at Frank with surprise.

"Yeah, okay. Get on." Kevin nods his head to the ride.

Without hesitation Frank opens the Exit gate.

They're all stunned and a little scared to follow him in. A judging "*what's wrong with you all*" look from Frank gets them all walking toward the ride load-in.

Eva doesn't look over at the disgruntled people who were properly waiting in line while they've been allowed to cut in ahead. She won't let her anxiety over inconveniencing others win this time. She can be selfish this one time.

Frank's behavior helps distract her as Eva watches him reach over the metal bars and give Kevin a forceful hug.

Kevin's face goes bright pink.

Frank quickly releases him and jogs to his seat.

"What the hell just happened?" Hyun asks Eva.

All Eva can do is shrug in answer. How's she supposed to know? She really missed a lot when they were separated.

Clare sits down first, and without much thinking Eva takes the seat next to her. She keeps glancing around, unable to believe this could be that easy. Nerves prickle up her chest, and she takes deep breaths to keep herself from making a run for it.

A calloused hand brushes against Eva's. Looking from under the restraints, she meets Clare's eyes. There's a sadness, but also a fear Eva wasn't expecting. Maybe it's the ride, maybe it's Javi's memory. She's not sure it matters. They're here together. That's everything.

They're ready and willing to have the shit scared out of them in Javi's name. That's what matters.

Kevin checks their restraints. Eva notices the pink on his cheeks as he walks to each seat.

"Don't start the ride!" A deep female voice calls out from the outside crowd.

It's Palchuck, and she's running as fast as she can towards The Big Drop.

"Holy shit," Bless exclaims, which surprises everyone.

"You cuss now?" Hyun asks.

"I will for that!"

"Now! Now! We have to go *now*!" CJ exclaims.

Kevin, in a flurry of movement Eva's never seen from him, runs over to the controls and begins the process of safety checks and button presses for the ride. Everyone must've taken their quickness pills because Palchuck is hustling through the crowd, followed closely by her team of guards.

"Kevin," Eva says, voice booming from her chest. "I hate to rush you when you're trying to ensure we don't die, but—"

"Then don't!" Kevin's voice is muffled by his back turned to them.

Restraints secured around her, all Eva can do is sit and stress.

The riders in line shout and look around, angry they were skipped, calling to Palchuck to fix this injustice.

And then Palchuck actually hurdles over the Exit gate.

A loud clunk and their seats jerk.

Eva's stomach drops. They're not going to make it. She's going to make Kevin stop the ride.

Their seats start their excruciatingly slow ascent.

Eva could imagine Palchuck leaping up and grabbing onto her foot, forcing the ride to stop.

Instead, Palchuck runs past them and grabs hold of Kevin.

"Stop the ride!" Palchuck yells. Eva sees the spittle coming from her mouth.

They're several feet off the ground, slowly going up. Could she really stop them now?

With his most deadpan face and uninterested shrug, Kevin responds. "Sorry, can't stop it once it's started."

"Yes, you can!" Palchuck pulls him closer by the collar.

He points at the manual nearby. "Per the guidelines, I can only stop the ride due to serious malfunction or safety issue. Furthermore . . ."

They're up so high Eva can't hear the rest of their conversation. The breeze blows past her ears, the music and noise from the other rides and games obscuring all other sounds.

Hyun and CJ whoop loudly.

"Hell yeah!" She hears Frank scream in his deep voice.

Eva, observing the confrontation, notices Kevin's self-satisfied smile and shrug.

Palchuck lets him go and turns to glare up at the teens on the ride. She crosses her arms over her chest. They'll have to deal with her once they get down, but for now . . .

"Eva! Clare!" Bless calls from the other side. "Your turn!"

"Turn?" Eva tries to crane her neck to see her, limited by the restraints.

"We don't have ashes to drop, but say something!"

"*Something's* gonna drop either way." Greg's terrified giggles are contagious.

Clare nods, hair whipping as the breeze becomes stronger the higher they climb. She takes a few deep breaths as if getting ready for a big jump.

"I think what I'm most scared of is that there's never going to be anyone like you, Javi. You were funny, caring, and you challenged me to be stronger.

Clare continues, voice louder. "You broke my heart, you jerk!" Eva feels a tighter squeeze against her palm. "But I have a way to fix it."

Eva sobs, wiping her tears on the restraints and then regretting it.

"Javi—" His name chokes in Eva's throat.

Oooh, wait. They're *really* up high. She can't remember a single word she'd rehearsed for this moment. All that comes out is, "I can't believe you finally got me on this thing!"

Somewhere, she can almost hear his triumphant laughter.

"I miss you like hell!" Eva shouts at the top of her lungs, which is echoed by everyone else.

Eva clutches the metal of her shoulder restraint and squeezes Clare's hand as if it'll keep her afloat. The Big Drop feels even taller when actually riding it.

Now that she's facing the hundreds of feet of height, every thought and fear is overshadowed by her stomach flopping at the realization that the ground is too far away. Almost worse than the height is the fact that they're moving upward so slowly. There's no ripping this Band-Aid off. You have to sit through the whole slow process of the unhurried climb to the top of the ride's tower.

Eva's heart pumps double-time. Her feet dangle over all the other rides, all the buildings of the fair grounds. No, don't look down; that's a rookie move.

God, she misses Javi. She wishes he were here to tease her about how scared she feels. She would've ridden this stupid ride a thousand times if it meant he could be here to make fun of her even once.

Her eyes flood with tears she can't stop. *Breathe, breathe.* In through the nose, out through the mouth. It's really hard to ground herself when there's no actual ground underneath her. Wow, she's never been able to see the whole park like this. Is this what Javi liked about being so high up? Feeling like you could see more than your usual perspective? Like seeing your small part in the whole. It's scary, but she can understand it. No one could've stopped him from going on his climb. It's no one's fault.

A warm, gentle thumb brushes her wrist, and Eva's eyes snap to Clare's.

She's crying too, cheeks wet from tears she hasn't wiped away. *It's okay*, she mouths at Eva, lips quivering, but the wind, fairground sounds, and Eva's own heartbeats drown out the words. She doesn't need to hear them to feel them.

Eva's hand squeezes Clare's tighter, like it's her only lifeline. Clare returns the squeeze, their grips crushing each other. Eva's never felt safer.

Clare, who didn't deserve what Eva did to her and yet is here. Helped her and helped everyone. They've started fixing whatever it was between them. And maybe they'll never fully get to where they were before, but something tells Eva they'll always be a part of each other's lives.

They both lean in at the same time and press their lips together. It's awkward and strange. They're confined by their seat restraints, lips meeting only at a specific angle. It's still the third-best kiss Eva's had, full of promise and strength, comfort when it's most needed. And, most importantly, forgiveness.

Clunk. The ride stops, and Eva's stomach feels weightless as she sits back.

This is it. They're at the very top, above even the palm trees.

The biggest smile spreads across her lips, and she sees it mirrored in Clare's face. Eva can't wait to kiss her again once this is all over.

"Oh my god," Greg calls out. "There's no line at the bumper cars."

Eva bursts out laughing because *of course* there isn't. She hears it chorused by the rest of her friends.

Gears whine again.

Clare squeezes her hand.

A *pop* as something unlatches.

They all scream as they fall.

EPILOGUE

one year later

3:53 p.m.

EVA LIES FACE UP, cool grass tickling her arms, bomber jacket bundled up as a pillow under her head. The orange sky is peaceful, not a cloud in sight, the night already chasing off the Southern California heat.

Perfect time to visit the county fair.

Which she's not doing today. She's banned from not only the Los Angeles County Fair, but any event hosted at the Fairplex—forever. Although the court proceedings did not take long, the verdict was very clear about that.

It said nothing about her sitting on the golf course across from the Fairplex, though.

She glances at her phone and smiles at the lockscreen picture, the same one she's had for over a year. In it, Javi's in the center, smiling so big his eyes almost crinkle shut. His right arm wraps around Eva, and his left around Clare, pulling them both tightly against his sides. Restoring the photo to its rightful place and framing felt right.

According to the time, it'll be a few minutes before anyone else will get here.

Good. She needs some time.

She closes her eyes and listens for the familiar sounds of the fair, which she can't quite make out over the sound of passing cars. If she could hear it, she might imagine herself there tonight.

Quiet steps approach, and a large shadow settles above her. She opens one eye to see Clare standing over her, hair pillowy large and blocking what's left of the sun.

"You gonna take a nap?" Eva's girlfriend asks with a teasing half-smile. The way the dimming afternoon light halos around Clare's curls twists something joyful in Eva's chest. Like a trapped giggle she wants to keep forever.

"Enjoying not being late this year," Eva says with a smile, stretching her arms out above her head.

"Lots different this year." Clare gently taps her toe against Eva's side. "I was actually invited, didn't even have to crash."

Eva laughs and bats her foot away. "You ever going to let that go?"

Clare grabs Eva's waving hands and hauls her up easily as if Eva weighs nothing. The thrill bubbles the giggles out of Eva's chest, an embarrassing level of giddiness that can't hide how much she enjoys Clare's strength.

"Not for as long as I keep getting make-up kisses." Clare smoothly pulls Eva to her side and wraps an arm around her, pressing a kiss to her lips.

Eva laughs through her nose as she returns the kiss. After the fair last year, it took them awhile to talk everything out, work through the built-up negativity to find their way back to the feelings they had had for each other before everything happened. Eva's feelings were buried by grief, needing careful prodding and excavation by a gentle, understanding archeologist. Clare had kept hers as if they were covered by a sheet of the thinnest paper, and the moment Eva was ready, affection came at her full force. It was a lot all at once, exhilaratingly frightening.

Eva doesn't deserve Clare, but she wants to. Fortunately,

she's better at talking things out to her mom, her therapist, and her friends. She has a place to release all her fears that she'll only ruin things again eventually. She's working through it.

"Eva!"

They turn as CJ and Greg step out from some nearby bushes. Greg's shirt features the Looney Tunes wearing baggy '90s clothing, faded enough it's probably passed through several owners. CJ's in sweatpants, fluffy boots, and a tank top—a part of her warm, a part of her cold as she likes to be.

"You beat us here this time!" CJ laughs as she pulls Eva into a hug.

"It's easy when Mom can give me a ride." Eva laughs into CJ's shoulder.

"CJ! CJ!" A muffled voice comes from CJ's hand. "We can't see!"

"Hang on!" CJ pulls back and holds her phone up, revealing Hyun's smiling face in one square, and Bless calmly waving from her own square.

"Heeeey, Hyun and Bless!" Eva grabs CJ's hand and moves too close to the camera on purpose. "You both made it!"

"Done with classes today, fortunately," Bless says, her purple coordinated dorm room behind her, a stack of binders and books visible next to her.

Hyun holds up his hands covered in potting dirt. "I took on seedling duty so I could sit in one place and chat." His camera slides and he falls off frame. "Dammit! Right into the compost."

Greg shoves himself in front of the screen. "What are your parents planting this year?" Eva takes the cue and hands him CJ's phone. She tunes out during plant talk, though fortunately Bless seems to enjoy it.

"Thanks for coming," Eva says, smiling at CJ.

"What, you think I'd miss this? Never." Her best friend wraps an arm around her shoulders and turns to face in the direction of the fair. The lights shine brighter the darker the afternoon grows. Eva can almost hear some music and noise over the whoosh of cars. "Not as fun from outside, gotta say. Almost makes me want to try to sneak in."

"Oof, no," Clare says immediately, shaking her head. "Most of us are still paying our fines off."

They all groan and nod their heads. Eva tells herself that at least no one was arrested, nothing on any sort of record that would carry extreme consequences. A very bright side. Even the community service was fun since they all got to do it as a group. Made it feel more like another hangout where they just happened to also be cleaning up trash. Who knew illegal activities could bring friends even closer together?

"'Sup." A deeper voice calls out, and they turn to see Frank walking up to them. His tall, lollipop-like frame somehow balances him perfectly as he walks over the uneven ground, carrying a small stack of colorful striped cups. His steps are lighter even if his face remains as sullen as ever. It must be carved that way.

"Hey, Frank's here! Whatcha got there?" Greg asks, the first one intrigued and walking over to help him with the cups.

"Lemonade," Frank answers, as if this was the expected thing to bring.

"*What?*" Hyun squeals through the phone. "*The* lemonade?"

"Yah." Frank hands the cups out to everyone, holding one close to the phone camera.

"Unfair!" Hyun bemoans, swinging his dirt-filled hands over his head. "How'd you even manage to get some when we're not allowed in there?"

"Kevin." That's all Frank says, but it's all he has to say. The entire group exchanges looks and knowing smiles.

Eva tries very hard to keep a straight face, despite being aware how often Kevin joins their group via Frank invite. She doesn't like the teasing looks she gets about her and Clare, so she's not going to pass that onto Frank. Even though she completely understands why people enjoy being jerks about it.

"Ooooo, Kevin!" Bless apparently has no such qualms. But she's also the only one who seems to have a free pass to say anything she wants when it comes to Frank.

"How's he doing?" Clare asks, taking the lemonade cup out of Greg's hands once he's had a few sips. No one wants a repeat of his sugar high from last year.

Frank shrugs, his eyes narrowing at Bless on CJ's phone screen. "Says the fair's boring this year without us."

Eva can't see Bless, but she can hear her making kissing sounds from Clare's phone.

"I'm muting you." Frank taps the screen a few too many times to be actually trying to hit the mute button. Hyun yells at him not to while Bless makes even louder kissy noises. CJ tries to hold the phone away from him but Frank's reach is too long for her.

Even though they couldn't all make it in person, Eva can't believe they're still together. She'd been so worried that Javi was the only thing keeping them from floating away. She hadn't seen all the ways they could make those connections stronger without him. Which also hurts in its own way. Eva's learning to hold two opposite things in her mind at once.

"Alright, alright," Eva says in her best settle-down tone. She reaches into her messenger bag. "It's only going to get colder so let's have a moment."

She pulls out Javi's water bottle. Still dented, still covered in old stickers. One side has a new addition: secured with clear tape is the physical County Fair ticket CJ bought last year. She tried her best not to cover too many of his old stickers, but it deserved to be among the special places he loved to visit.

"You don't . . ." Hyun says, voice slightly worried. "He's not . . . in there?"

Eva lets the dramatic silence hang for longer than she needs to, then laughs.

"No," Eva says, shaking the water bottle near CJ's phone. "It's empty." She holds it close to her chest, the metal surface chilling her fingers. "But still a part of him, so I felt like it needed to be here."

Clare loops an arm around Eva's waist, thumb brushing warmly against the fabric of her T-shirt.

They stand together in the grass, arms linked or bumping against each other, some form of contact as they all face in the direction of the fair.

A line of cars continues to pass through, making their way to the fairground's parking area. A breeze blows past, ruffling their hair and clothes like a faint caress. They don't say anything; they don't have to. They get to feel now, to be around each other in that quiet way only people who've been through the same difficult event together know how.

Slowly, the sounds from the cars seem to quiet around them. Eva's bangs dance in the breeze and tickle her forehead. She closes her eyes.

She can hear it.

Pop music mixing with rock, mixing with Tejano and country.

People singing, laughing, talking.

Greasy smell of sizzling fryers.

Whirrs and clunks of machinery.

Screams from riders falling on the Big Drop.

"We miss you, Javi." Frank's voice is so soft and low Eva almost didn't hear it. Clare rests her head against Eva's.

Frank holds his lemonade cup out and spills it.

"Nooooo," Hyun moans from CJ's phone.

"Hey!"

They all turn toward the gruff adult voice. A man in a security uniform and a walkie-talkie fast-walks toward them, feet stomping through the pristine golf course grass.

"Shit," CJ breathes.

Eva quickly shoves the water bottle into her bag.

"What's happening?" Bless asks as CJ disconnects the call.

"You're not supposed to be here." The man points an accusatory finger at them. "This is for members only!"

"You think they'd actually arrest us this time?" Greg asks in a panic.

"Back through the fence!" CJ yells and takes off.

Strong arms tighten around Eva, and she feels herself lifted off the perfectly manicured grass, surrounded once more by the familiar scent of Clare's cherry blossom moisturizer.

Eva laughs, a loud barking sound, the excitement of fear, as she and her friends run back to the hole in the fence.

ACKNOWLEDGMENTS

OUT OF THE WHOLE book, this might be the hardest part to write. How do I thank and acknowledge everyone who had a hand in making this book what it is and who guided me toward the best version I could write? Without writing a whole other book about it that is, ha-ha.

First, this book wouldn't exist without the Golden Crown Literary Society's Writing Academy staff and fellow students. I have a screenwriting background, but tackling prose and a novel for the first time felt daunting, and I couldn't get past the first three chapters when I tried on my own. The class gave me structure, deadlines, and the tools to turn this idea into a proper novel. I'll always be grateful to Tammy, Kim, Finn, and the rest of the staff and teachers who work so hard to support sapphic writers and stories.

With that, thank you to my Writing Academy mentors. Jamie, you very tenderly took me through my first mentor experience and gave me so many things to consider as I was still figuring out what I wanted this story to feel like. (You better have saved that Target receipt where you wrote down notes for me. I want it!) Carrie, your thoughtful and passionate approach helped me hone in on the specifics that made this story so special and truly my own. And thank you for your guidance through my first experience with the publication process (Ah! Scary!).

To all the people who read early drafts and gave the notes they could: Emily, Haley, Sara, Lony, Sarah, and my mom Nuria. You're all my guinea pigs where I got to test how things were working (or in some cases not working).

Thank you to the Bywater Books team—to Ann, Christel, and Salem who were excited about the book, believed in these kids and their journeys, and whose enthusiasm and dedication fed the fire I needed to keep my deadlines.

My developmental editor, Anna, who took this entire cake and added the frosting to make it complete. I've never felt more understood than when you pointed out exactly what I was trying to do with this book, and had the best notes to make it even better. It's also an honor to get to work with one of my favorite authors!

June, you've been with this book from the very seed of the idea. You saw the pieces before anything came together, and you were a big, sometimes forceful, part in getting them all to fit. I could not have expected to find a beta reader better than you to point out all the things that worked, all the things that didn't, and who would argue with me until I figured it all out.

To my wife, Caroline, I always remember that conversation where I said "when I wanted to be a writer" and you stopped me and made me realize what I was saying. You gave me the space to figure it out and later, even more importantly, the time to do it despite our busy lives. You're my dream girl.

And lastly, you who's reading this (hopefully you got this far; otherwise, you missed your acknowledgment!): whether you love YA or rarely read it, I hope you enjoyed these teens and their adventure. Thank you for supporting sapphic authors and sapphic stories.

ABOUT THE AUTHOR

LYVIA MARTINEZ grew up in Puerto Rico where her love of stories was shaped through weekends binging Blockbuster movies and long afternoons reading during power outages. She studied filmmaking and screenwriting at Brigham Young University and Chapman University and is a graduate of the Golden Crown Literary Society's Writing Academy.

Lyvia has worked in film and TV for over ten years and loves stories in all forms. She currently resides in Los Angeles with her wife, a clowder of charismatic cats, and a revolving door of foster animals.

The Foreword INDIES Publisher of the Year Award was presented to Bywater Books for its twenty years of ushering in the "coming of age of queer literature."

> "In a year when LGBTQ+ communities faced renewed attacks and the names of DEI efforts were sullied by those in power, Bywater Books remained firm in its commitment to publishing titles that celebrate queer existence and that embrace diversity. Their world-widening books make us laugh, make us cry, and stand as enduring testaments to the breadth of love and the human experience."
>
> –*Foreword Reviews*

Bywater Books believes that all people have the right to read or not read what they want—and that we are all entitled to make those choices ourselves. But to ensure these freedoms, books and information must remain accessible. Any effort to eliminate or restrict these rights stands in opposition to freedom of choice.

Please join with us by opposing book bans and censorship of the LGBTQ+ and BIPOC communities.

At Bywater Books, we are all stories.

For more information about Bywater Books, our publishing mission, authors, and our titles, please visit our website.

https://bywaterbooks.com

www.ingramcontent.com/pod-product-compliance
Lightning Source LLC
Chambersburg PA
CBHW030345290826
50605CB00034B/414
* 9 7 8 1 6 1 2 9 4 3 4 7 3 *